Revolution

A Collide Series Novel

Book Four

SHELLY CRANE

Editing services provided by Jennifer Nunez

Printed in paperback and available in Kindle and E-book format through Amazon, Create Space and Barnes & Noble.

Printed in the United States

10 9 8 7 6 5 4 3 2 1

More information can be found at the author's website

http://shellycrane.blogspot.com

ISBN-13: 978-1479223138
ISBN-10: 1479223131

"They say before you start a war, you better know what you're fighting for."

- The Cab

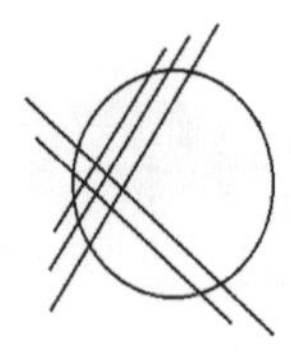

Acknowledgments

As always, my husband: Axel, you're amazing beyond words.

My boys: J & N, you keep my brain full of imaginative ideas. This job keeps Mom a little busy sometimes, but you guys are so good about it. I love you and couldn't imagine doing this without your daily inspiration of Cartoon Network commentary, Harry Potter and Phineas & Ferb jokes, and your hilarious accents of our Scottish Schnauzer dog, Scrappy. He is totally Scottish, don't EVER let anyone tell you that he's not!

My Hellcats and the most awesome group of authorly girls ever: M. Leighton, Amy Bartol, Georgia Cates, Quinn Loftis, Samantha Young, Rachel Higginson & Angeline Kace. You've made my life author enormously easier. Thanks for listening and all of your support!

My gals and bloggers: Jennifer N, Gloria G & Amanda C (Globug & Hootie), Mandy A (IReadIndie), Heather R (Supagurl), Donna (Passion), Jackie (Sated Faery), Books Books Books, ReadersLive1000Lives, Haley (Ya-aholics), Ellen (Always At The Heart), Mary (Booknerdsacrossamerica) and all the bloggers that I didn't mention, you guys rock my face off and I still credit you with lots of author success. It's totally true.

Where It All Began
Chapter 1

Merrick

I rode in the passenger seat of the busted Chevy truck. The man beside me smelled of musk and cigar that had long saturated the seats and his clothes. We bounced along the road and I tried to calm myself as I took in my surroundings and not think about the reality that I was going to meet Sherry for the very first time. And Danny, too, of course.

The pain in my chest was palpable to a human's heart attack. It was unreal the amount of terror that seethed its way through my guts in a rampant way, hell bent on destroying me at my very core.

Why?

Because I had waited and watched as the world was destroyed and taken over by the Lighters for far too long. We always waited until we could wait no more. Sometimes they just wanted to cause a ruckus, start a war or end a dynasty and then they'd leave and go back to where they came from. But every now and then, they'd come and a Taker would make its way into their ranks. When that happened, we could no longer sit back.

The Taker was here, and now so were we.

I almost broke every rule I've fought years to keep and come the other night to Sherry's rescue. Matt, such an idiot. If Sherry hadn't slammed the door on him, I would have been there in a heartbeat, jumped in the first corpse I could find and strangled him with my bare hands. But she always could handle herself and now, with my heart beating in a human chest, I felt ashamed for the first time in my life for not trusting her more. She was this incredible creature that had worked her way into my life without her knowledge and without my consent. And now, here I was, hitching a ride in a broken down pickup truck making a swift ride to her. Right to her door.

My hands shook on my lap and I stared at them in fascination. The human body was marvelous and annoying. I was…anxious. My body shook with almost a strange fright, and it did it against my will. That part I didn't like at all.

I asked the driver to turn into an abandoned parking lot and thanked him for the ride. He waved, bored and uncaring, and drove away with a sputter. I peeked through the shrubs just as Sherry's little Rabbit beat its way into the parking lot. I could barely see her through the glass because of the glare of streetlights, but her silhouette was enough to throw my heart into a pace that hurt and made me clutch this human chest. And when the door creaked open and I knew I'd see her for the very first time in real life with human eyes, I actually thought I might expire right there. My heart raced unhealthily and my eyes blurred…and then there she was, right in front of me. She fought and fidgeted with the items in her hands and I ached to help her, hold her, sweep her into my clumsy arms and take her away.

So even though Danny was my priority, or was supposed to be, I found my feet being propelled forward by nothing but the sheer need to see if her skin was as soft as it looked.

I stepped by the shrub and stopped so as not to scare her. I scolded myself, hearing my breathing loud and unnecessary to my body's function. It was a miracle in itself that she wasn't alerted to my presence from that alone.

She turned to me and stopped cold. Her eyes saw me for the first time and even though she was obviously scared of me, some strange man in her parking lot at night alone, I still couldn't wait for her to speak.

But she said, "Matt?" and stiffened.

I felt my eyebrows bunch in confusion and then it all clicked into a horrified reality. How had this happened? I was in Matt's body? I looked at her face and knew she was about to bolt. I did the only thing I could think to do. "Sherry, don't run. Don't be afraid."

I inwardly cringed at hearing Matt's voice come out of my mouth. She cringed, too, and leaned back a little. It hurt to see her retreat from me. This was not going how I had imagined, though I wasn't really sure what I thought she'd do. I was still a stranger to her, no matter than I knew every detail of her life.

"Matt, what are you doing here?" she asked me, jerking me from my thoughts.

"Sherry, listen, please. I know you're scared of me and I know this sounds crazy, but I need you to open your mind and just listen to me for a minute, ok? I need you to come with me."

We went back and forth and eventually, with wasted time strangling me with worry, I decided to lay all of my cards on the table, so to speak. "You don't have to fear me. I'm not…Matt."

Well that backfired when I saw her little cheeks turn red with anger. "Matt, stop it! It's not funny!" She breathed hard with fear. I hated that I and I alone had put that fear into her by coming here, even if I had done it haphazardly.

I reached deep for some sense of calm and comfort. Maybe if I just explained things rationally… "I'm not trying to be funny, Sherry, just listen. The strange things going on in your world..."

I saw her step. I couldn't let her get away, so I stepped. Her brow arched in silent challenge and it was so cute, I had to stop myself from taking another step toward her, but I knew that would just make her more upset. She stepped again and I countered. "Matt...died, Sherry. I know this is odd and unsettling for you and I'll explain everything later, but we don't have time. I'm here to help you and we need to leave, right now."

She bolted. It thrilled me that she finally caved, because I wanted to touch her more than anything and this gave me the excuse. I blurred to block her path and grabbed her tiny wrist, careful of my strength that wasn't quite human. My fingers tingled a bit at her touch, but I focused on my task as I spun her around and pressed her to the wall, covering her mouth with one hand.

Then all bets were off.

She smelled like vanilla and soap and it felt like it slapped me right in the face. I never could have imagined what she *actually* smelled like and now, I was being assaulted by it.

Her lips under my palm twitched and caressed my skin. Though she was giving me the look of death with her gorgeous eyes, I let my mind wander to her soft lips. I imagined what they'd feel like if she *allowed* me to touch them, instead of me taking that touch.

She then squinted her eyes and turned her face as if she expected me to hurt her. I felt my lips thin. I wished I'd come down and taken care of ol' Matt long ago. Though it would have made me break my oath to Danny, my oath to not intervene because she wasn't my charge, I wished as she looked at me and waited for Matt's wrath that I had done something.

She peeked at me and she must have seen how torn I was. We both were breathing loudly. I held in a groan just barely. Her breath, as it puffed through my fingers, was warm and a hint of mint made me have the strangest overtaking sensation to kiss her.

I licked my lips to stop myself from doing just that and instead focused harder. "Sherry, I'm going to uncover your mouth. Please don't scream. I'm not going to hurt you, I promise, that's not what I'm here for. I just need you to listen to me. It's very important and we don't have time for this. Can I uncover your mouth?"

I could see the smart mouthed comment forming, a hint of a smirk twitched at the corner of her lip as she thought of it. I wanted to smile, imagining exactly what she'd say at this moment. I moved my gaze across her features. Can you imagine seeing a priceless Michelangelo painting from far away for so long and finally getting an up close and personal look that seemed to be only for you? That's what this felt like. I'd seen her a million times over the years, but it was like I was seeing her for the very first time. It was like I was the only one to have this moment.

Her eyes were solid, no flecks or specks. Her cheeks looked soft, her ears cute and elf-like, her chin round and adorably stubborn, her neck curved and…kissable. I moved my eyes back up to her lips; pout, parted, and passionate.

I gulped and decided to try to keep persuading her. "I'm not Matt, ok, I need you to understand that. After everything going on, the moon and the visitors, I'm sure you can comprehend this. I'm not Matt. Matt died in a car crash about five hours ago in Orland Park. He was drunk and was out there by himself in his truck. I know your world has noticed the strange events taking place. I am a part of that and I'm on your side, but...they're coming. I need you to believe me and to get Danny. We have to go. Now."

I could see all over her face that she didn't believe me. She licked her lips and I felt a humming pain go through me. A delicious pain that warmed my body. I waited, bated and needy. It was embarrassing I was sure, if I knew how to be embarrassed.

She squirmed a bit, but it was easy to keep her there. She had spirit, always had. But I had a job to do here and we needed to get going and get out of there as quickly as possible. Then she began to lie. I wanted to be angry, or suspicious, but it sounded so much more endearing in person.

"Matt - I mean, whoever you are - let me go, and then we'll talk, ok? I'll go inside to get Danny and I'll be right back and then we can go. Ok?"

I wasted no more time and began my search of her. I kept reminding myself that I had to do this, to make sure she hadn't been compromised, that she was still on our side. Well, at least I hoped she still would be after I kidnapped her, which I was about to do.

I let my fingers crawl over her belly. I'd seen that belly so many times and had been objective, but this…her breaths moving under my hands, her skin quivering under *my* touch… I quickly removed my hand from her stomach and moved to her thigh.

Oh, gah, not better! Not better, Merrick! She must have thought so, too, because she gave me a look that told me she didn't appreciate me getting intimate with the area under her skirt. I felt a little ashamed at enjoying it so much, but it had to be done. I frisked all of my Specials…when I came to earth. Ahem…

I did my best to assure her of my sincere apology as I took the syringe from my back pocket and poked it into the delicate skin of her arm. She fell limp and I swiftly placed her in the car and blurred to the front door.

I knocked and Danny answered, all groggy and agitated as usual.

"What do you want?" he asked angrily. I took me a split second to remember that I wore that horrible man's face. I pasted on a sad smile and told him my little story. It wasn't as surreal as meeting Sherry, but Danny was animated and eager. He believed me right away, kind of making me peeved at him for it. He was too gullible, always had been.

He ran to the car and jumped into the driver's side. I explained that I had somewhere to take them and he drove us there quickly, breaking the speed laws I was sure. I would chastise him for such an act if the Lighters hadn't been so close to coming and getting Danny.

We arrived and I hoisted Sherry's small weight in my arms and led the way to the underground warehouse. Danny went off to explore and I tried not to explore his sister in his absence. I smelled her hair as I set her down in the chair.

Without any permission of mine, my body's hands took her face gently. I wanted to gasp at the feel of it. I had wanted to do that so badly that I had let my human emotions control me. Oh, well. She was aware and had already felt me do it, might as well keep going.

“I know you can still hear me in there. I’m sorry I had to do that to you, but I had to get you and Danny to safety. It’ll still be a while until you wake up. Listen, I know how this sounds and looks and I can explain everything to you both when you wake up, but I’m not Matt. Matt is dead and I’m sorry to be the one to tell you that. I’m not here to hurt you or Danny. We’re underground in a warehouse with only one way in and one way out. The elevator and I have the key. I promise you, I’m not going to hurt you. I’m here to help. We are going to be here together for a while so it would be nice if you’d get use to the idea... Sherry,” I breathed her name with every ounce of reverence in me.

I inched closer and once again stopped myself from letting my lips touch her forehead. Instead, I did the stupidest thing I'd ever done. “I can’t believe I’m actually here, actually touching you.” I let my thumb rub back and forth over her cheek to let her feel, even for just a second, the power of my words. “You don’t know how long I’ve..." Enough, Merrick! "Just try to get some sleep. We’ll go over everything together later. By the way, my name is Merrick. I’ll be around when you wake up.”

I let my fingers slide reluctantly from her face and stood. I gulped and left her before I made an even bigger fool of myself. I went in search of Danny and just hoped beyond hope that when she woke, she'd at least listen to what I had to say.

I was remembering…

The past, from when I first came to get them all those months ago. One of my favorite memories because all of my dreams became real that day.

All of a sudden, there was this strange light blocking my way. Cliché and bright and beckoning for these types of situations. I didn't remember there being a light before when I thought back to what had happened that day.

I took a deep, thinking breath. The light barreled toward me and I just let it engulf me. I remembered the bunker, I remembered the Lighter, I remembered the knife, I remembered Sherry's face as I fell, my Lily.

I didn't want to go into that light, it felt final and pulling, but I couldn't stop it from taking me…

A Love So Deep
Chapter 2

Sherry

I could feel the wind on my face as Merrick and I drove down the highway. The top on the Rabbit was down, and my cheeks were getting wind burned in the Chicago chill, but I didn't care. I leaned my head back on the scratchy leather and soaked it all in.

"Are you happy?" he asked me and smiled as he waited for my answer, his gaze switching from me to the road and back again.

"Yeah," I sighed with no hesitation. "You're so good at driving now." I giggled. "It's pretty funny."

"What's that, sweetheart?"

"How you were so, so bad at it before."

He mock scowled at me and then smirked. "You're lucky you're cute."

"Why?" I said coyly and fiddled with my necklace. "What would you do to me?"

"Something fun…for me." He grinned at his humorous threat and I laughed, throwing my head back and leaning over to rest my head on his shoulder. He pulled me the rest of the way with a hand on my thigh and then slung his arm over my shoulders. "Well, I'm happy." His fingers squeezed affectionately and he kissed my temple and spoke against it. "God, thank you…I'm so happy here with you."

"I'm happy about that." I looked up at him, seeing the glow of joy on his cheeks. Not that he could lie to me anyway, but still. "I don't know if I ever told you this or not, but I'm so glad that you broke the rules. I'm so glad that you came here to save Danny…and me. And I'm so glad that you want me, with all my weirdness, brokenness and shortness." He snorted, but I kept going. "I just can't wait to be at our cabin in the hills, away from everybody and everything. Be normal. Watch Lily con you out of everything she ever wanted."

He laughed. "Oh, that'll definitely happen."

I smiled at him and then looked back to the road…just in time to see Mrs. Trudy standing in the road. "Watch out!" I yelled, but I wasn't sure who I was yelling it to.

She didn't move, just watched us stoically as Merrick slammed on the brakes and came to a stop inches from her. I looked at her and back to Merrick. He was smiling. He leaned down to me, nose to nose, and let his fingers run a path across my cheek. "No matter what happens, baby, I love you more than I ever thought was humanly possible. Sometimes, my heart hurts from being too full. Know that. If nothing else comes of this day, know that I loved you so much that I could never be sad again, wherever I am."

"Merrick?" I asked in confusion. "What do you mean?"

"I love you, baby. I will always love you."

"I love you, too," I answered even though I wasn't sure of his confession or what Mrs. Trudy was doing there. I looked back to Mrs. Trudy and she waved. Then she pointed to her watch and lifted her eyebrows in a 'hurry up' motion.

I was more confused. I mean, not five minutes ago I was looking down at Merrick. He was bleeding on the floor, the life literally draining from him as I held in my shaking hands. And now, we were cruising along the highway…and…

Wait. I gasped awake.

I looked up and pushed Cain's hand away from my neck. I scrambled up and away from his lap, where I'd been laid out like I was the one dying. He must have caught me when I passed out. I put my hand on Merrick's cheek and failed at stifling a sob at seeing him so lifeless all over again.

He'd told me he loved me in the dream. He said he was so happy, no matter what happened… Had he known he wouldn't see me again? Had I met him in some dream place and he was telling me goodbye, or was it all just wishful thinking?

Lily still had her hand on Merrick's arm and her face was calm and anticipatory. She was waiting for something. I looked around and everyone else seemed to be waiting for something, too. I looked back at my very life, my love, my soul mate and husband who risked everything to be here with me, who changed the very core of my being. I waited.

Cain once again rubbed my shoulder. "Sherry," he tried, but I didn't want to be placated or soothed. If this was it, if Merrick was slipping through my fingers, I wanted to see it all and not have any doubts about the realness of it all later. I would torture myself with this memory for as long as I lived.

And then…his fingers twitched. I heard more than felt the gasp that invaded my throat. I sat stunned as he opened his eyes slowly with flutters and blinks.

He looked around the room as if looking for something specific. He smiled at Lily and touched her cheek. Then his eyes settled on me and he stilled, his smile slipping away. He frowned as he leaned forward and held my face in his hands. My skin felt the familiar tingle of his touch and I broke wide open with sobs that ripped my chest in two.

"Ah, baby," he soothed and urged me onto his lap. "You thought I was gone," he guessed. His brow bunched as he thought about that. "I *was* gone. I remember. There was this light and then we were driving…the car ride…and Mrs. Trudy." We both peeked over at Lily who looked extremely proud of herself. He looked back to me and pressed his forehead to mine. "I was gone, but I'm here."

"How is this possible?"

"You can't get rid of me, it seems even with death," he joked.

I wasn't amused. "Don't joke," I croaked and sniffed. I whispered, "I watched you die."

"And I'm so, so sorry," he said with conviction, his voice deep and rough.

I sniffed again. "Do you feel different?"

He shook his head and palmed his chest. "No. I feel like…me."

"That's good." I sniffed again and someone handed me a tissue. I locked my arms around Merrick's neck and sighed into his warm skin. "Don't ever leave me again."

"Never," he promised, his arms tight around my back and he sighed his words into my neck. "Never, honey, I promise."

"Merrick," Jeff said and cleared his throat. You could tell he hated to interrupt, but there was still a crap load of things to figure out. "Sorry. Um…but we've got issues here, man. Ellie and Marissa said there's an army coming. And what should we do with this?" He kicked the Lighter's boot. "Is it still just a Lighter or is it a human now? He didn't burn up when he died so…"

It made me pause. That's right, no lightning…

"Please, Jeffrey," Merrick said roughly and didn't take his eyes off of me. "Be the captain for a while, huh? I just…can't right now," he confessed and gazed at me with barely veiled agony as he let his hands cradle my face. "I just can't do anything but be thankful to still feel the buzz from the touch of your skin," he whispered only to me.

"All right," Jeff replied and seemed almost happy with Merrick's response. "Marissa, can we have a timeline, sweetheart? When are we looking at?"

"I can't tell," Marissa said and gulped. Jeff reached his hand out to her. "I just know it's soon. Within the hour."

"Ok," he soothed her and ran a hand down her arm.

Merrick sighed and stood as he said, "I need a minute with Sherry." I bumped into Cain, who was still behind me. He smiled in relief at me and patted my arm before walking back to Lillian.

"You're leaving now?" Josh said. It was at that moment that we all noticed him. Like *really* noticed him. Josh was supposed to be dead. He sacrificed himself for Racine. He jolted at all of our silent stares on him and straightened his back. "That's right. I told you already that I wasn't Josh anymore. I'm Simon in here and this is my body now, so get used to it quickly so we can get to work."

I felt my jaw drop. It felt different with Simon. With Merrick when he explained being in Matt's body, it was foreign, but not unpleasant. But with the cut of Josh's death so fresh and there not even being any time to mourn him yet, it was too much. I turned and buried my face in Merrick's neck, not wanting to see Simon wearing Josh's face. I felt Merrick's head shake and an angry breath leave him.

Then Simon said as he glared at Merrick, "Have you forgotten the real reason we even came here?"

"Simon," Racine growled, low and dangerous. "How could you?"

I jolted my eyes back to them. I looked at Merrick and saw him gritting his teeth. What for? I swung my gaze back to Josh…or, uh Simon…and waited. Racine continued as she made her way to him. "How could you!" she repeated louder. "Did you think about this for one second or did you just snatch the first body that was available and not give a thought to the consequences? What if I jumped in Cain's body after he died and you had to face me every day?"

"I can help in this body where my old one couldn't-"

"You're wearing my charge's body!" she shrieked and choked on a sob. "Did you not think what it would do to me to see my dead charge walking around, constantly being reminded of how I failed at the one thing I was put on this Earth to do?"

He blanched a little and I felt right about that. Shame on Simon for being so selfish and only thinking about himself.

"I didn't think, no. I just reacted. I knew that I could do more good in a body that wasn't hindering me like the other one and-"

The crack of her hand across his cheek was loud. He looked at her blankly, as if he understood that he deserved it. "I hope that one day I can forgive you for this, Simon."

"I hope that as well. I'm sorry, sister. This decision was for the good of all, and I sacrificed the good of the one. I'm sorry to have caused you pain."

"I understand," she said sincerely. She turned and took in the room. "Please try your hardest to call him Simon and not…Josh." She gulped.

We nodded and she went to sit on the couch, burying her face in a wad of tissues. Could she not see that Josh sacrificed himself for her because he was fond of her? Because he cared about her? I for one was proud of him. Racine would grow to be one day, too.

"All right," Miguel drawled and stepped up to the front of the room beside Jeff. "We know they're coming. We need to buck up and push all this trivial crap to the side and figure out what to do."

"Yes," Jeff and Simon agreed in unison. Jeff scowled at Simon, but looked back to Miguel. "Outside perimeter?" he began his plotting and it seemed that Merrick and my reunion would just have to wait.

"Might as well," he agreed with a sigh. "No point in waiting down low. They know we're here." He grinned evilly. "May as well meet them and gain the upper hand. They don't know that *we* know they're coming."

Cain nodded and said, "Ok, let's pull the old 'women and children in the cellar' bit and get this thing started."

"Now hold on a minute!" Lillian said.

"Do not argue with me on this one, L," he growled. "Really? You almost died yesterday or may have even *actually* died and you want me to let you out there for another try at it? No."

She gulped and to my surprise, nodded. "All right."

He blinked his own surprise. "Ok, good." He slowly turned back to Jeff and Miguel. "Ambush style. Let's go."

"Sounds perfect," Miguel said and winked at Rylee, who growled at him, as he made his way to the kitchen. "I'll grab some grenades."

Cain and Lillian began their goodbyes and that started the flood for them all. I refused to look at Merrick. I'd just gotten him back minutes ago and now he was being put right back out there on the front lines again. It seemed childish to pretend that this wasn't about to go down, but I just couldn't force my chin to move his direction.

But he knew what I was doing and took my stubborn chin in his hand. My Merrick looked at me knowingly and gave me a sad, small smile. "I'm so sorry, honey. I wish…Well, you know what I wish."

"I wish that, too. It's ok. I'm used to the whole song and dance by now." His smile grew. "You go fight while I stay and pine for you like the lovesick puppy that I am."

"That sounds great actually."

"It sounds like crap," I argued making him laugh out loud. He framed my stupid little useless wet cheeks in his hands and I tried to steady my quivering lip.

"I love you more than I can ever get to you to understand, and I'm sorry that we can't have our little reunion right now." He reached forward and bit my bottom lip gently. He made a growly noise in his throat. "Mmm, I'd love nothing more than to drag you to our room right now…caveman style." I laughed. That was totally something Cain would say. "But I'll have to settle for this until later."

He slammed his mouth to mine and I felt the pleasurable hum all the way to the ends of my hair. I let my arms circle his neck and bring him closer to me. His hands pawed and pulled me so close and tight that it was hard to breathe.

Not that I was breathing anyway. I was too busy being breathless.

When my fingers weaved their way through his hair, he pulled back with a groan, grabbing my hands gently and pulling them to his mouth. He kissed them and exhaled his frustration in a warm puff against my fingers. "You can't do that," he chastised. "I'll never leave if you do."

I made mock pout lips which caused him to laugh in a rumble.

"Can't you stop being adorable for just two seconds?" he said wryly. He kissed my forehead, then my cheek, then my lips. He sat there with them pressed to mine, just absorbing and not moving, before pulling away with a puckering sound. I sniffed once more and let him set me to my feet. This was it. No more stalling.

"I love you, Finch."

"I love you, Sherry." I jolted a little. He hardly ever called me Sherry anymore…unless I was in trouble. It was always baby or honey or gorgeous. He laughed at my expression. "I miss saying your name sometimes. I know you hate it, but I love it. Your mother may not have named you Sherry for the right reasons, but I don't care. You're my Sherry."

"What do you mean 'the right reasons'?"

His lips twisted a little. "She refused all the girl names your father suggested. And on the way to the hospital she passed a graveyard at a stoplight. She picked the first female name she could find and…there you have it."

"What?" I said, disgusted. "How do you even know that? Danny didn't come along until later."

"She confessed it to your father once, when Danny was born. Your father was upset that he couldn't help name either of you and wondered where she got the names from. You were a graveyard, Danny was a burger place." I gave him a 'Huh?' look. "Danny Boy's Burgers on Fifth Street. True story."

I just shook my head. My mother was a psycho!

He pressed his mouth to my ear, wrapping me in a tight, final embrace. "I've got to go, baby."

"Be careful. And you better come back."

"Always," he promised.

With one last kiss that ached with sweetness, he went to Jeff and Miguel to plot our ambush of the Lighter's…ambush. Could this day be anymore screwed up?

I held in an explosive sigh and turned to Lily. She was playing with her doll, Joy's, hair. Twisting it into a messy braid that had no pattern or order. She was so innocent and yet, not. There was a new air about her, one that I didn't have time to think about. I squeezed my eyes shut tightly and took a deep breath, holding it in so long it hurt before blowing it all out. When I opened my eyes, Lily was standing in front of me. I jumped and then laughed. "You scared me, bug."

"Sowwy. Are we gonna go hide in the closet again?"

I pressed my lips together. "Yeah. Probably. That ok?"

"Can Calvin and Fwankwin come, too?" she said and swung from side to side as if this all was no big deal.

"I think that's a good idea." I took another needed deep breath and prepared for Merrick's outrageous look at what I was about to say to everyone. "Ok, I think me and the kids and anyone else…Ellie, at least, need to come with me to the back room, right? We'll lock ourselves in."

True to my knowledge of him, Merrick's eyes bulged, and then his face softened into gratitude. He mouthed 'Thank you'. I nodded. I understood that he hated for me to fight him every time on whether I was going to fight or not. But as morbid as it sounded, I learned that stupid accidents and enemy attacks can happen right in our living room and he'd be safer not worrying about me and Lily. I almost smiled. I was making massive progress in my mind. It was hard - so, so hard - to let go of control.

Before I even realized it Merrick was nose to nose with me. I did smile then. He pressed his lips to mine before lifting Lily and giving her a stern look. "Stay with Mommy."

"Mmhmm." Then she gasped. "Oooh, let's bring snacks!"

Merrick guffawed at her before kissing her forehead. Then he kissed mine and went back to plotting. I went to gather a few snacks just in case we were bunkered down for a while and told Lily to get together some games or something.

I heard them plotting. Miguel, Merrick, Cain and Jeff would lead the attack outside with a group and Pastor, Max and Daniel would lead the one at the door of the bunker in case anyone got passed, which they were thinking was likely since they were sending so many. And then Marissa, who agreed to hold down in the bunker, but refused to be locked in the backroom, along with a few others would be in the door waiting for anyone who got through, if that were to happen.

It was then that I realized how much this could affect us. This could be *it* for us. It made me feel strange to be so calm about it. We'd been through so much, not just lately, but for months. We'd fought so many Lighters and been locked up and beaten down…but we always came out on top. Was that why I felt this way? Did I have some cocky notion that we were unbeatable?

But when Pastor called everyone's attention and asked us to listen to him for a minute, the shakes started. This was real. This was happening. The Lighters were coming for us and they were bringing a new enemy we'd never seen. I knelt on the floor next to Merrick and decided not to hide how scared I'd all of a sudden become. But I knew this: if we died, we'd die together, a family, an army of resistance.

We wouldn't lie down. We wouldn't let them rule us and turn us against our kind. We would not be their puppets to our own demise.

This was a revolution, whether the enemy knew it or not.

Amen and Aman
Chapter 3

Sherry

"Friends, acquaintances, family." Pastor looked at his daughter as if she were five years old again. "I just wanted us to take a few minutes to collect our thoughts. I know these minutes are precious for planning our attack, but we need this. Whatever religion you are, whatever you believe in or don't believe in. Whether you believe there's a man who sits in the clouds and watches us like ants or a Heavenly Father, it doesn't matter. We're all the same. We're all human…" His brow lifted as he looked at Jeff, then Merrick. "Of sorts."

"Human works just fine, Pastor," Merrick said and smiled, squeezing my arm. "Go on."

"Ok, well, whatever we are. Humans, angels, aliens, we all have humanity. We all want what's best for this world. We all want to…survive." He looked around at us. "And we need all the help we can get. So I'm going to bow my head and ask the big man to give us a little hand up. You make your own decision as to closing your eyes or not, but you be respectful," he said sternly. He knelt down on one knee and took his hat off. Everyone else followed suit and I wasn't surprised when everyone closed their eyes as we huddled there in the commons room.

"Lord," he started low, "we could sure use your help today. With every conflict comes an opportunity. We can show these devils that we won't be stomped under their feet, but the opposite. We can show them that the human spirit in us all that you created won't be taken so easily. And the Lighters? Well, I think that hell misses their sorry behinds and it's time they went home." I heard a few 'Yeah's and

'Mmhmm's. "Give us strength beyond our bodies, swift and cunning hands, and nimble minds, Father. Amen and Aman!"

"Amen."

And we all opened our eyes and stood. The knot in my throat was smaller at his words, but still lodged and causing my eyes to water a little bit. But then Cain's next words made everything else stop.

"Pastor, uh..." He looked back at Lillian and grinned this smile that said *I hope you're ready for this*. "Do you think...you could marry us?"

Lillian gasped and covered her mouth. Her eyes instantly watered. Billings grumbled something from the corner about being stuck with one woman forever, but everyone ignored him.

"Right now?" Pastor asked easily and looked at his watch as if the time piece could tell him when the Lighters were coming. "I sure can, lickety-split like."

"Me, too," Jeff called, and took Marissa stunned hand. "Come on, sweetheart. You know you're not getting rid of me. Marry me so Merrick will stop gloating."

Merrick chuckled and squeezed me to him with Lily smooshed between us. Marissa burst wide open, but Jeff just smiled and hugged her to him gently. "Of course I'll marry you, silly!" she said laughing as he palmed her flat belly.

"All right, let's get to it," Pastor said. "We need to get into position outside before they get here."

"Agreed," Miguel said gruffly from the corner and looked at everyone like they were nuts.

Danny stepped up and laughed as he said, "Don't be a stick in the mud, Aussie." He took Celeste's hand and yanked her forward with him. "Marry us, too, Pastor." He looked over at Celeste with a grin. For once, Celeste was speechless except for the surprised smile. "If something were to happen to me, I want to know that I at least got to marry my girl."

Though morbid, his words were the sweetest I'd ever heard out of his mouth. I knew I was beyond shocked when Merrick reached over with a chuckle to close my dropped jaw with his finger.

"Bloody h-" Miguel looked at Lily and rolled his eyes at his inability to curse right then. "Get on with it then. We've got a war to fight, if you all remember?"

"Why don't you just shut it," Rylee barked at him. "This may be all they've got and if they want to be saps, then just let them!"

"Ginger, you almost sound like a sap yourself," he goaded.

She started to unload on him, but her father stopped them. "If we don't get on with it, no one will be getting married, so shut your yaps. If anyone else wants to get hitched, come on up here," he said and laughed as he rubbed his hands together.

Jeff and Marissa, Cain and Lillian, and Danny and Celeste came forward. And Pastor got right down to business. "These folks wanna get hitched. Any objections?" Everyone chuckled, but stayed silent. "All right, men do you wanna marry these gals?"

"Yes," they all answered.

"I do," the pastor prompted.

"I do," they repeated.

"Gals, do you wanna marry these men?"

"I do," they said, but Celeste said, "We do, uh, I mean, I do."

Everyone laughed again as Pastor went on, "By the power invested in me, yada, yada, yada, I now pronounce you men and wives. You may kiss your brides."

They did. Cain held Lillian's face gently, Jeff was still rubbing Marissa's belly and Danny bent Celeste down all *Fred Astaire* like.

When we stopped clapping and laughing and whistling, reality crashed back down, but it was a lighter load. It seemed that we all had more than one reason to live now. We had more reasons to fight like hell.

I turned to my Keeper and kissed his chin. "Stake a Lighter or two for me."

He grinned. "Oh, I will." His grin melted into sweetness. "I love you so much."

"I know," I answered and bit my lip. "Just go before I break down, ok? Love you."

He nodded and I could practically feel his resistance as he stepped away. He blew Lily a kiss instead of giving her some long goodbye. And I loved him all the more for it. She didn't need to know that our whole world as we knew it could be ending right then.

I squeezed my eyes shut tight to block that thought and then tried for a smile as I grabbed Lily's hand. "Let's go pack some snacks, bug."

"K!"

I fretted about the food. We didn't have enough to feed everyone for very long. Thank you, Piper, and if I had been a cursing kind of person, I'd have been cursing up a hurricane. We almost had two bags packed when Lana came in with a sulking Calvin. She tapped me on the shoulder and signed 'Make Calvin help you while I help them'.

'Ok,' I signed back, 'Are you making grenades?'

She nodded and gave him a stern look. Then she pointed to the ground and mouthed 'Stay'.

He signed and said, "Yes, ma'am." As soon as her back was turned he huffed and hoisted himself onto the counter. "I am not a baby anymore. You guys have got to stop treating me like I'm a walking, talking toddler."

"You guys?" I asked. "So I'm lumped into that broad analogy?"

"You know what I mean. And yes, you do still try to keep me from fighting," he said softly. "I've grown a lot in the last few months, you know."

"That's only because you had to, Calvin," I told him as I stuffed the last bag of cashews in the bag.

"Exactly!" he yelled, but immediately held his hands up. "Sorry. It's just really frustrating that the Lighters treat me more like an adult that anyone else does."

"Why are you so eager to fight?" I asked in exasperation. I was getting a little tired of this same conversation with Calvin.

"Because…they took your parents, Miguel's wife, Mrs. Trudy…" His eyes turned glassy as he spoke her name. "They took Josh's parents." He blanched. "They took Josh, for that matter. It's not right, Sherry. It's not fair and we need to use every resource we have. I wouldn't have been given these hands if not for a reason."

I licked my lips. "You're right." And I realized that he truly was right. But I also realized that I wasn't about to plead his case when we only had minutes until battle. "I promise you as soon as all this is over, we'll make them understand for next time, ok?"

He started to argue, but I stopped him. "Pick your battles, Calvin. Now do as your mom said and help me carry this stuff."

"Ok," he agreed reluctantly. He jumped down and hoisted both bags, carrying them into the doorway. It was then that Marissa gasped, causing us all to freeze.

"Showtime," she said and everyone scrambled. I yelled for everyone to follow me that was going into the back room. Everyone else grabbed their weapons of choice and made their way to their battle zones.

I gave one more peek to Merrick as I turned the corner to the back hall. He was creeping up the stairs and turned back just in time to lock eyes with me. An eternity's worth of love and words transpired in that gaze. He mouthed, 'Always' and I smiled as the wall cut me off from him. I kept right on smiling even as my body tried to betray me and crumple. Lily needed me there and Merrick needed me to be strong for her.

Calvin threw himself on the couch dramatically and sighed loudly. Franklin joined us and everyone else who wasn't fighting. I almost welcomed Margaret and Pap's bickering because it took my mind off what was going on upstairs. Ellie worried her fingernail between her teeth and rocked herself slowly. Ann looked back at me as she clicked the lock into place.

I clicked on the lantern as she doused the lights in the room. We stuffed a comforter in the crack at the bottom of the door to keep light and sound in hopefully. I explained to Lily, Calvin and Franklin that if we needed to, they'd have to get in the closet and be as quiet as they'd ever been. They all agreed.

Franklin's mom was there along with Calvin's mom, Lana, but the dads were doing grenades, she said. She looked worried. I silently told her to join the club.

Lily asked Calvin to play dolls with her. He reluctantly joined her on the floor, but it soon became Chuck Norris meets Joy doll and she was going down repeatedly. Lily, scandalized, pouted, but began to retaliate. "Oh, no you don't, Chuck! I'm Piper, psycho Barbie!"

Everyone's eyes snapped to her before we laughed. It really hurt to try to hold in laughter when it was literally busting your gut. I wiped the corner of my eye and tried to scold her. "Bug, you can't make us laugh right now, ok? But that was awesome, nonetheless."

"Ok," she whispered and kept going with her assault in hushed, but forced tons. "Take that you sissy!"

I turned my attention from her to keep from laughing more and focused on the wooden door that was the only thing keeping the ones on the outside from us. Our fate was being held together with some seriously tattered cloth today. One moment of weakness and it would rip and we would be gone forever.

I shook that thought away and worried my heart pendant between my fingers. I saw Ann's heard jerk a little and she focused on a spot on the wall. I knew the Keepers were talking to her. "What, Ann? What?"

She looked at us all. "They're here."

A Feat of Massive Proportion
Chapter 4

Merrick

"Jeff, she's fine."

"Don't start in on me," he barked back and shifted the crow bar from one hand to the other in agitation and readiness. We waited just inside the back door of the store, the first line of defense for when the bastards arrived. "She's…I'm going to have…" He stopped and looked at me. "There's going to be a baby. Marissa's and mine. I'm going to have two people to look after now." He grinned a weird sort of grimace. "And I just know it's going to be a girl. I just know it."

"How do you know?"

He grinned wider. "That's my punishment."

I laughed. "It sounds like a reward instead."

"What would they say?" he asked seriously and nodded his head toward the heavens. "What would they think of what we've become?"

"I don't know," I answered honestly and sighed. "I can't say they'd be proud, but I hope they would understand at least."

"This time is different," Jeff insisted. "All the other times we came here, it was different. I feel like I've let them down…but I also wouldn't do anything differently."

"You're fine with not going to the After?" I asked. It had been on my mind a lot lately, with death knocking louder on our door every day.

"I…am," he said finally. "I really am. I know that the After is what was destined for us, but I feel like my destiny had changed. Marissa…"

I waved him off. "You don't have to explain to me. I know."

"Are you ok with not going?"

"Yeah, I am, but I would like to have seen it, just one time."

"Yeah, me, too. I'm glad you're still here. Um…where did you go? When you died?"

"I didn't go anywhere," I remembered. It was hard to believe that was all just a few minutes ago. "It was like I was waiting to see if it was real or not before I moved on."

He sighed and jerked, hoisting his crow bar in his hands. "Sense it?"

"Yep," I gripped my stake tighter. "Game time."

We waited. When we heard the crunch of snow under boots, we went for it. We blasted the door open, knocking the Lighter from his feet. The snow was slippery and melting, and the hot air from the blazing sun around us almost made me dizzy. I quickly staked the Lighter. The satisfying lightning shot up, and I hoped that the other Lighters saw so they'd know we meant business.

We looked around, but saw no one. I could still sense them, though.

They're still here.

Yep.

What game is this?

I think we're being ambushed. Above us on the roof, one o'clock.

I didn't turn, we just waited. When I heard his descent, the small cracking of shingles as he pushed from the roof, we both turned, stakes raised. We both skewered him and I had to turn my face away from the lightning since he was so close. But when my eyes reopened, we saw them. It looked like a hundred of them. They came over the roof, they came from around the building side, they came from the sky.

Ok, you can call them now.

Brothers, now. Like right now.

Max, Billings, Daniel and Ryan ran to the door with all of our cavalry in tow. I didn't want this anymore. I was so selfish, but I wanted to live my human life making love to my wife, playing with my daughter, eating with friends, bickering with Danny. I had chosen to give my Keeper life away, and it was worth it, but I didn't want to spend it this way. I didn't want to waste both of my lives.

Even as the thought coursed through me, I still found myself raising my stake and moving forward as they piled out of the store door. I ran to the forefront and Jeff followed me.

"Well?" I said to the waiting Lighters who watched. "What are you waiting for?"

That was all it took and they descended on us rapidly. I just hope we lasted long enough to keep the ones inside safe. That was all I wanted right then.

Danny slapped them on the face as he forced his compulsion on them. He must have told them to play dead because everyone he touched fell to the ground like a lump of coal. And I followed behind him and staked them each in turn. Billings and Jeff were tag-teaming them. Cain was blasting them into the building side and Ryan was trying to get to them before they could get up. It seemed that we had the upper hand.

But thinking or speaking too soon was never a good thing.

"Look!" we heard and saw another wave just like the first; over the roof, around the sides and from the sky.

Waves! Jeff said. *They're trying to tire us out!*

Well, it's working! I staked another one and groaned at the ache in my shoulder from one of their hits. *If they keep the waves coming for something bigger, we won't make it!*

What do we do?

Keep fighting. No choice. I'll call Miguel. Maybe a few grenades will make them slow their roll.

What in the worlds does that mean? He glared at me from across a Lighter's back. *Why are you constantly talking like Cain and his non-English gibberish?*

I laughed. *I just mean maybe it'll make them think twice if we have some tricks up our sleeve. Miguel! Grenades, now!*

I know I couldn't wait for his reply because there would be none, but I hoped he got the message and was on the way. The Lighters kept coming and we kept staking them and what not, but it wasn't enough. I saw the back store door swing open, but flames were what I saw. Then Miguel with his wolfish grin and swagger. "We improvised a bit!" he yelled and laughed as he threw a grenade, but it was trailed by a flaming rag of some sort that was stuck to it.

When it landed on the Lighter's chest, he engulfed in flames and within seconds, burned up with lightning. I heard Jeff in my mind.

Ok, this sucks, but it's still the same old Lighters. This isn't new. What were Ellie and Marissa talking about?

I shrugged and bumped into Daniel. He looked upset or agitated about something. "What?" I barked wasting no time.

He shook his head before looking at me with his now silver, human eyes. "I can't sense them, and they seem to not be able to sense me. I'm just a human to them now."

I sighed. "Look, that's a good thing in my book. It means you're not the enemy anymore."

The Marker's screech was loud and brazen. I turned in utter shock. Markers never came out in the daylight. Ever. I thought it had been a rule or law of their nature, but apparently not. Was this what she had meant? That we'd see something we'd never seen before. I hoped so.

Behind you!

I turned just in time to duck. The Marker's foot swiped my arm and we both yelled at the contact. I tried to tame the writhing and glanced at my arm. That bastard! It was like he didn't even care that he was going to injure himself by injuring me. I looked up to see Jeff staking him. He looked up confused and shrugged his shoulders.

I groaned as I got up, the venom from the Marker was relentless and plagued you for long minutes after the touch. But our little group didn't have minutes, so I pushed through the pain and pounced on a Lighter's back who was attacking Racine. Once again my skin grazed his on my wrist and we both jolted and groaned.

It seemed that I was just as desperate to save my people as they were to save theirs.

The rules were changing for us. I wasn't sure I liked that idea or not. But then the howl of a beast rang through the melting snow and debris scattering the yard, making us all stop in our tracks. I glanced around to look for it, but came up with nothing. The Lighters all looked at each other and then shot into the sky all at once, leaving us confused in the yard. We huddled together in a circle with our backs to each other's .

"Look alive," Jeff said to everyone. "This isn't over by a long shot."

"What was that? A freaking werewolf?" Cain barked.

"I don't know," I answered. "Just wait."

A loud thump resounded. It sounded like a giant's footsteps, as childish as that was. "There!" I yelled as a man came around the corner of the store.

He was normal looking enough, but his steps were deep and loud beyond their capability. He smiled at us from across the yard and even from that far distance I could see that his grin was too wide, his teeth too long. He took another step and it shook the ground under our feet. He kept coming and I could practically smell the fear wafting from our group. I was sure that our new guest could, too. I wished we had a few minutes for a pep talk, but time was up.

He got closer and clapped his hands, just once, but it was so loud that we all winced and covered our ears. He watched us and we watched him. He grinned once more and then blurred quickly to Jeff on the other side of us. He smashed his fist into Jeff's stomach, sending him crashing through us and skidding in the sludge of mush and snow. We picked ourselves up, but Jeff was slow moving.

What is that thing, Merrick? I've never been hit that hard in my life.

You got me, brother.

I felt my conscience zing in warning and looked up to see the thing moving his way to Danny, who was attempting to use compulsion on it. I blurred to Danny, throwing myself in front of him, but Danny kept concentrating. The thing slowed to a crawl pace before shaking, as if to shake off the compulsion. Danny screamed and grabbed his head before looking up in awe. "Ah, man. He threw my compulsion back at me."

Miguel threw a grenade at it, but it just blurred out of the way and… smirked?

"Get back," I told Miguel and Danny. "We need to regroup."

But the *thing* was already looking at Daniel. He spoke and his voice was painful to our ears. It was like grating metal. "Hello, traitor."

"What are you?" Daniel asked it.

"I am the balance. You switched sides, and not only that, but in such a traitorous way that evil was rewarded a new species. Me." He grinned, his gums dark and blackened with only God knew what.

"I…" Daniel looked back at us, his face impossibly white with terror. "I did this? But-"

"You and only you did this," the thing said. "How does it feel to know that your treachery to us is what will be all of your demise?"

"Don't speak to him again," Jeff ordered. "Let's kill this thing and be rid of it."

Daniel nodded and said, "I'll take my punishment. I deserve it."

"Not you, idiot! I'm talking about that thing!" Jeff barked in exasperation and pointed his stake at the new beast. It just laughed at us with a metallic crunch to its voice.

"And you," the thing said and appraised me with deep eyes. "You have death all over you."

"I have life all over me!" I yelled and charged it. I blurred and hit it in stomach with my shoulder. He was made of lead, or may as well have been, but he at least fell to the ground. With my ego intact with that fact, but bruised, I raised my arm to finish him with a fist. He opened his mouth and howled this howl that caused me to see stars it hurt my ears and head so badly. I fell to the ground beside him and covered my ears fully expecting blood to come seeping out.

Cain stepped forward, with Josh…uh, Simon right by his side, and blasted him with his palms out, but the thing just flew back a bit then back flipped back into a standing position. Cain gawked and looked around at us. This wasn't working. We needed to think.

It couldn't end like this. After everything…it just couldn't be the end this way.

Hot Hands
Chapter 5

Ryan

I watched as Jeff crumpled to the ground, taking another hit from the *thing* we had yet to identify. I ran my hands through my hair with frustration at having absolutely no idea what to do. My human brain just wouldn't think.

I began to feel the tug and buzz of my conscience. I cocked my head to the side, and hoped and prayed that Calvin wasn't doing anything stupid. He had begun to be aggressive in his efforts to help us and fight, but there was no way in hell or on this Earth I was letting that happen.

And when that thought hit me, so did another. My conscience…it wasn't buzzing because Calvin was in trouble, it was buzzing because this was Calvin's task. In all the hustle of fighting and trying so hard to keep our charges safe, we'd forgotten the most important thing. The reason the Specials were special and needed to be protected was to keep them safe until their task was presented to us and could be fulfilled.

I looked across the field to see Merrick shielding Danny and it all fell into place for me. I gulped down my petty fear and ran. I saw Miguel eyeing me as I ran passed him, like he couldn't believe I was being the coward I was.

But he didn't know what I was up to.

I yelled to let Marissa know it was me and she swung the door open. I ran past her without explanation right to the door that I knew Ann was guarding on the other side. I stopped for just a second and took a breath. Please, please, God, let me be right.

Ann, it's me. Open up.

Did something else happen? What are you doing down here.

Open the door, Ann.

She opened it with a scowl that quickly morphed into horror as she read my thoughts. "No! Ryan, what are you thinking?"

"He's my Special. Move." I deposited her to the side swiftly and went to Calvin. I tried really hard not to glance at Ellie, because I didn't want to deal with two things at once, but I still couldn't stop from glancing her way. She stood, her mouth slightly open, and watched me. Calvin looked up, shocked to see me and even more shocked when I took his arm and said, "Come on, champ. You're getting your wish."

He grinned and made a noise of excitement, but then Sherry stopped me with a hand on my arm.

"Ryan, what's going on?"

"He needs to do this," I said low. "I've been so blind lately, we all have. They're Specials for a reason, Sherry. This is his job, his *task*," I emphasized. Her eyes went too round and she bit her lip. She looked at Calvin with a look that a mother would give. I felt her pain, literally, it hurt me to think about this, but it had to be done.

"O-ok," she stuttered. "I mean," she turned to Lana, "he's not my son."

Lana was a different kind of woman and mother. She was perceptive beyond what most people were capable of. She gave me this look that told me she understood. She smiled and broke at the same time and signed 'What I wouldn't do to change things, but they are what they are.'

I bowed to her slightly in thanks and pulled Calvin's arm. He came willingly and said, "Yes! Finally! I've waited so long for this that I was starting to feel like it would never happen unless I *made* it happen."

I stopped in my stubborn, inhuman tracks. Was that a message directly for me or was it? I turned to Ellie, who still looked at me with a longing that I had known was there for a while now. She was shy, like me and my human self. I had kept her at a distance because I feared hurting her. If this all ended today, could I give up the After to stay here and die a human? What if I fell in love with her, would that change my decision? Merrick and Jeff were pretty adamant and sure of their decisions.

Could I risk breaking her heart to explore that?

My body answered for me as I found myself propelling across the carpeted floor to her. She let her arms fall to the sides and closed her eyes, squinting in a way as if I'd hit her instead of kiss her. I plowed into her, my arms going around her like I'd seen the other men do so many times. My lips took their first taste of female flesh and I felt a growl work its way into my throat. But she whimpered and that halted all movement, until she gripped my neck and tugged me closer. I felt clumsy and awkward, but she didn't seem to be complaining, and when she opened her mouth to me and I felt her tongue reaching for mine…

I pulled back and licked my bottom lip. I could still taste her there, smell her. Gah, I had to get out of here. I hugged her to me and spoke against her ear. Something in me that I didn't understand was extremely satisfied when she shivered. "I'll be back. I just couldn't go another minute without knowing what that felt like."

"I'm glad you did," she said breathlessly and laughed as she leaned back and touched my chin. "Please come back, because I really want to do that again."

I felt myself smile and stole one last peck before sprinting toward the door with Calvin. We'd wasted too much time already and I knew that I was going to have a fight on my hands with the other Keepers.

"Thanks, Calvin," I told him as we rounded the corner and clapped him on the shoulder.

"For what?" he asked.

"For making me brazen."

His face scrunched up. "You mean I said something to make you want to kiss Ellie?" He turned back and thought. "That was *not* my intention."

"That I know," I told him through a laugh. We went through the back door and he gasped as he looked around. "Still want to help?"

"Yep," he replied and gulped. "Let's do this, Ry."

I felt a ping in my gut. "Ry?" I asked and looked over at him. He was almost my height now.

"Yep, Ry. It suits you, man."

I chuckled, but sobered as a Lighter looked at us and started to inch toward us. "Stay close."

"*You* stay close. I'm ready to bar-b-que some Lighters."

"Calvin, be serious. This is…serious," I mumbled and tried not to question my decision. Then I heard Jeff in my mind and wanted to just block him and push him out. But I didn't.

Ryan, what are you doing?

It's what's right, Jeff. My conscience was buzzing. It's time for the Specials to start fulfilling their tasks.

Are you nuts! He got hit in the arm and swung around with distraction. I winced, but he just sat up and glared at me. *Our job is to protect them.*

Our job is to protect them until they can fulfill their task. This is Calvin's and I'm done talking about it.

I turned to Calvin. "Calvin, you ready?"

"What is that thing?" he leaned back and said. "It's wicked."

"Yes, it is. Do you feel anything?"

"Like what?"

"Like a…buzzing or a sense of purpose?"

Calvin laughed and gave me a strange look. "What are you talking about, Ry? Are you asking me if there's a bee in my pants?"

"What? No. I'm just asking if you feel anything different."

He laughed and clasped me on the shoulder like he was the adult and not the other way around. "You mean like if I'm supposed to be doing this or not? Yeah. I feel that. Stand back, Ry." He held his hands up in front of him just as the beast turned to grin at him. "I'm sick of this thing already."

I gawked and felt my teeth grind together at the injustice of the whole situation. Why was I given one purpose and one only, to watch over a boy, and then to have to turn him loose to find his own way against a beast? It felt so right in my gut and conscience, but so wrong in my human head.

I watched, as did we all, as Calvin and the thing went head to head. Calvin's hands burned and blazed. The beast smiled and cocked his head to the side in contemplation. "You sent a child to do the job," he mused. "A hot hands Special with an unjust ego the size of a Buick."

I stared at him. He seemed so…

"Human?" he finished my thought and grinned. "I am. I am the best of both worlds. Lighter part to read your thoughts, Taker part to deflect your gifts, human part to catch you off guard and my true nature, the Graphter, to end you all once and for all."

"Never heard of it," Jeff barked in his way that was becoming his own. "Sounds like a trick to me."

"Only the ones with the lower hand need to use trickery, Keeper," the thing mused with a smile. "You can call me the new Taker if you like, for I and others like me will continue to come and share all of his traits."

Calvin bolted toward him. I felt the gasp settle in my throat like a lump, but he apparently had a purpose. He ran straight to the things back, let his hands touch the beast's back and let his gift loose on him. He yelled, "If you wanna be the Taker, then die like the Taker!"

And he did, but not without one final look over his shoulder as he burned. It was as if he knew this was going to happen…and he was happy to make the sacrifice. I felt everything in me cringe and become uneasy.

Right as the lightning began to build, he said, "We know *right* where you are. We'll see you again."

And the lightning took him with a blast that knocked us all down on our butts. I coughed and sat up, staring at the spot that he had just been. Did that really just happen? I found myself blurring to Calvin, who had been knocked back the furthest. I leaned over him and shook my head when he leaned his head up to grin at me. "That was so awesome!" he yelled. "Did you see that?"

"No, Calvin," I chuckled in exasperation, "I had my eyes closed."

"You did not. You totally saw!"

"Yeah, I saw. You kicked butt."

"I can't wait to tell Mom!" he said excitedly.

I turned to Jeff. "Did you hear what he said?"

He groaned. "I heard. We better start packing everybody up."

I sighed and looked at Cain as he slapped his stake into his palm over and over in frustration as he said, "You mean we have to leave the store? After all the work and everything we've done-"

"Can't be helped," Jeff cut him off. "You heard that thing. Let's get this show on the road. The sooner we get out, the better."

He huffed and groaned as he and the rest of them beat a quick path back inside. I slung my arm over Calvin's shoulder as we followed them. "I'm proud of you, Calvin."

"Thanks, Ry. I'm kinda proud of me, too." He grinned and bounced excitedly. "Let the record show that I saved your behinds."

I shook my head and felt a smile tilt my lips. "Sure thing."

As we descended the stairs, I was plowed into by a sweet smelling thing that made my smile even larger. I wrapped my arms around her and felt the question I kept asking myself , 'Would I be able to leave when and if the time came?' spring to my mind, but I pushed it to the back.

This girl, this human female, had wiggled her way into my heart somehow. It happened without my consent, really. I'd tried to talk to Merrick about it once, about how his feelings for Sherry seemed to be all consuming. He didn't really know how to explain it to me. I could see exactly what he meant now. If you asked me how this happened or why, I would have no words to describe it.

Confused would be a good word.

I pulled back and looked at her face. She was fighting tears and I realized…those tears were for me. This human cared for me and though I struggled to understand the whys of it all, I understood one thing perfectly.

This girl had been sent to me, given to me really, for a reason and I intended to guard and look after her as if she were my own charge. She made me feel strange in my belly and chest, a buzzing that had nothing to do with my conscience. I felt warm and...content when I was with her. Content was something I hadn't felt since we arrived on Earth and the fact that she gave me a small slice of my old self back was a gift all itself.

I saw in her eyes as she tilted her face back that she wanted me to kiss her again. And this body wanted to as well. No, that was a copout.

I wanted to.

Me.

I wanted to feel the rush of blood that her kiss induced in me. So I did.

With my fingers wrapped gently around her upper arms I pulled her closer. She came surprisingly easy and then lifted on her toes to reach me. I felt her nose on my cheek first and then her lips. I let my body take over and was surprised when I once again put my arms around her and then lifted her feet from the floor in an embrace. But she just held on and it felt incredible.

For now, all those *What Ifs* would just have to wait. Today, I was taking my prize. When she tugged at my hair and pressed closer, I realized she was doing the exact same thing.

Smitten Kitten
Chapter 6

Cain

An eager L was waiting for me at the foot of the stairs and I let my newfound vulnerability fly like a flag and ran to her. It actually was a little liberating. The fact that I been crying like a chick just yesterday was not the issue on trial here. It was the fact that I liked that L and anybody else that wanted to take a gander could see that I was smitten.

I smirked as L smashed herself to me and leaped, wrapping her legs around me. She pressed her face to my neck and exhaled. I exhaled, too, and dreaded telling her the devastating news; that we had to pack up our crap and get the heck out of Dodge. She pulled back a little. "You're worried about something. I thought it was all over?"

"No," I sighed. "No, my little smitten kitten, it's not over."

She smiled, but stopped. "Not over? What do you mean?"

"Let Jeff explain. I'm more than willing to let Keeper boy take the fallout."

She gave me a weird look, but turned to look at Jeff. He must've already told Marissa because her hand gripped Jeff's so tightly that his fingers were white. Lillian looked back at me with alarm, but I gave her my best reassuring smile.

"All right," Jeff started, but plopped himself down on the bottom step and groaned, running his free hand through his hair. "It seems… Well, we took care of-Calvin took care of," he corrected and continued, "the new beast that we encountered. But it seems that they aren't finished with us. They know we're here now and will be back. We've…we've got to leave the bunker."

"What?" Sherry gasped. She was the only one who spoke, everyone else just stood stunned. She looked destroyed. She'd been here from the beginning and I could imagine she'd have lots of attachment to this place. I felt that familiar tug for me to go and hug her, make everything right again, but I held back. Poor girl had been through hell lately. Screw it. I tugged Lillian along with me and went to Sherry's side. I gripped her fingers and that seemed to jolt her. She looked up at me and the tears forming at the edges of her eyes made me ache. She squeezed my fingers and I squeezed back. Then I squeezed L's fingers and she squeezed back, too. I looked down at her, my wife, and I let my breath come out in a long puff.

This next step for us was going to suck something fierce, but we could do this. We *had* to do this.

Danny wrapped his arm around Sherry's neck from behind and we continued to listen to Jeff as he explained that our home was no longer our place of residence. The pastor went on about his place being a good replacement. Miguel argued that his place was destroyed.

"Yeah, no thanks to you!" Rylee told him, hands on her hips. "You and your bunch of Neanderthals ransacked the place!"

"We did no such thing! We didn't break your place, a Lighter did. We almost died trying to get out."

"Now, now," Pastor soothed them both. "Trouble has befallen us all, but that's no reason to go at each other's throats." He gave Rylee a hard look. "The fact that our place was destroyed is all the more reason to go back there. No one will think someone was staying there or would know there was a basement underneath. It's not as comfy as this place, it'll be an actual bunker, not the lovingly titled one you've coined this place as, but we'll be together and we'll be safe."

"Let's do it," Merrick said and his worried face turned to Sherry. "Let's go as soon as possible."

Max, who had been awfully quiet in the corner, stood. Then Patrick and Ann stood. Then Simon, A.K.A. Josh, stood. They seemed to be doing that silent agreement thing. Merrick gulped and nodded at Jeff. Jeff looked at his now wife and in a rare show of affection got down on his knees and pressed his ear to her belly. She giggled out of surprise and nervousness as she combed his hair with her fingers.

"I'll do anything to keep you safe, little one. Don't you worry." He looked at us all without getting up. "Let's get going. Bring only what we need. Every person needs to get a bag together, but only what you can carry. We'll leave at daybreak."

That seemed to be everyone's cue.

We scattered in a haste to pack our pathetic little lives into bags and boxes. I dragged L to her room first and helped her stuff her clothes into a pillowcase. Then we went next door and I put all my crap into my duffel.

I pulled her down with me and figured we'd pick up our bedding stuff to bring with us tomorrow. This was it. It was sad that my whole life fit into one duffel bag, and the sad little beat-up guitar next to it.

"Are we going to be ok?"

I wanted to just say *Yes,* I was just too tired to not be honest. "I don't know."

"This is it, isn't it? This is the beginning of the end. Everything that happens from now on is going to be life or death, stay or go, win or lose."

"Uhuh," I answered and rubbed my chin on her head. "It looks that way."

"So…this is our last night of peace? And privacy?" she said with a funny tone.

I frowned. "Yeah, guess so."

She lifted up to lean over me. She bit her lip and gave me this fluttery eyelid look and…holy… I gulped as the meaning of her actions hit me. I didn't gulp with fear, but with *finally!*

"Well, you are my wife now," I said, my smirk ear to ear.

"I am," she agreed and kissed my chin. "Make me forget that the world's ending, Cain."

My heart ached a bit at that, but I complied with a willing mind and body and even grinned as I said, "Anything you want, L."

I wasted no time yanking - yes yanking - her shirt over her head. It was at that moment that I realized just how long it had been since I'd been in this…position. With everything going on in our lives, it was like my body just forgot to care about sex, but with her under me and wanting me, it cooked me like a brush fire. I feverishly finished disposing of the clothes that hindered me and when my rib cage touched her sweet belly, a loud, embarrassing growl reverberated through me. It didn't matter that I could feel her ribs because she'd gotten so thin, as had we all. It was still *her.*

She giggled and rubbed her cheek against mine; scruff against softness. "I'm already yours, you Neanderthal. No need to stake a claim."

"Sorry," I said sheepishly, which pissed me off, in fact.

"Don't be sorry," she said and then took my lip ring between her teeth. I panted. "It's very cute."

"I don't want to be cute right now," I insisted and buried my face in her neck. She laughed again, but it was a breathy laugh of surrender. "I just want to make the world disappear, except for this little, tiny room."

"Please," she begged, her cool fingers pressing on my back.

And so I did, finally, slowly, fiercely and happily.

Oh, Happy Day.
Chapter 7

Sherry

"I'll keep watch tonight," Miguel announced. "Everyone else go to bed. Tomorrow, we're outta here."

No one put up any fight. We all drifted up and away. I saw Riley from the corner of my eye as she went to stand beside Miguel with Jethro. She was keeping watch, too.

I peeked over to see Lily had conked out on the sofa end. Danny reached down and picked her up gently. "I've got her. Go to bed." He glanced between us. "You need it more than any of us. Glad you're back to the land of the living."

I fought to not roll my eyes. "The death jokes are too soon," I snapped.

He nodded and smiled small indicating that he knew that. He and Celeste took Lily, and Merrick lifted me up in his arms. He carried me to our room and as soon as the door shut, it was like giving my body permission to freak.

I immediately started to shake and heave. He took us to the floor and wrapped his arms around me as I cried all over his shirt. He pressed me and squeezed in that reassuring way of his, up and down my body in waves. I lifted my face and slammed my mouth to his out of necessity. He let me know that this was what he needed, too, by gripping my legs and pulling me over him. With deft hands he pulled my shirt over my head and pressed me against him. The sigh that escaped his lips was full of relief as his hands wandered me as if he was checking to see if I was still really there in his palms.

I knew this ordeal had shaken him, too, not just me. I couldn't imagine what it must have been like for him to go through that. I'd ask him about it, but for now…

His face, from not shaving for days, maybe even a week, was coarse, but it just added to my pleasure. It grated the skin of my neck and the tickly sting ignited me.

He let his hand run up my ribs and I sucked in a breath. He spoke against my temple. "When I think about never touching your skin again…about never feeling your breaths against my neck…never seeing your pout face again." I chuckled sadly and accepted his kiss on the corner of my mouth. "I can't think about it. It hurts too much."

"Then don't think about it, Merrick," I coaxed and pulled his shirt over his head, too. "Just don't think at all."

He took my mouth deliciously before rolling us and placing me under him so I could feel his weight, the heaviness that I never thought I'd feel again.

This wasn't sex. This wasn't just making love either. This was about being as close as humanly possible. Not only was he careful and slow as if we had all day and night, but he was hungry yet sated in a way that I'd never seen before. One second he was a gentle starving man, the next he was a happy and serene guy with touches more gentle than I thought possible to still feel them.

After some hours - hours! - and lips tender from kisses, we lay akimbo on the mat, both breathing deeply and soundly. We listened to each other's breathing for a long time, switching positions and repositioning. Both of our sighs were telling of the inability to sleep for some reason. It wasn't that I wasn't comfortable or happy or…sated. I just couldn't turn my brain off. Eventually, after I'd rested on Merrick's chest for a while and neither of us had gone to sleep yet, Merrick sat up with us. "Put your clothes on, honey," he urged.

I looked at him blankly in the dark and he helped me put my shirt and jeans on. Then he took my hand and led me into the dimly lit hall. It only took a second to realize where he was going. When he slipped into Lily's door I smiled at the big sap.

He pulled me down with Lily in the middle of us and we both wrapped our arms around her. She stirred. "Daddy?"

"Right here, Lily bug."

"Daddy, you're hogging the blanket."

We chuckled, but I soon heard Merrick's sigh as Lily wrapped her little arms around my neck. I pressed as close as I could get, Merrick's arm squeezing my waist gently as I was encumbered with warmth and love.

Finally. We all slept as a family. One big, happy, glorious, special, unconventional, beautiful family.

"Oatmeal, bug. We don't know when we'll eat again. It might be a while until we get there," I urged her. I was packing up food in the kitchen and had Calvin and Franklin getting the food from the one pantry with food in it. I looked around the room. Mrs. Trudy's handmade apron that I still wore sometimes was hanging there by the fridge. My engraved wooden spoon that Danny made for me, that table that held good and bad memories.

Phillip being flipped over the top by Jeff, Merrick and my morning after breakfast, getting to know Marissa, Lily eating her noodles… So many dinners and discussions. So many things that would be so hard to forget.

I shook my head and turned my necklace charm in my fingers. It was warm to the touch as if telling me something, a signal maybe. That everything would be ok and that everything happened for a reason.

I took the two canvas bags I had and placed them by the stairs. Everyone was bustling about through the commons room and hallway. I watched Max as he perused the bookshelf. He looked sad on a whole new level. I understood. Trudy had been his charge and now we were leaving the only thing he had left of her. He made his way to the old record player and ran his finger down the length of it.

I went to his side and picked up the Etta James album we'd played over and over again. I put it on the turntable and let her loud croon distract me for a few seconds. Everyone else stopped, too, bracing themselves on the walls and stairs. We just listened and it seemed that though our lives were splitting at the seams, there was hope on the horizon.

I laid my head on Max's shoulder and felt a loud sigh go through him as *At Last* played.

I found a dream that I could speak to
A dream that I can call my own
I found a thrill to rest my cheek to
A thrill that I have never known
And you smile, you smile
Oh, and then the spell was cast
And here we are in heaven
For you are mine at last.

"I miss her, too," I told him. "I miss her a lot."

"But once we leave this place, she'll be gone for good," he mused and looked around. "At least here, I was surrounded by her things. When we leave this place, it's like my failure of keeping her safe will be unbearable."

"Max, what was her task?"

"I…I don't know," he stuttered. "Why?"

"How do you know her task wasn't to stab and distract the Taker?"

"I would have felt…" His brow bunched. "I mean my conscience was buzzing, but that was because she was in danger."

"Maybe," I mused back. "Either way, you and I both know that you didn't stop Mrs. Trudy from doing anything that she wanted to do."

His lips twisted. "I know. I just wish things would have been different."

"Don't. We. All." I gave him an awkward sideways hug as *Witchy Woman* by The Eagles began to blare out of the speakers. I looked over to see Danny wink and give a cheesy thumbs-up. I sighed and pushed his arm with annoyance playfully.

I went to finish up the packing, but stopped with a thought. "What are we going to do about Piper?"

Everyone stopped once again like my voice had some siren qualities. Max just looked straight ahead and eventually said, "Doesn't matter. We leave her here."

"Ok," I answered carefully. Everyone got back to work and in my book that was as good as agreeing. I had beef with Piper, but the Keepers had major drama. They were the ones who needed to decide whether Psycho Barbie got a get outta jail free card.

"Psycho Barbie?" Max asked with brow raised.

"Did I say that out loud?" He nodded and a ghost of a smile sat on his lips. "Daggumit! I have got to stop doing that."

I heard him chuckle in confusion as I walked away. Merrick came back with a couple of bags from the pantry. "That's all of it."

I winced. "All of it?"

He hesitated, as if that hesitation would spare me the heartache of his answer. "All of it."

I sighed and felt my body sag in defeat. Even my feet and toes seemed to not give a flip anymore and refused to hold me up any longer. I collapsed, all dramatic like into the chair and covered my face with my hands. Merrick came to stand behind me and rubbed my shoulders in a soothing motion. "Everything will be all right."

"Saying it doesn't make it true," I mumbled through my fingers.

"Actually, you're supposed to speak *only* good things. Never speak out loud the things you wish to not happen. You give those words power that way."

I peeked up at him, impressed. "Where did you hear that?"

"Well…God said it. I paid attention in Sunday School sometimes." He grinned.

"Who did you watch that went to Sunday School?" He ticked his head to the side and I guessed. "Orville."

"The one and only."

"It comes back to him a lot doesn't it. Maybe you should have married him."

"Maybe," he mused and leaned down to let his lips touch my ear. "But then I wouldn't be stuck on the run with my wife who makes me happy just to be alive." His fingers brushed my neck with the intention of soothing. "Everything I've ever gone through was worth it to be here with you right now. Nowhere else I'd rather be."

I gulped. I was already an emotional wreck and then Mr. Sap had to go and say something like that? I sniffed to try to stop the tears. "All right, you. Stop or I'll cry."

He pulled me up and held my chin so I had to look at him. "Where's my optimistic girl at this morning?"

"She hasn't had her coffee yet," I joked.

His face cracked with a gorgeous smile. "Well, we better remedy that."

He set out to make a pot coffee and for once, I just let him. It felt nice to have someone take care of me for a minute. The years of always looking out for everyone else and being the happy go lucky gal were catching up to me. I only hoped that when this was all over, there was a piece of my former self left to salvage.

A little bit later, I slipped away to have one final look at the Keeper who had it out for me from day one. She may not have needed or wanted closure, but I sure did. I needed to look at her human face and know that the Keeper inside was misguided and unhappy. That she wasn't evil, just the most unhappy and angry that one could get to drive them over the line of sanity.

I had to believe she was insane and not just someone not only capable of such acts, but plotting and enjoying them.

I stopped in front of her locked door. Crap, I'd forgotten. So I wouldn't be able to see her, but I could hear her. And she could hear me. I had one very important thing to say.

"You horrible witch."

I heard movement on the other side of the door. "Well, Sherry, Sherry quite contrary came to see me in the flesh. Not going to just leave like the other cowards, huh?"

I leaned on the opposite wall with my back. "I had something to say to you. The others didn't. That simple."

"Is Merrick all right?"

"Don't ask me if he's all right. It's your fault he was hurt in the first place."

"He's fine," she said and I almost heard her sigh. "If he wasn't you wouldn't be so calm about it. What did you have to say to me?"

"That I feel sorry for you." I heard a sound that sounded like scoffing. "No, really, I do. To be so pathetic and go to the lengths you went to ruin lives…it must be dark and bitter inside your head."

"I didn't ruin anyone's life. You all ruined mine!"

"No, we didn't. We can't help it that you were born a Keeper, that you had responsibilities that none of us can imagine. It wasn't my fault that Merrick fell in love with me either."

"Don't talk about him," she muttered. "I never want to hear that traitor's name again."

"Said the pot to the kettle."

"I betrayed humans, he betrayed our kind. It's different. Something you will never understand."

"You're right. For the life of me I can't understand why you'd betray humans when those other Keepers out there," I pointed in anger though she couldn't see me, "have charges that are human still. Your charge was human."

"My charge was stupid."

I took a deep breath and sighed. "Ok, we're done."

"That's it? You came down here for that?"

"I told you what I wanted to say. No matter what you did, no matter who you hurt, no matter all the damage you caused, we're still here, Piper. Still fighting for our lives, still together as a family. Your little stunts didn't stop anything, especially not Merrick and I."

"I still have faith that one day he'll come around."

"Useless wishes of a useless Keeper." I shook my head. "Goodbye, Piper."

"You're leaving?"

"We're leaving."

I heard her slam against the door. "I thought you were just bluffing a response out of me. You're really going to leave me here?"

"You killed Polly, Piper! You got Merrick stabbed and put everyone in jeopardy."

"Please don't do this to me!"

"Is that what Polly said when you fed her to the Lighters?"

Silence.

Good.

I walked away from the woman who tried with everything in her to destroy my life, and never once looked back.

Wherever The Road Goes
Chapter 8

Merrick

The snow was long gone by the time we started to load the vans. The mush and sludge of the sandy mud was making the trip back and forth from the door interesting. We had a little assembly line going and things were getting done quickly. Miguel and Jeff were both standing guard with rifles in hand and eyes to the sky. Whatever that thing had been, that Graphter, it wasn't something I wanted to meet again.

Miguel interrupted my thoughts. "Oi, I've got a bad feeling, mate."

"About what? This whole thing?" I guessed and he kind of nodded. "We've all got a bad feeling, Miguel."

"But this one's in my guts," he justified and tapped his belly. "I got a feeling like…like this might be the turning point. Like the last wave of the war is headed our way and it's make it or break it time."

"I think you're right about that." I stopped loading bags and boxes for a second, using the end of my shirt to wipe the sweat from my face. "I think that whatever happens next will determine everything."

"Straight from the Keeper's mouth, eh?" he mused and chuckled, his accent extra thick when he laughed. "So, hey, uh….I'm glad you're not dead and all that."'

"Thanks," I said wryly. "That just means the world, Miguel."

"Look, don't have a piff. I'm just saying is all. Things would be less… interesting without you around. Cain and Danny wouldn't have anyone to pickle with."

"That's true." I glanced at him sideways. "They do like to…pickle me."

"You know what I gettin' at. Come off it!" he feigned anger and punched my arm. "I'm not about to cry on your shoulder, mate, I'm just saying…glad you're not dead."

"Well, I'm glad I'm not dead, too. Thanks." I hoisted another box and asked, "So, that Rylee is a hellcat, huh?"

"Hellcat?" he scoffed. "Pfft. She's a pussycat, that one. All meow and no bite."

"Her teeth looked pretty sharp to me," I ventured and peeked at him to see his look of pondering.

"Well, I guess she's all right. She's prickly, but aren't all gingers that way?"

"Never met a redhead except for Kay before. I have no idea."

"Well, I've met loads of them and it's all in the genes. Like I said, she's harmless-" Miguel "oomphed" when a box slammed into his chest.

"Standing around doing nothing, Aussie? Wow." Rylee clapped. "I won the bet. Chivalry *is* dead. Hey, Jethro!" she yelled, cupping her mouth with her hands. "You owe me five bucks!"

"Listen here, Red, I'm doing plenty." He shoved the box into the back of the van all crooked and out of order. I rolled my eyes and fixed it as he went back to bantering with Rylee. "I'm keeping my eyes glued to the sky watching for something that might come and take your pretty little head off."

"Aw, you think my head is pretty," she said in her best girly voice and batted her eyelashes. Miguel was turned from me so I couldn't see his face, but he didn't say anything. Eventually her playful smile turned down and then she…blushed! She turned quickly and practically ran back inside the store.

Miguel looked at me with awe etched on his face. "Did you see that! Her cheeks were as red as that gorgeous hair."

"What did you do?"

He coughed. "Nothing. Just, uh, I was thinking of what to say, is all."

"And what did you come up with?"

He sighed. "I didn't. I couldn't stop staring at her freckles."

I laughed and he glared at me. "What?" I defended. "I remember being a babbling idiot once."

"Babbling idiot? What you mean by that?" he barked.

"You've got a thing for Rylee," I said slowly. "It's practically tattooed to your forehead."

He laughed, exaggeratedly. "Ha! Good one, Keeper. Me, like that red headed cactus? Nah."

"You sure are protesting a lot, Miguel." I loaded the last box in and slammed the doors shut, thankful that they shut without jamming from the full load. "She is pretty. Are you telling me she's not?"

"She's pretty enough."

"Pretty enough for what?"

"Someone else!" he barked and started to walk away, but stopped. "Don't tell Sherry about this, ok?"

"Ok, Miguel. Your non-existent but totally there crush on the red head who wants to serve your spleen on a platter is safe with me."

He grinned. "Thanks, mate."

I laughed as he walked away and peeled my sweaty shirt from my body. I threw it over the van top to dry hopefully. It was so hot, it should be criminal. I hoped that since the snow was gone that the new basement we were headed to wouldn't be too hot to stay. We needed a break. We need one thing to go our way.

I looked over at Jeff and saw that his shirt was off, too, and he was yelling at Billings to hurry up and quit 'lollygagging'. I'd never understood that expression.

I heard the radio start downstairs. The hatch door and store door were wide open so the sounds drifted to me with a slight echo. I heard Billings yell, "Yeah, Billy Joel! About time you played something decent around here."

I had no idea who Billy Joel was, but it sounded nice enough.

No one had brought me any boxes in a while, even though the van was full, they didn't know that. I trotted through the door to see what was up. Rylee, Ryan, Miguel and Max were going at it about when we should leave.

Apparently, Max and Rylee were for waiting until nightfall, and Miguel and Ryan were trying to get them to understand that we needed to go right then.

"Lickety-split!" Miguel yelled. "You really think they are going to give us the whole day to regroup and not try to ambush us before the day's over? You're loopy."

It sounded weird to hear the fighting over Billy Joel's cheerful words. "*For the longest time. Whoa, for the longest time*."

Rylee yelled back. "You don't know anything about strategy!"

"Ginger, leave this to the big boys, ok?"

I felt my mouth open a little at the look she blazed his way. The steam coming from her ears wasn't even the worst part. She walked right up to him and grabbed his shirt front. "You listen here, buddy. I am not some little sweet girl to be tossed in the back with the women and children. I will wield a knife just like the rest of you." Her lip quivered a bit as she went on. "I *deserve* to earn my revenge, just like the rest of you."

Miguel caved, just like that. He pulled her to him and wrapped his arms around her. She put up a fight just for show. If she wanted to displace herself, she could've. "I told you, don't pity me."

He smiled down at her, and it was a smile I'd never seen on him before. I felt instantly like I was intruding, and judging by the awkward looks on Ryan and Max's faces, they agreed with me.

Miguel said low, "So, a guy has to be full of pity to want to put his arms around a pretty girl with spirit?" She looked stunned in that girly way that shows that a guy completely surprised her. He put his hand behind her head and pulled it to rest on his chest. "Just rest here a bit. And don't you worry about those bastards, love. You and me are gonna make them pay if it's the last thing we do."

She sighed as if the weight on her shoulders had been lifted and closed her eyes. I'd never seen her face relaxed like that before. She looked so fragile and tired that way. I guess that's why she never let herself show that. She had this hell bent flag to carry that said she was too strong to be affected.

He leaned against the wall at his back and they just stood there, the shadow from the stairs above covered their faces.

Daniel leaned over and asked, "What's a ginger?"

"Redhead," I answered, knowing what he was going to say next.

"Why not just call her a redhead?"

"Humans have an affinity for nicknames."

He looked puzzled, but shrugged and walked back to the hall. Ryan and Max beat feet to get out of there, so I went to find Sherry and see if she was almost ready. Instead I found Lily. She was in the back corner of the commons room and she was crying. Her arms reached for something that she couldn't touch and she jumped and stomped her foot. Then she started to climb the shelf.

I blurred to her and caught her up to me. "Whoa, what are you doing, baby?"

"My doll," she whined and pointed. "My doll, Miwey, is up there."

I looked up and saw the doll's leg sticking out of the shelf from behind a book. I reached in and grabbed her. A small stack of books fell to the ground. I just looked at them. It was pointless to worry about it or clean it up. This wasn't our home anymore. I held the doll out and Lily took it, sighing with relief. With all of Lily's newfound talents - bringing people back to life, healing Daniel and Lillian, seeing Trudy - it was easy to forget that she was still just a child.

I kissed her cheek. "Who gave Miley to you?" The poor doll was still missing a leg and ragged.

"My sister." She stroked her hair lovingly. "I love Joy, but my sissy gave me dis doll and said she had super powers. She had to leave me and said that dis doll would pwotect me. And it did, Daddy!" She looked at me excitedly. "Uncle Jeff and Uncle Miguel found me when I was getting her outta da twash can."

I felt a hard tug on the organ in my chest. It pumped sympathy out and made me squeeze her to me. She patted my neck like I was the one who needed comforting. Maybe I was, but then she said, "Daddy, you're squeezing me."

"Sorry, baby," I apologized and leaned back. "You keep your super power doll with you until we get to our new home, all right?"

She nodded like it was serious. "I pwomise."

"Good girl. Let's go find Mommy."

"She's in the kitchen," she said matter-of-factly and swung her arm while holding my hand with the other. "She said it was filthy!"

I chuckled. Leave it to Sherry to worry about the kitchen being clean during the possible end of the world.

Sherry was wiping the counters and then bent down to scrub the cabinet doors. She bent directly from the waist and I felt my lips twist even as I twisted my head to check her out. Those jeans were looking pretty good on her right about then. Though she was getting so thin, she still was gorgeous. Lily ran to the table and snuck a small pack of Raisinets. She saw that I caught her, but I nodded and smiled as she took off.

I inched to Sherry quietly and palmed her warm behind. She jumped, gasping, but smiled when she saw it was me. I bent so she could reach my neck and she wrapped her arms around me. I wrapped mine around her slim waist as well and then palmed her behind again. She giggled and squirmed. "What's gotten into you?"

"Those jeans," I said and heard the low notes in my voice. "That's what."

She didn't laugh, but smiled at me like she understood. She brought her hands down and rubbed my bare chest, my bull tattoo actually, with her fingers. He fingers inched to the red mark on my arm; my reminder that Markers and Keepers don't mix. "I am going to miss our little room."

I chuckled. "Me, too. Never thought I'd say that."

"Me either. But it's true." She sighed and bit her lip as she looked up at me. "I wish…we had time for one more go, ya know. With privacy."

I felt the blood jolt in me. "Mmhhmm." I leaned down to nuzzle her neck. "Who says we can't?"

She laughed and pushed me back a little. "That one says."

I peeked behind me to find Lily covered in chocolate. Knees to face. I smirked guiltily, but Sherry just laughed and called Lily to her. She hoisted her on the countertop and cleaned her up. Then she let Lily run off to play and came back to me. She pulled me down again and kissed my lips gently. "Love you."

"I know," I sighed in happiness.

"I know I need to stop cleaning." She looked around the uselessly clean kitchen. "I just can't imagine Mrs. Trudy leaving it any other way." She licked her lips. "Max is having a hard time."

"I know. I heard, but there's not anything to do about it. He's acting really strange lately anyway."

"Yeah," she half heartedly agreed.

"Hey," Danny said from behind us and jumped to sit on the counter. "What's up? We heading out or what?" Wow, that kid looked weird with a beard and shag head. He wasn't as hairy as the rest of us, but for someone who had shaved twice a day before, he sure looked different now.

"We're heading out," I said with certainty. Max nor anyone else was going to stop me from getting my family the hell out of here. In fact…

I don't know what the hesitation is about, but we're leaving today. It's the best thing to keep everyone safe. It's daytime, they won't be expecting us to move in the day. Honestly at this point, I don't care if someone decides to stay or not; we're going.

No one has a problem with leaving now, Jeff intercepted. *Who has a problem?*

Max sighed. *I have my reasons. I think I'm the only sane Keeper in this group anymore! Everyone else's heads are crammed up some human's butt.*

Now hold on just a minute! Kay yelled, making me squint. *Maxwell, just because your charge is gone doesn't mean that we're wrong for still being close to ours.*

I didn't say that!

I butted in with, *Listen, I wasn't trying to start the great debate, I'm just saying, my family and I are leaving with or without you. I hope you come, but don't try to talk us into staying. We need to get out of here as soon as possible and I'm not going to wait around because someone's trying to change everyone's minds.*

Duly noted, Max barked.

I let my eyes focus again and Sherry was watching me with a curious expression. "It's so weird how your eyes are still open, but you blank out like that when you talk Keeper talk."

"Sorry. I just remembered something I wanted to tell everybody."

"No, it's fine."

Danny said, "Well it's not cool with me. Rude, man." He grinned and then laughed when Sherry slapped his leg.

"Where's Celeste?" Sherry asked.

"She's crying in the second room."

We jerked to look at him. "What?"

"Yeah," he sighed. "She's pretty upset. She doesn't want to leave, she's scared, she'll miss this place 'cause Mrs. Trudy was here...and her mom."

"Well then go and hug her, you idiot!" Sherry yelled and glared.

"I did!" he defended and dodged her swat. "She said she was fine, that she just needed a minute."

We heard a loud sniffle from the door and turned to see Celeste. He was telling the truth. She looked wracked.

"Celeste," Sherry sighed and opened her *Mother Hen* arms up to her. She went right into the semi-circle her arms were making and I stepped back a step to give them some room. She sniffled again and let Sherry stoke her back. "Now, what's wrong?"

"Well, Mom…" She didn't finish.

Sherry hugged her for real and I ticked my head to Danny to follow. He pressed himself to Celeste's back and whispered something in her ear. She nodded and he kissed the side of her neck before following me out.

"Dude, this sucks."

"Yep," I said, letting the 'P' pop to show my annoyance. "I'm just ready to get you guys out of here."

"I'm right there with you, Pops."

I looked at him sideways with my *What The* face. I knew what the little twerp was getting at. "I am not your father."

"I know." He chuckled a little bitterly. "*You're* here."

"Danny, look." I stopped us. "I know things are rough right now and everybody seems to be going down memory lane, but I've got to tell you, I need you, man."

"Ok," he said and crossed his arms. "What's up?"

I sighed in a groan. "We are going to have to trek it back to that dilapidated dying facility with all the girls and kids and Specials, right there in the open daylight." I hoped he understood my urgency. "One wrong move, one person who thinks something's out of the ordinary, one thing. That's all it will take and we're done. I need you, you get me?"

"I got you," he said strongly. "I get it."

"Good. Now go get Celeste and make sure you have everything." I turned to go make sure everyone was ready. "Because we aren't ever coming back," I called over my shoulder.

Right Place, Right Time
Chapter 9

Sherry

Lily was on my lap as Jeff cranked the engine and began to pull away. She wasn't buckled in, but I could've given a rat's patootie about that right then. If we got pulled over by the cops, her seatbelt would be the least of our worries.

Besides, we were all crammed into the vehicles like disgruntled sardines anyway, there was no room for law abiding citizens anymore.

The Enforcers were in full swing, but Billings, who was in the front seat making a Marissa sandwich with Jeff, had conveniently worn his uniform and said he'd tried all he could to deter them if we did get caught on the way there.

I couldn't help myself. I turned in my seat to watch as the store got smaller behind us. It was just a stupid gas station. An eyesore, a place that held some of my worst memories…and some of my best. It was bittersweet with a side of heartache to leave it.

I felt Merrick's hand on my shoulder and I turned to look at him. He had that look on his face, like he could read my thoughts. "The new place is even better."

"Really? I thought you destroyed it?" I teased.

"Kind of," he said and grinned. "Actually it was your brother's fault."

"I'm not surprised," I quipped and leaned my head on his shoulder. I peeked as a car passed us. It was Cain and Ryan along with their ladies and Calvin in the Jeep. Show off.

"It'll be great," he said with as much spark as he could muster. "It's the perfect hideout, plus Pastor and the others had quite a stash of supplies we had to leave behind there. It should help."

"Food?" I asked excitedly. I felt the pulse jump in my neck.

"Yep. A couple crates if it."

I sighed and sagged against him. "Oh, thank God. I was so worried about feeding everyone. That helps some." I turned my head to lay against his, my side to his front. He rubbed his nose against my forehead, breathing me in.

We heard screeching tires and looked up. The Jeep was swerving and braking swiftly. I gasped as it went up on two wheels trying to avoid whatever was in the road. Merrick pressed me to the seat along with Lily with his outstretched arm.

Jeff cursed and slammed on the brakes, too. The van behind us did the same. The stench of burnt rubber filled the van, but I was barely breathing waiting to see what was going on. Merrick and Jeff both cocked their heads at the same time. Ryan was talking to them. Jeff cursed again and yelled, "It's a trap!"

Merrick nodded, his eyes unfocused as he listened or spoke Keeper talk. I held my breath. Cain's door opened, then Ryan's. That was when I saw the dark object on the pavement. It was a body…

Then people jumped out of the ditch with guns, yelling and pointing, crouching as they barked orders like a military mission. The body from the pavement lifted fluidly and bounced on its toes. It was a girl, or woman I should say, and she was smiling. She trailed her fingers across Cain's chest in a cocky *Nana Booboo* motion, but that was so stupid. I held in my cringe when he grabbed her around her neck and swung her to hold her hostage against his chest.

The ditch men traded glances that said *Is she worth the fight?* What was this? Some elaborate, but apparently horribly thought out plan to what? Rob us? I rolled my eyes and huffed. Idiots. I guessed people were just desperate.

But when they started moving toward the van, toward Lillian and Ellie, Cain was done playing. He tossed the woman aside, probably because they didn't seem too worried about her anyway, and clotheslined the guy closest to him. Daniel blurred passed the van to help Cain with Max on his tail.

"Ah, crap," Jeff complained and opened his door just as Merrick was opening his. "Stay here with Billings, sweetheart."

"You, too," Merrick said to me and they both blurred to Cain's side. Ryan had jumped out of the Jeep, too, and was already helping keep the guy's friends off Cain. Though he didn't seem to need much help. He kicked one guy in the guts and then punched another in the throat. They both went down and the other robbers looked around in question. The Keepers yelled back and forth with them, probably trying to get them to join us or something.

The knock on my window startled Lily and I both. I glared at Danny before cracking the door to talk to him. "Don't sneak up like that."

"Sorry. What's going on?" he asked and looked at the fight as if he wanted to join them.

"Someone tried to rob us or something," I mused and squeezed a sleeping Lily on my lap. "What are you doing?"

"Just seeing if they needed help." He glanced at Billings. "Why aren't you helping?"

"Woman and children duty," he said calmly.

"Uhuh. Well, I guess I'll- oomph," Danny cut off and I looked up just in time to see him get tackled. I scrambled to the window to see and saw Danny slap the guy's face and compel him to roll over and play dead. He got up furious. "Hell's bells, man!"

Merrick blurred to us and puffed an aggravated breath. "Sorry. They didn't believe us. They think we're trying to trick them into showing us where they're staying. I don't know what we're going to do with them."

Billings leaned over Marissa and yelled, "Hog tie 'em"!

Merrick and Marissa shared a look before she said, "For once, I'd go with what this one says. Let's just secure them and leave them."

"I take offense to that, but I'll help anyway," Billings spouted indignantly and got out.

"She fell asleep, huh?" Merrick asked, looking at Lily.

"Yep. Girl can sleep through a freight train."

"Good," he said wryly. "She needs to learn to sleep with fifty other people in the room with her."

"Me, too," I grumbled. I looked out to see them tying the guys, back to back. "What was up with them?"

He huffed and leaned his big tan arms on the window. "They thought we were part of the Enforcers. They think you guys were prisoners and we took all of your stuff. They were about to pull a Robin Hood act and steal it for themselves and the other misfortunates."

"Others?"

"They claim to have a big pile of people somewhere. Whether it's true or not, we can't risk trying to join forces. We just need to get where we're going and settle in first."

"Yeah." I shook my head. "Wow."

"Let me make sure everything's situated and then we'll go."

I nodded and stroked Lily's hair. When it was a common, mundane event to have to tie up strangers and leave them on the side of the road, you knew things had gotten bad.

We pulled up in front of a seriously busted up wooden warehouse looking… thing. Merrick was right. Danny had destroyed the place. Jeff and Pastor went first to make sure that no one had found the basement and all the resistance goodies they'd been collecting.

I hugged Lily's sleeping body to mine. I wondered how all of this was going to work. As I stepped out of the van with Merrick's help, I looked toward the town to see billows of black and gray smoke hugging the sky. Cain and the rest of them followed my line of sight and we all gawked at the sight.

Then I gasped when a Marker came into view in the distance. Then another. Merrick grunted and strained to see better. Was this real? Markers flying right over the town, not even trying to hide?

I looked up at Merrick for answers, but I could tell by his face that he had none. I felt my arms tighten on my precious cargo out of instinct. Things really were going to hell.

Jeff and Pastor gave the all clear and we all eased out of the vehicles and climbed a ladder to the roof. Merrick took Lily from me and jetted the ladder with ease. It was impressive to say the least.

We got a better look at the city now that we were higher and it didn't make it look any better. The smoke and haze covered it completely and it was wide and encompassing. "We'll talk about it," Merrick said and urged me to his side as he woke Lily to get us into the tunnel. "Let's do one thing at a time and get all this stuff inside first."

I nodded and made myself look away from the destruction of Effingham. All those people. Something bad was happening. No wonder those people tried to rob us. Things were way worse off than we thought.

We followed them over to the elevator and took turns going down. The stairs were a sore subject it seemed and Danny's face turned red and angry when I asked if we could just take them instead. So I didn't bring it up again.

It was quite a trip and once we arrived, I wasn't really impressed, as bad as that sounds. I thought there would be some semblance of rooms or separation, but there literally was none. It was one big room with a couple of doors that I assumed were closets or storage sheds. Merrick immediately went to the stairs and began to put stuff in front of it to block it. He laid a chair sideways and then threw a broom and box on top of that. He turned to look at everyone. "No one goes on the stairs under any circumstances."

"Duh," Rylee spouted and then yelled at someone for messing with her 'things'.

"Now, Rylee," her father admonished. "Just because we lived here first doesn't mean you can claim everything as *yours*." She huffed and pulled the chair away from Ellie anyway. She plopped herself down and crossed her arms violently. "Ok, home sweet home," he announced and sighed as we all looked around. "We better just be happy to have a roof over our heads, yeah?"

"Even if it could collapse at. Any. Moment," Rylee said looking at the roof with disdain. We all glanced up. It looked sound and safe to me. I got it. She was speaking figuratively. Ah…

"All right," Jeff said and swiped his face with a hand, "it's been a long day. Let's get settled in, guys."

Merrick was walking all around the crates in the middle of the room. They were marked "Canned Goods" and "Explosives". There were lots of them. "Where did you get all this stuff from?" he asked Pastor.

"Well," he drawled and smiled, "the Lord provideth."

"So you're not going to tell me," he remarked and scowled.

"Oh, I'll tell you, but I don't think you'll believe me." He laughed. "We were walking down the road toward this place. Well not toward it, just walking. They were more of us then," he said sadly and then went on. "We had just about used every resource we had. No food was left and we were basically looking for a place to die peacefully. And then there they were. They were sitting smack dab in the middle of the road."

Merrick frowned, a deep groove in his forehead that meant he was really thinking about something. Everybody else had stopped to listen. "In the middle of the road? Weren't you suspicious that it was too easy?"

"Sure we were. But you know what they say about a gift horse."

Rylee butted in, "That you don't leave it in the middle of the freaking road."

Pastor went on. "We cracked them open and it was exactly what it looked like." He smiled and lifted his dirty hands. "Manna from Heaven."

"Can we cut all the religious mumble?" Billings said and crossed his arms. "Let's get back to what's in the crates."

Pastor took his hand and ran it under the word "Canned Goods" on one crate. "Canned goods," he said sarcastically. I wanted to laugh.

"Ha. Ha. What about the rest of them? You mean to say that you found crates in the middle of the road that really had guns and explosives in them?"

"That's what I'm saying."

"Well then!" he yelled and laughed. "Let's go door to door to the enforcement facilities and give them a little 'Hey, how you doing'."

"We can't do that. There are innocent people in there!" I said and found my chest heaving a little with anger. I knew what he was saying, I understood, but I had been one of those people just days ago.

He sighed and twisted his lips. "Sorry. You're right. I'm just shooting in the dark to find a solution here."

"I know," I answered back and waved off Merrick's look of concern. "I know."

"Sherry's right, of course," Pastor continued. "We can't do that. The reason I kept it was because I knew there would be a right time. That one day, there would be a moment of weakness or bloated egos on their part and we would be able to take advantage of it."

"You got a TV in here?" Cain asked. "We need to see if our little blip at the hospital and then the store and all made the news. Hadn't thought about that until now." He looked at Jeff and Marissa. "I bet they've got all kinds of people looking for us."

"Sure," Pastor said. "It's small, but it works." He went to a small cabinet on the wall and opened the doors. The nine inch TV sat there, dusty and beautiful. He flipped it on and we watched as the non-stop news played us a story about Malachi's recent 'good work' - even though he was dead as dead could be - at the new enforcement facility near there. They'd taken over someone's house to use as headquarters since we'd demolished the jail there.

And then a man came to the podium at some sort of press conference, and he looked pretty irritated. He coughed dramatically and then explained that they were now upping the ante on the rewards.

"Due to the circumstances that have risen in the past few days, we have decided to increase the reward for anyone who catches and brings a rebel to us or gives us information regarding their whereabouts. The reward is now twenty thousand dollars for the capture…"

The rest of his words were lost on us. I sat in disbelief. Well it explained why the town was in disarray. Everyone was looking for rebels. Miguel bolted and turned off the offensive TV. Billings started laughing hysterically. "Twenty thousand! Twenty thousand! For twenty thousand I'll turn my own self in!"

"Billings," Cain warned, but he was on a roll.

"We don't stand a chance now. It was bad before, but now we've lost the store, we've lost our privacy, we're losing people left and right, ambushed every time we turn around, we've got no way to gain the upper hand now, and on top of all that? We're being hunted by money hungry desperate people." He laughed once more, bitterly and angrily. "We're gonna die."

I took a deep breath and looked over at Lily, who had woken in my arms. She was looking at Billings like he was some sort of alien.

"You have to bewieve in it, Mister Biwwings," she spouted.

He looked at her. He sighed, his chest deflating with sadness. "I'm sorry, Lily. I shouldn't have said that, ok?"

"Why you so sad?"

He smiled. "Cause I feel like everyday it's raining on us."

Calvin busted through Ryan and his mom and started belting out, "*If you walk away, everyday it'll rain, rain, raaaai-a-a-ain! Ooooooh!"*

We all stared a little before laughing at him. It was obvious what he was trying to do, so when Franklin joined him and they continued singing as Lily squealed and ran to dance with them, I was pretty proud of the kid.

"Don't you say goodbye! I'll pick up these broken pieces 'til I'm bleeding if that'll make it right! 'Cause they'll be no sun light, if I lose you, baby! And they'll be no clear skies, if I lose you, baby!"

Calvin held Lily's hands and danced with her as they sang. She didn't know the words, but twisted her legs and hips to his tune. Cain grabbed Lillian and started dancing with her, too. It reminded me so, so, so much of the bunker.

And it made me realize that home is where you make it. Yes, the bunker was a good spot and convenient and we'd been there so long it just seemed wrong to leave. But my home was my family. And we were all right here together. And dancing to Bruno Mars without a bed to our names or a shower to bathe in, but we were smiling and alive.

To me, that was everything these days.

Everything.

Blade of Fire
Chapter 10

Merrick

I didn't dream often. I have no idea why, but it just never happened or I never remembered them. So to have my first nightmare was brutal. And to wake up sweating and panting, having Sherry fuss over me, was worse.

"Are you ok?"

"Fine," I answered gruffly.

"Merrick, don't placate me!" she hissed and I turned to look at her in the dark. "I know you had a bad dream, I heard you. Now what happened?"

I sighed long and loud to show her I absolutely didn't want to tell her. But I did anyway. "I had a dream about leaving you."

She stiffened all the way to her bones. "What?" she squeaked.

"No, not leave you that way." I eased her to my lap and wrapped my needy arms around her. "Leave you like…death." She gasped. "When I…died," I said, because that was exactly what I had done, "I saw this light. Cheesy, I know, but it was all encompassing and it was just for me. Though I knew it was meant for me to go through," I pressed my lips to her temple, "I just couldn't leave you."

I thought she would cry, get sappy, make me console her, but no.

She laughed.

I felt my eyebrow reach my hairline and leaned back to see her face in the shadows of the big room we were all camped out together in. Lily slept on a sleeping bag on my other side and the room was quiet and oddly peaceful.

"And what's so funny?"

She giggled once more and then wrapped her arms around my neck. She let her legs straddle me before whispering in my ear. "I think I'm a little slap happy. I can't sleep, and you telling me that you defied death and refused to leave me was just suddenly funny." She leaned back. "I'm sorry," she said, but she didn't look sorry. She looked like she was about to have another giggle fit.

I found myself chuckling a little, too. "Honey," I whispered, "I don't know what I'd do without you. I'd be a very lonely and disgruntled Keeper without you here to keep me laughing and happy."

"Good," she said in return and pushed me down. She lay down on my chest and sighed deeply. I rubbed her back and loved feeling her heartbeat through our shirts as our chests pressed together. Within a minute she was asleep, breathing deeply. I chuckled again, the movement shaking her a little. She was something else.

I let sleep claim me as well and this time, I dreamed of our unreachable future, not the horrible past. I didn't know which one was worse.

In the morning, we all woke and decided that some arrangements needed to be made. Everyone piled randomly on the floor at night wasn't going to work for me or anyone. So Sherry, Lillian and a few others started putting up clothesline rooms; little nooks along the walls that were separated by sheets on clothesline wire. And the rest of us got to moving the crates and going through it all. Making some order to the chaos.

It took us pretty much all day to get everything 'livable'. There was no running water for showers. The ladies pitched a fit about that one. So we rigged a closed off space for taking 'bowl baths' Miguel called it. None of us really understood how good we had it before, I guessed.

There was a toilet. As in one toilet in a small toilet closet with no sink. I shook my head as I looked at it. Could be worse. There could be *no* toilet.

"Where is the food?" Sherry asked. I turned to find her eager, red face behind me.

"Haven't you done enough today?"

"Nah," she said and wiped her cheek with the back of her hand. "I need to see how we're doing on food so I can have a little piece of mind."

I grimaced. "Well…"

She stopped and ticked her head to the side. "What?"

"There was a crate of canned food," I hedged.

"Yes," she dragged out.

"But it was a whole crate of green beans."

"What!" she shrieked.

Miguel passed us and laughed. "I told you not to tell her."

"Beat it, Aussie." I put my hands on the tops of her small arms. "Baby, it'll be fine."

"How? Explain how the only food we have plenty of now is basically just water and won't help to keep us full or alive, is fine."

"We'll just have to do food runs again. No way around it."

She groaned. "Oh, my gosh. We can not get a break!"

"Sherry," I whispered and put my arms around her, lifting her to my level. She sulked and refused to meet my gaze. "Sherry," I sang, taunting her.

"What?" she muttered.

"Look at me." She did immediately. "We'll be ok. I didn't defy death just to die of hunger, ok?"

She sighed dramatically. "Fine."

"Fine?"

"Fine!" she laughed. "Fine."

"Good." I kissed her forehead and then let mine rest there as I set her feet to the concrete. Her tingling touch was my constant reminder of everything I would've missed if I wasn't on this earth any longer.

"Oi!" Miguel shouted. "You hear that?"

We all stopped and listened. Katie shushed Sky who continued to cry, but we could still hear it. Trucks. Big ones. Did it mean something?

"We need to go scout," I told him and he nodded. "I'll be back," I told Sherry. She nodded and hugged Lily to her as she gripped her leg. Calvin and Franklin followed behind me with stakes in hands. I turned and gave them a look.

Calvin said, "We're with you. Let's go scout."

I glanced at Ryan who was on our tail and he nodded as he passed us. "Let's go!" he called over his shoulder.

"Sweet!" Calvin chimed and went past me, too. I sighed and looked at Laura and Eli. They watched as Franklin followed Calvin. "I'll keep an eye on him. We're just going to get a look."

He nodded as any parent would in that situation. Reluctantly.

Daniel started to come, but I waved him off. "You can't sense them, but we don't know if they can sense you. Just stay here, ok?"

I ran to catch up and we rode the elevator up to the roof. Jeff and Miguel had come with us, and Billings, too, apparently. I could hear him cursing about the soot from the roof on his boot.

"Get down!" I told Calvin and pushed both of their heads down. There was a long line of big trucks roaming around the highway. They were going back and forth. Not necessarily looking at the warehouse, just the road in general. I felt a little better about it.

But then I heard the familiar screech of a Marker and peeked to see one coming the opposite direction. "Search is in full swing it would seem. Good thing we left the store when we did," I told Miguel. "They would have caught us coming down the highway."

"Bloody right," he muttered and ducked lower. He caressed his leg over his pant leg, the Marker's scratch. "You think they're looking for us or just searching for rebels?"

"Anyone's guess." I looked around. "But they aren't moving along. Let's get back inside. We need to talk about making a food run in the morning. Everybody's getting pretty thin these days. We don't have much left and hardly any protein at all."

"Good," he said and motioned for us to follow him down.

But we all stopped dead when we heard the bark of a dog.

A dog…

I leaned over the side in shock to see a dog barking and putting his paws up on the building side as if asking for permission to come inside. I gawked. A freaking dog.

Dogs were extinct as was every other animal. So how the heck was a dog sitting in front of us?

Franklin couldn't handle it. He yelled and leaned over the side. I heard the wings beat just before the Marker grabbed his shirt back. I wasn't fast enough before he had him fully over the edge. If I had grabbed him then, he would have fallen to the ground below.

Miguel went to shoot it, but I slammed my hand into the butt of the gun to make his shot miss. It did and he scowled. "You want him to drop to the ground from that height? Not me. Let's go."

We made our way down the ladder and followed the Marker with Franklin out into the parking lot. I knew we would probably draw the attention of the trucks full of Enforcers, but what else could we do? I'd just told Eli and Laura that I'd watch out for Frank.

Miguel and I stopped under them and waited for the Marker to make his move. Miguel once again grabbed at his leg and groaned a little, his scratch burning from being near the Marker. A blaze of fire flew passed us to the tree near us. Calvin. A large burning branch fell from the top and came plummeting toward the ground, toward the Marker. He lowered to keep from getting hit. I braced myself and took my one chance. I jumped on its back, knocking it sideways and making it release its hold on Franklin. We all slammed to the ground, but we were alive.

I felt my body writhing and my teeth gritting as the Marker's skin made contact with mine. The searing pain wasn't something I ever wanted to feel again, but I'd do again to save him. Just like I'd done for Sherry and that memory played behind my eyes. I felt my breath return slowly as his venom receded.

He screeched and made a huge fit over it before Miguel ran him through with the barrel of his shotgun through the Marker's chest while he was down. He burned up and I groaned as I sat up. "We've got to get outta here," I told him through a wheeze.

"Mate, what-" he was cut off by Franklin's screams.

I turned to him, a prayer on my tongue that he hadn't been scratched by the Marker. No answered prayers this time. His eyes were glazing as he groaned. The scratch on his wrist was small, but powerful.

I wanted to curse and scream. Sherry was right. There were no breaks for us.

Ryan hauled him up into his arms and then hoisted him over his shoulder. We all ran to the warehouse and climbed the ladder. When we reached it, I'd forgotten one thing.

The dog.

It waited patiently there, at a loss of what to do with it. We couldn't afford to give it food. We could barely feed ourselves. Calvin gripped my arm. "Just bring it with us and stop trying to find a reason not to. Franklin wanted it."

"That doesn't mean we should keep it," I said low, biting back a groan at the pain in my neck from the Marker's touch.

"Yes, it does! It's the reason he got taken by that thing. If he woke up and saw that the dog wasn't there after all that trouble, he'll flip his lid, man."

"Whatever," Miguel said and gingerly picked up the dog around his middle like a soiled baby. "Nice doggy."

"It's a Jack Russell, Miguel, not a Doberman."

"Does it have teeth?" Miguel asked as he held it to his chest and grimaced as he climbed the ladder. "Then it's a Doberman for all I care."

Billings laughed as he climbed and I wanted to punch him. There was no time to laugh. He had no idea the hell that boy was about to go through. Only two people really understood what it was like. Sherry and Miguel.

Sherry…she was going to be devastated and pissed and angry. I growled and groaned as I jumped from the edge and wobbled to the elevator.

"What's up with you, mate?" Miguel asked.

"I jumped on the Marker to get him off Franklin."

He hissed through his teeth. "Oi, I heard about that from Ann. She said it sucks balls. That true?"

"Dude," I complained and chuckled in pain at the same time. "Shut up."

We emerged and I held my breath at the chaos about to erupt.

"Laura!" Ryan yelled. Franklin was out for the count still and Laura's eyes bugged. She ran toward us.

"What happened?"

As Ryan explained to her what exactly had happened…and what had to be done, Sherry ran to us, too. She covered her mouth shaking her head and glanced at me. I nodded and she squeezed her eyes shut tight for a second before standing straight. She took a deep breath and then yelled, "Marissa!"

Marissa, who'd been standing back giving them space, rushed to Sherry's side. She gasped at the dog, calling Sherry's attention to it. She balked at it, but shook it away and focused. Sherry grasped Laura's arm and said, "Laura, go with Marissa."

Laura shook her head, but Sherry stood her ground. "Laura, I know, ok? I know. But you don't need to be here right now. What they have to do him, you won't want to see, trust me."

She looked at her funny. "Why?"

"I had this done to me," Sherry whispered. "He'll be ok, I promise, but we need to help him now and you need to go so as soon as we're done, you can be there for him."

Laura looked at Eli and he shrugged, wiping his face to remove the look of anguish. He failed though. Marissa took Eli and Laura to the back. There was no way to remove them from the room, but they didn't need to see it at least. I took Sherry's hand. She jolted at my touch and I realized how worried and focused she was.

The girl who had taken Mrs. Trudy's place, and then in the past few days had lost her way a little, was back. She was back big time. I squeezed her hand and we pushed everyone aside. "Miguel, Jeff, Ryan, come on. Let's take him to the makeshift bathroom."

"I'm coming!" Calvin yelled and fought against Ryan's back. "I'm coming, too!"

"No, you're not," Ryan told him harshly. "This isn't your fault, Cal, no matter how much you want to believe it is. I'm not letting you come and torture yourself. We'll be done in a little bit and then you can sit with him."

"It was my fault. He wanted to come along because you let me help last time and I bragged about how cool it was. He didn't want to be left behind again."

The dog barked and yelped at Calvin's screaming.

Ryan sighed and placed a hand on his shoulder. "I know, Cal, but you can't come. I'm sorry."

Calvin huffed and sat down right there in the middle of the floor, his stake laid across his lap. The dog licking at his ear and arm.

We all gathered around Franklin, who had yet to wake up, and knelt at his side. Ryan pulled the sheets together so we'd have visual privacy, but no one was safe from the screams that were about to come from the kid.

"Where's Jeff?" Sherry asked.

"Right here," he answered and pushed the sheet away with his back as he came in. He had a knife in his hand and he was getting the blade red with a Zippo.

Sherry grunted as she put her hand on Franklin's forehead. "It's going to be ok, big guy. Hopefully he stays asleep."

"No one can sleep through this, love," Miguel said and looked her in the eyes. "Right?"

She nodded, her tears begging to be released, but she refused them. Miguel reached over and took her hand. "His scratch is so small. It'll hurt, but there's not much area to cover. It'll be quick for him." He leaned back. "He's a big boy. Let's get on with it, Jeff."

Jeff took steps of a man that wanted no part in what he was about to do. I agreed with him. Sherry held Franklin's head. I took his shoulders to stay near Sherry. Though I was worried about Franklin, I hoped this wouldn't cause problems for Sherry, flashbacks or whatever.

"All right," Jeff said and leaned close and he pulled the Zippo off the blade. "Here we go."

What's This Life For?
Chapter 11

Sherry

I cleaned the wound and maneuvered around Laura as she gripped his hand and sat there in the chair. It creaked every time she moved, making me want to sigh with the bleakness of it all.

Franklin had woken up doing our…procedure. Oh, yes, he had. And it had been agonizing and ugly. I hadn't thought about using Lily's gift until that moment. But she told us that she couldn't 'fix' that kind of wound. That she only fixed human inflicted wounds, not supernatural ones. I thought back and realized that was true.

I could hear Marissa trying to stop Franklin's parents from coming in. I could hear Calvin saying, "Ah, man, ah, man," over and over and over again.

As soon as we were done, I left to tell Frank's parents to come in and then went straight to Calvin. He was huddled against a wall with Lana and that dog. She had her arm around his shoulders and his head was resting on his dirty jeaned knees. I sat on his other side and took his hand. He lifted his head. "He ok?"

"Yep. He'll be just fine."

"He was screaming," he whispered.

"It hurts to fix what happened."

"They did that to you, didn't they? When you were scratched. I remember hearing you scream like that."

I turned to see his dirty face, his fingernails caked with grime underneath, his neck lined with sweat and dust. The dog was asleep on his lap. "Yeah, they did that to me, too. I'd have had them do it to me again if I could have kept Frank from having to have it done to him."

"I know you would. I would, too. I feel really guilty."

"Don't. Frank can make his own decisions."

He twisted his lips. "Can I see him now?"

"You can, but he's asleep. Miguel is using the last of our medicine that we stole from the hospital on him, so he'll be asleep for a few days." I sighed and said more to myself than him, "We're going to have to make another run for medicine, too."

"Can I come?"

"Not this time, Calvin," I told him, a bit harshly. "It's too soon. We need to all make a few hard decisions and figure out what we're going to do, but we need to be smart about it. We need to use strategy, not revenge, if we want to keep surviving and beat them one day."

He nodded, "Yeah, ok. I'm gonna go see him now."

"Ok." He laid the dog on the floor and I watched him go, before turning to Lana and signing, '*Poor guy. I wish things were different, Lana. I wish he could be safe.'*

She signed back and smiled, '*No one's safe anymore. Even if the Lighters left tomorrow, we still wouldn't be safe. The world will never be the same. All those desperate people will have to try to get their lives back together, like they are trying to do now. Desperation brings out many emotions in people.'*

I nodded remembering those people who tried to rob us on the road.

I told her I needed to see about making some dinner and went to do so. There had been no schedules made yet or lists. We really didn't even know how some things were going to be done yet. Like laundry. I guess we were hand washing them in tubs now.

And the food. There was no kitchen, no stove, no sink. We had to cook everything over a fire in a brick pit the guys had made of debris and leftover building supplies. We had a few things to burn, but soon enough, we'd have to start going out to get firewood. And with it being so hot at the moment, it made it pretty toasty in there when I cranked the fire up.

It was an endless cycle of suck.

But we'd get through it. We always did and I had no inclinations to start giving up now. I even managed to snag Mrs. Trudy's apron in the getaway. Wistful was one word to describe my mood as I slipped it on and looked at the five large cans of beans I was about to open and cook. We were all going to turn into beans if we kept this up. Why had Piper gotten rid of the good stuff? Of all the things to leave behind, beans?

I gripped the old metal handheld can opener and went to cranking. Beans and beans and people dying and kids being attacked and beans… Merrick came up behind me and took it from me. "I've got it."

I refused to let go. "No, I've got it."

He put both arms around me from behind. "Baby, let go."

I did and he set it on the counter. I knew what he was doing. I didn't want to be consoled right now. I wanted to stew and be mad. I wanted to throw the can opener across the room and curse and yell.

His arms went around my stomach and he rested his chin on my shoulder. We just sat there for a minute like that, not saying anything. My anger began to melt away and it turned into something else as his skin pulsed electricity through mine. It became calm. Not peace by any means, but calm.

I turned and let him engulf me in his warmth that was warmer than normal, but comforting to me. I let my sigh escape against his chest and his arms tightened. "Better?"

"Yeah," I answered and leaned back a bit. "How did you know?"

He smirked. "That poor can opener was sure getting a workout." He nodded to the can I'd been desecrating. I had kept on going after the top was off and began ripping the liner and grating into the can rim.

I grimaced and felt my nose wrinkle. He ran his finger down the length of it and tapped the end gently. I just let him hold me for a long time. He murmured something about us being ok. I knew it was true.

I had to believe that to be true.

For the next two weeks, we pressed repeat on the days and waited for something. Anything. Our existence had become trivial and innate, primitive and surviving at all costs. We ate our stupid beans, we took our lame bowl baths, we slept in our sleeping bags on the concrete in our little makeshift rooms, we were bored beyond measure.

But we were alive.

Franklin was better and up, but still sore. Calvin never left his side.

The dog was a conundrum. We had no idea how he'd survived when all of the other animals had killed themselves or been killed. Franklin got to name him since he was the one who 'found' him. The dog was aptly titled, Bones, because he was pretty much skin and bones anyway.

The constant noise of the place was…well, constant. It never ended. There was no escaping Pap and Margaret's yelling, or Miguel and Rylee's fighting, or the kids playing with the dog or groaning about being bored, or Danny and Celeste's canoodling because they had no shame. But there really weren't places to canoodle anymore.

I was going through some serious Merrick withdrawals. Serious.

And judging from the way his eyes followed me around, I assumed he was missing our alone time as well. I raised my eyebrows at him when I caught him staring again. He smiled at being caught and shrugged. I laughed and turned back to working in the 'kitchen area' we'd blocked off with Marissa and Lana when Cain came in and plopped two large cans of beans on the counter. "I know you don't want to hear this," he started.

"Oh, Lord! What now?" I asked and laughed.

"We only have 10 cans of beans left, 2 bags of rice, a couple cans of cream corn, all those green beans in the crates and one box of brownie mix."

I chuckled, almost hysterically. "But there's no grease or butter or eggs, so that does us absolutely no good." He shrugged. I wrenched my necklace violently. "Great. No more shampoo, no soap, no toothpaste, nothing to wash our clothes with, no medicine." I sighed. "We're screwed."

"We'll just have to make a run." He came and put his hands on my shoulders. "There's nothing else to do. We just didn't know how good we had it before."

"We had to leave so much stuff behind," I mused. "I wonder if we could go back and-"

"Nix on that. There are watching the store, I'm sure of it."

"Ok, fine." I stood taller and felt the dog bumping my leg with its tail. I glanced at him and back to Cain. "Why don't we have a meeting and let them know that we'll be going on a run then."

"We? As in you and me?"

"Yep. I can tell if they're lying and you can blast 'em if they come after us."

"You know Merrick's not gonna like-"

"We have to!" I gave him a look to tell him I was done playing. "We have to. This isn't about shampoo anymore, this is getting scary. You can't survive on beans alone. We have to do something!"

He thought, playing with his lip ring with his tongue, and then nodded. "Ok. Let's go, shorty."

"Really?" I said stunned. I glanced at Marissa who was giving us the *'You're gonna get it'* look. "That easy?"

"Yep. You're right. There's nothing else to talk about. It's not like we can go hunting for food. Unless the dog is some indication that the animals are coming back. I doubt that." He reached down and rubbed the dog behind the ears. "I think this guy just got really lucky."

"Yeah. Well I'm sure the Keepers have something cooked up. Merrick's been doing that Keeper talk thing a lot so they probably have a plan of some sort."

"Oh, they do," he said. "Simon's been plotting all sorts of things with his new face." He grimaced. "He seems to have forgotten that they can still sense a Keeper regardless of what face he's wearing."

"My ears are burning," Simon said. He was perched at the edge of the 'kitchen area' with arms crossed and brow bunched like the sneaky man he was.

"It's true, is it not?" Cain rebutted. "Don't you have something planned?"

"Maybe," he said and turned away.

"Showtime," Cain said and grabbed my hand as he bolted out of the kitchen, dragging me along. Simon must've called the Keepers in his mind because they were all present and accounted for.

Cain crossed his arms once more and studied them. "We know you've all got something planned, but it's not going to work."

"*We* don't have anything planned," Merrick said and nodded to Jeff. "Some of us still have our heads screwed on right."

"I know they can detect me!" Simon yelled. "Are you just going to let your charges die of starvation?"

"Of. Course. Not," Merrick growled. I left Cain and went to his side. He smiled at me a little and then went back to glaring at Simon. "But running out there all cocky because you've got a brand new body isn't going to solve the problem. We've done runs before. We know what has to be done."

"And what has to be done," Cain cut in, "is that Sherry and I are going on the run."

Merrick stiffened, his arms tight and angry, and looked down at me. "What? Now who's plotting?"

"I wasn't plotting," I insisted, but backtracked, "I mean technically I was plotting, but not all sinister like. We just need me to go and you know it. If Cain and I go, I can lie detect and he can blast them if we run into trouble."

Silence engulfed the room like the smell of stale coffee.

I knew they were all waiting for Merrick to blow up. So was I for that matter. His eyes were tight and calculating. It wasn't hard to notice as we all stood around how scruffy and unkempt everyone looked. The girls' hair was a mess of ponytails. The guys had beards and shags. Everyone was so thin and...unhealthy looking. We *needed* to do this.

I raised my eyebrows at Merrick in contest when he remained silent. He let a breath out through his nose and said, "We were planning to send Miguel and Simon - though Simon was completely against what we wanted - to get food, supplies and medicine. They were going to be gone for two days to get everything. We hadn't said anything to anyone yet because for one, we don't think Simon should go-"

"You've said that," Simon barked.

"And for two, we knew you or someone else would try to think of a way to go instead."

"Ok, well, Simon? They're right. Keepers couldn't get two feet inside a store before a Lighter sensed you. They are everywhere now. And -"

"Wait. Wait, wait!" Ellie yelled and smiled at us like we were all idiots. "I can go. They can't sense me."

"But we need you here to keep the ones looking for us away from the Specials and Keepers. They would be able to sense us if they were close enough."

"Oh," she said in deflation. "Well what about Cain? He's a Special?"

"Cain's never been detected by them before," Ryan explained and smiled a little at her across the room. "That's why…Cain and Sherry going is a good idea," he eased and then looked at Merrick, waiting for his reaction.

I smiled at Ryan, but let my smile slip away when Merrick turned his gaze to me. My old Merrick, the one from the beginning where he was constantly worried about my safety and threw fits over it, was in full swing. But he was trying to rein it in. I inched toward him and put a hand on his chest. "This isn't me trying to be all rebelliony like before." His lips twisted. "This is me doing what needs to be done for everyone to survive. You know there's no one else who can go who has the best chance to-"

He put his hands up to my cheeks, effectively stopping all my thoughts and words. He leaned his forehead to mine. "You'll be the death of me," he murmured.

I smiled. "Thank you."

"Thank him for what?" Rylee asked and huffed. "For *letting* you go?"

"Shut it, Rylee," someone said.

I leaned back to see him. "Cain will take care of me."

I know that. Once again, you just don't understand how hard it is to just let you go and hope for the best. Things are worse than ever now.

"I know. Thank you for understanding that you can't be selfish with me." I laughed at his scowl. "You are being a very good Keeper right now."

"Yeah. And a horrible husband," he whispered against my forehead.

I didn't say anything else. I tried to take my victory with grace.

"So we're going," Cain said and clapped once. "Awesome. Let's go a.s.a.p. because if I have to throwback one more meal of beans, I'm gonna go ape crap."

Calvin laughed and then stopped when no one joined him. Simon, the ever annoying Keeper lately, had to say something. "Take this seriously, Cain."

"I'm dead serious, Simon." He held up two fingers. "Two things I'm always serious about. Missions and food."

"Cain," he said in exasperation.

"I got this," he rebutted harder. "Stop worrying so much." He looked at me. "It'll be best if we leave first thing in the morning."

I nodded. Lillian, who was behind him the whole time, grabbed his hand and looked at me. There was some silent message there that I didn't get, but I nodded anyway. I would watch Cain's back like he watched mine.

That night when everyone was asleep, I lay awake and tried not to think about the morning. Merrick didn't understand when it came to this part of me. He thought I was trying to be stubborn, but it was more than that. I didn't want to go, I just felt like I needed to.

Sleep refused me, so I started singing really low. The lack of radio or piano was wearing on me. Gavin Degraw seemed upbeat, but melancholy enough to fit my mood. "*We got two tickets, but they're one way. And I went with it so I can't say, no. I lit a fuse I can't stop. I opened doors I can't lock. Still I never meant to be this close, and let it slip away. I keep stumbling until I finally missed the last train. She's ready, I'm not ready. I run every time."*

"Who's that?" Merrick whispered. "His logic is sound."

I laughed. "You're such a goofball." I rubbed his scruff. "Everything will be ok."

"Mmhmm," he muttered. "It better be. Or this world will have to deal with me." He leaned over me in our small tented space. "Be careful. Be smart. Be quick. Don't recruit anyone. We have enough mouths to feed."

"I know. I promise, in and out quickly, just what we need and nothing else." He sighed and laid his head on my chest. His fingers caressed my ribs and I wiggled under him. "Lily is with Danny and Celeste tonight," I whispered and ran my hand through his hair. "I can be very quiet."

He kissed my chest through my shirt and looked up at me. "I just want to hold you. Is that all right?"

I nodded and continued to rub his head and shoulders as he laid his head back down. My poor Merrick was going to worry himself into an ulcer. I knew he would be like this until I came back.

So I vowed to come back soon and in one piece.

Duct Tape
Chapter 12

Merrick

"You've got your food packed, right? And the credit cards? I'm not sure if they'll still work or not. You might have to try a few of them for gas or whatever-"

"We've got it," Sherry assured me and rubbed my chest. "We've got everything we need."

I did this half growl half groan thing. I knew I was stalling, but I just couldn't seem to stop. Cain and Lillian were trying to be discreet in their goodbye. She was wiping her eyes even as he kissed her teary cheeks and hugged her. I rubbed my face. I needed to stop being such a pansy.

I jerked Sherry to me and squeezed her with all I could muster without hurting her. She laughed happily. "This was all I wanted."

"I worry. That won't ever change," I defended.

"I wouldn't change one thing about you. If you didn't worry about me, I'd be worried about *that*." She smiled. One of those smiles that was solely to placate me and make me feel moths in my guts and googly eyed, as she called it. It was totally working.

I just kissed her. To feel her breath as she gasped into my mouth, to feel her warm fingers as they gripped my arms like she was hanging on for life, to feel the buzz she caused me, like being drunk without the hangover. I kissed her good and long and dangerously.

When I finally released her, she had that glazy eyed look that made me want to drag her to our room…but we didn't have a room anymore. I sighed. Things were so different now. I kissed her forehead and said, "Gah, I love you, baby."

"I love you, Finch," she whispered, the slight hitch giving her away.

"I love you more."

"Unfathomable."

I smirked at her inability to let me win. I peeked up to see Cain waiting for Sherry, but trying not to watch us. I nodded to him and he sauntered over, putting a hand on my shoulder. "We'll be back before you know it."

I turned to give him my full attention. "I know you'll take care of her," I lowered my voice, "but I promise you I'll murder you in your sleep mafia style if-"

He laughed. "Dude! That was awesome! Say it again." Before I could say anything he continued, "I get it. You'll murder me dead." He chuckled again. "You *know* me. You and Sherry are family. I promise you I won't let anything happen to her."

"I am standing *right* here," Sherry said and smirked at us both.

"Where?" Cain joked and looked over her head. "Can't see a thing."

"Down here, turd."

"Turd? I'm wounded. Is that even a real word? If I were writing a novel right now, *turd* would be underlined in red," he goaded and laughed as she slapped his arm.

"Turd," she repeated and reached up to hug me. "Please don't worry so much. Make sure Lily brushes out her hair because if you don't it's a rat's nest."

"Ok." I touched her cheek. "Bye, baby."

"Bye."

One side of her mouth rose in a half smile. She let Cain lead her to the elevator, a beaten messenger bag over her shoulder. Not everyone was up yet, but there were plenty of us awake to see them off. Lily wasn't one of them. Sherry said it would be too much to see Lily upset about her leaving so we let her sleep.

We'd been over and over the rules and things they needed to remember. They were well equipped to handle this, taking the Jeep and clean clothes so they didn't look like rebels.

Simon pouted by the elevator doors, but I barely saw him.

The elevator doors closed and Sherry and I both leaned until the little sliver of each other through the crack was gone. I swiped my face with my palm and plopped myself onto one of the bean crates. Gah, this sucked.

"Sherry is a smart girl," Jeff told me. He was attempting to un-knot a shoelace from his sneakers. "And Cain is perfect for this."

"I know that," I said a bit harshly. I was tired of everyone making out like I was overreacting.

I don't think you're overreacting. I'm just trying to offer you some comfort.

I'm afraid there's none to be had, brother. How's Marissa?

Good. His smile was proud. *Really good, if you don't count morning sickness. Her belly is starting to stick out a little. It's...awesome knowing what's inside there.*

Delivery isn't going to be fun.

I remember Katie. He stopped what he was doing and looked at me. *I know it seems cruel to bring a baby into the world like this, but I still can't help but be happy about it. It makes sense to me; to bring life into the world when so much life is leaving it.*

I nodded and smiled. *You're getting wise in your old age, papa bear.*

I'll take that badge and wear it proudly.

I bet. Hey, uh...what are we going to do about Simon?

He's sure cocky, isn't he?

I grimaced. *Yeah, he is. I don't get it. Josh was cocky, but this is insane. He's reckless.*

We'll keep an eye on him. Cain's gone, so he should tone down a bit the next couple of days.

Don't remind me. Cain was gone and so was Sherry. *Why don't we make ourselves useful and figure out a way to make a clothesline and get a pipe to run water to the kitchen. Sherry would be happy to find that when she got back.*

Deal. He got fed up and cut the shoelace straight through with a knife.

"You know we don't have replacement laces for that, right?"

"They were knotted. I'll just glue it."

"Glue it?" Billings said and took it from him as if to examine it. "You can't glue that! Try some duct tape."

"Duck tape? What's that?"

"Duct tape," he corrected, enunciating the 't'. "It's…ah, here." Billings pulled a roll from a compartment in his cargo pants leg. We gawked at him in disbelief. He shrugged. "What? You never know when you're going to need duct tape."

Catnip
Chapter 13

Cain

I opened Sherry's door to the Jeep like a true gentleman. She climbed in, a little sulky and pouty. It was pretty cute. I got in my side and cranked the air conditioning. "Wow, it feels weird to be going on a run. Especially with you, no offense."

"None taken," she said lightly. "Everyone underestimates my size and assumes I have nothing to offer. That's why I'm so good to go on these runs." She turned to look at me. "I didn't mean you, I just meant….in general."

I chuckled. "It's ok. And point to you, well played."

She tried to smile, but it was a horrible imitation. I knew what was eating her. It was eating me, too. Leaving the spousal units behind. I felt my brow come down to reach my eyes. What if she knew about the crush I used to have and feels uncomfortable? I glanced at her. She looked normal enough, but would Sherry have the guts to call me on it? But there wasn't anything to call on anymore.

That was history of the best kind; the kind that was rewritten with something even better.

So I'd stop worrying about it like a sissy and get down to business. "Now," I started, "we play the usual bit. We're married with three kids, getting some groceries, a little peroxide, a random package of rectangle size bandages, maybe a blow up mattress or two. What do ya think?"

"It's brilliant, Cainy boy." She tried that smile again that hung all wrong.

"What's the matter, huh? Don't want to be seen with me?"

"I know we have to do this, but we're not going to get enough to feed everyone. You know that right? Next week, we'll be right back in the same boat."

"We'll do what has to be done," I said sternly. "We survive, we fight back. What else is there anymore?"

She nodded and took a curl between her fingers, her eyes distant, but focused. Some Coldplay song came on the CD player from my mix tape and she jumped forward to turn the radio up. She smiled, a real one, and her fingers moved on her lap a little like piano keys were playing underneath them.

"You miss it, huh?"

She looked at me and then at her hands. Her smile grew. "Yep. I miss it very much. But not as much as you miss a real meal, I bet."

"Oh, good Lord, don't get me started." I felt my stomach on instinct and wasn't impressed with the bones there." We're all skin and bones," I mused.

She lifted her arm and grimaced. "Mmm," she muttered unsatisfied. "I'm not worried about me so much, or you for that matter, no offense. But the kids…we all look pretty ragged, but the kids are scrawny."

She wasn't wrong. And Calvin and Frank were so active, always running around, they never kept weight on when we were eating good, and now…

"*Lights will guide you home. And ignite your bones. And I will try to fix you," s*he softly said the words. She leaned her head back on the seat and I focused on the road.

I wasn't exactly sure how I was supposed to act around her now. She and I had always been connected in a way that was different than other girls. I thought it was love before, and it was, just a different kind of love. I bit on my lip ring and smoothed a hand down my shaved chin. None of us had been shaving since supplies were so low, but to go into the Need Warehouses, I had to look presentable.

It felt so good to not feel like a wildebeest anymore.

She kept on humming and leaned over the small console to lay her head on my shoulder. She looped her arm through mine. She glanced up and grinned at me playfully. She rubbed my chin with her knuckles. "You look so much better when you're not sporting a food catcher."

"Food catcher… Oh. Ha, ha." I smiled and remembered Lillian's grin at finally seeing my face again this morning. I rubbed my phantom beard before patting her knee. "You're hilarious."

"I *am* pretty hilarious," she joked and put her head back on my shoulder. "I've missed you, Cainy boy."

I smiled that her calling me that no longer sent me into orbit. "Cainy boy," I mused. "You know you are the only person I ever-"

"Let call you Cainy boy. I know. I like it that way," she laughed her words. "Just like no one can call Merrick Finch, but me."

"Finch?"

"Long story."

"We've got a long ride," I coaxed.

She sat up grinning. "Ok. Well, he proposed and we were trying to find a last name since he didn't have one to give me…"

I listened as she talked about my best friend. Her eyes glistened when she told me about Pastor and marrying Merrick in that little church. I listened. And I was truly happy for her.

"What a waste," I muttered as we passed the Taco Shell. They weren't serving tacos anymore. Now it was just dust.

"Yeah, a waste." She laughed. "I would just about maim and murder someone for a taco right about now."

"And I'd be there right beside you, a willing accomplice."

"Accomplice doesn't suit you, Cain."

"Usually not," I agreed. "But today, I'm your accomplice and you're mine, little one."

She chuckled at my jab and poked me in the ribs. "Shut up, husband."

"That's a good little wife," I said, miraculously with a straight face. Before she could respond, I slammed on the brakes.

I stared at the Enforcer and put my hands on the wheel; ten and two o'clock like a good little compelled citizen. I glanced at Sherry to see her demeanor was like mine; frozen and waiting patiently. "Good girl," I muttered under my breath.

"Sir, please roll down your window," the Enforcer said. He was so young. So young and pliable and stupid. I felt sorry for the guy for being so gullible. I rolled my window down slowly and gave him an expectant look. If he thought I was stating my business without asking, he had another thing coming. He huffed and crossed his arms. "You know the drill. State your name and the reason for crossing the border into town."

I said, deadly calm, "Cain, and my wife, Sherry, and we're headed to the Need Warehouse. We're crossing the border because we live out of town."

He chuckled. "What you want to do a thing like that for? Hardly no one lives outside the borders anymore."

I smiled a little, unable to stop it. "We're just rebels, I guess."

The idiot actually laughed and waved us on. "Stay safe now and happy shopping."

"Back at ya, buddy," I yelled and rolled my window up. I peeked at Sherry. She was biting her lip, but her chest was shaking with a laugh. I joined her again and it felt so good. My chest had missed the jolting of a laugh.

"I can't believe you did that!" she said and wiped her eye with the side of her hand. "I can not believe you said that!"

"Hey, I'm not a good liar. He asked for the truth, so I just gave it to him."

"You sure did!" She wiped her eye again and laughed. "Oh, gosh. I needed that."

"Me, too. 'Cause we're here."

She sobered and blew a long breath. I parked in the middle and flicked it into park. We sat for a second to gather ourselves. I looked around and saw all the people heading inside or coming back with their baskets full. Everybody seemed so normal. So peaceful. If only it were true and not a horrible façade.

"Ready?" she asked, her voice surprisingly steady.

"Yep." I jumped out and ran to get her door. She was already half out, so I shut it for her. She straightened her shirt and stroked a curl nervously. I took her cold hand in mine as we came around the back of the truck. "In and out, easy peasy, got it?"

"Mmhmm," she answered and people watched as I had done.

I pulled her face to look at me with a hand on her cheek. She looked up at me, her big brown eyes so trusting and waiting and honest. It took me back to another time and I grimaced a little. She frowned.

"Am I doing something wrong?"

"No. I was just…thinking." I cleared my throat. "Listen. Don't worry about all of these people, ok?" I glanced around to make my point. "We're here to save our family. These people can't be saved, ok?"

She nodded. "I already got the *Don't be the hero* talk from Merrick." She smiled a little. "Am I that glaringly transparent?"

"Absolutely." I grinned, too.

"Look at them," she said sadly and watched a man and his wife enter the doors. They looked like neatly dressed zombies. "Can you imagine living like that? Just a sheep, a follower of something you didn't even understand or know about?"

"Or being aware of everything and having to witness it all and not be able to do a daggum thing about it," I countered.

"I don't know which one's worse."

"I do," I said. She looked a little quivery lipped so I kissed her forehead and wrapped her up in my arms. "In this case, ignorance is not bliss. They're miserable, they just don't know it."

"Yeah," she replied softly against my chest and sighed. "But they aren't hungry."

"True, sweetheart. True." I leaned back. "You ready to rectify that?"

She nodded and let me take her hand again. We reached the Enforcer guarding the entrance and I knew it had begun. No turning back.

We had arrived at the Lion's den.

"Ears!" she yelled loudly, and for a second, I had no idea what she was talking about. Until Sherry pulled her hair back to show that she wasn't a Keeper. Oh, yeah. That's right. I did the same and she waved us on with the disdain of any customer service employee.

The next one jerked Sherry's arm and said, "Smile for the camera."

She jerked her head to the monitor and told us to flash our IDs at it. We did and she pushed us right along.

It was exactly like it sounded. It was a big warehouse and they carried out baskets or buckets - most people had rectangle laundry baskets - and proceeded down the line. The attendant put one of her items in your basket for how many people you had, except for one thing. We didn't have a basket. We should've known to bring a basket if we were coming to the Need Warehouse. Crap.

One of the attendants saw us looking lost. She charged us with a frown that reached her black rooted temple. "Where's you basket?"

Sherry burst right into loud, girly tears. I gawked at her, but when I turned to see the attendant, she had softened like melted butter. "Oh, honey. Now what is it?"

"I'm pregnant!" Sherry blurted and hugged me around my waist. "It was my fault. I forgot the basket! I forget everything now. I'm so…" sniff, "forgetful."

"Oh, honey," the lady repeated. "You wait right there."

She ran to the wall opposite us. I looked down at Sherry. She winked through her pout. It took all of my strength not to laugh or smile. The woman brought us a basket and whispered, "You're not supposed to receive any food without a basket." She took a marker out of her pocket and marked "Wanda" on the side. "There. You tell them Wanda said it was all right this once."

"Thank you so much." Sherry sniffed again. "I'm so sorry."

"Don't you worry about it." She smiled at us as we began to walk away. And then, "Oh, miss?" We froze and turned. "Since you're pregnant, you get an extra ration. Remember to tell the attendants that you're pregnant."

We nodded and waited in line.

"An extra ration," Sherry mumbled. "Great. All of our problems are solved!"

"Hey, now, ho hum. We'll take what we can get. Especially considering that you're freaking awesome!" I spoke in her ear from behind. "You played her like a fiddle."

"I panicked," she said like an apology.

"You panicked good."

She smiled and then it was our turn. "I'm…I'm pregnant," she blurted out again. The lady rolled her eyes and smacked her gum as she shoved three cans of tuna into our box. I felt a little of my smile melt away. Crap, Sherry was right. It was something, but three cans of tuna would feed three people. And we had over twenty at the bunker waiting for us to put something other than rice and beans in their bellies. We needed to do something, anything.

I followed Sherry closely in line, listening to her say over and over again that she was pregnant, though I knew that would never be. I tried to think of a plan. She shopped and I plotted.

It was eerie and started the thinking process for sure. The fluorescent lights were so dark, they were almost blue in tint. The radio above was playing some crackly version of Johnny Cash's *Ring of Fire* and the windows above were so coated in algae and condensation that it was impossible to see or let light in. It was like they were purposely trying to set some depressing mood on everyone.

We went to our next attendant. Her apron was dirty and her nametag said Buffy. She caught me staring at her nametag and must've thought my gaze was directed elsewhere…in that general vicinity. She grinned, showing a golden side tooth and a *Come Hither* sway to her neck began as she nodded toward a door to the side. I imagined it was a closet.

I gasped loudly and put my arms around Sherry. "And in front of my wife!" I scoffed and pushed Sherry along the line. "I'm a happily married man!" I yelled over my shoulder and then tried to hold in my laughter. She flustered and covered her mouth, looking around to see if anyone else had seen. No one was paying attention to us which made it even funnier to me. I pressed my mouth into Sherry's shoulder from behind and smothered my chuckle.

She chuckled, too, and shook her head at me. "Poor girl never stood a chance."

"What do you mean?" I said, still laughing.

"You have this…" she thought and moved her hand in the air, "thing about you, Cain. You're catnip."

I choked on the air I was laughing with. "Catnip?"

"Yeah. Catnip." She grinned at my grin. "Smirking catnip."

I laughed out loud at that. "Oh, boy. Let's get out of here before you get us into trouble."

"Well, my middle name is trouble," she mumbled sarcastically.

"Actually, you're middle name is sarcasm."

"Ha. Ha. Ha. I forgot. Trouble is my first name."

I smiled at her. She was in a better mood at least.

I hoisted our box at the end, and honestly, I wasn't impressed with the weight of it. Also we took the smaller box of 'necessities' they gave us. It contained toilet paper, toothpaste, shampoo and soaps of all variety for the household. They literally gave you what you needed to survive the week and nothing else.

The thought just rammed into my brain out of nowhere.

I was certain the Lighters and their dead prince had stashed a nice amount of food for him. I was sure of it. And now he was dead. I wondered if the Mayor's mansion had been abandoned. I remembered Josh talking about the pantry when he was doing his search for Lily and Calvin that time. It was huge and full of food. Now it could be completely bare, but I was willing to risk it to take a peek and hope for the jackpot.

I slipped my arm around Sherry's shoulder while one-arming the box against my hip and tried to think of a way to keep her from freaking or whatever. I didn't want her to get hurt, but we had to do something.

I took her to the Jeep and put the box in the back. Ugh, we didn't even have a whole lot of room for much. A few boxes more and we'd be all full up. I beat my fist on the back door and groaned at the sting. It all just seemed so hopeless. We were just biding time until there was no more time to steal. We could only go one so long until the food ran out.

I was scrubbing my head with my hands and biting my lip ring when a conversion van screeched into the parking lot. It swung around and fishtailed until the back door was pointed toward the warehouse entrance.

I could only stare at first as three men piled out of the back, their faces covered with bandanas…and they opened fire on anyone who was between them and the food inside.

Taste Buds
Chapter 14

Ryan

The room was too hot. I rubbed my eyes and rolled over…only to find that I wasn't alone in my 'tent'. I didn't need to squint in the dark to see it was Ellie. I sighed.

We had not done anything since that day that I kissed her. Nothing in the way of 'us' anyway. We'd all been too busy. When we were together, there were twenty people in the room with us. It was bad timing for someone who might want to say something to another person.

Like say…that he wanted to kiss her again just to taste her. That he wanted to kiss her so hard that she clung to him for mercy. I didn't have any idea where the thoughts were coming from, I just knew that she was precious to me. Like a charge was for me, but more than that. And I wasn't really sure…what to do with her. Or if she even wanted me to think about her that way. So I kept my mouth shut and so had she.

But the looks across the room were unavoidable. If I caught her looking at me, then she knew I was looking, too, and vice versa. So why were we tip toeing?

"Ellie?" I asked, my voice hoarse from sleep.

She whispered, "Please say it's ok if I just lay here."

"What happened?"

"Nothing. I just…miss you. And my bed is right by the elevator and I don't like it."

"Uh, sure," I told her, hating the gruff grate of my voice.

She lay down again. The only part of us that was touching was our knees as we lay on our sides facing each other. I could see her, but there was no way she could see me. I studied her face. She was so young. I knew my body was young, but I felt old inside.

I looked at her porcelain face, so pale, but in a way that made her features stand out and be beautiful. Her long dark hair, a curtain that worked perfectly for the shy girl. Her neck was smooth and… I felt my throat tighten. The notion that I had absolutely no idea what was going on in that human's head about me was infuriating.

She could have made any manner of conclusions, all of them wrong. Or all of them right and maybe that's why she kept her distance this past week.

The brushing of the sleeping bag I was laying on made me pause. She was leaning up and sitting on her legs. "You can see me in the dark, can't you?"

"Yes."

She nodded and seemed disappointed. With me? With my ability? I sighed in frustration some more.

"What?" she asked and squinted, hearing my displeased grunt.

"I just…don't understand you." Her face took on this fallen look that made me feel like a jerk. Was my statement offensive? "I mean that I just don't know…what you want from me."

Again that look, but worse. She rolled over and her breathing accelerated. Then she was up and out of my tent before I could even say anything else.

What just happened?

I lay there and tried not to listen to the sounds of everyone else awake on the other side of the warehouse. I wasn't in a mood for people right then, except maybe for Ellie. Though it was exhausting to be around her, and not know what was really going on, I enjoyed her company. I enjoyed her shy smiles and the way she seemed completely lost one second and then completely sure the next.

Ellie, my conundrum.

I wondered if it was prudent or dutiful to go after her. But if she left, she wouldn't want me to follow, would she? Unless she was a woman that wanted to be chased.

I sat up in the dark and gripped my hair in frustration. I was such an idiot! Of course she wanted to be chased! All human females had this need to feel wanted and needed. I'd snubbed Ellie with my own self consciousness without even meaning to. She thought I didn't want her, that I had rejected her, when in my cowardice, I was asking her the same thing.

Did I want her? Was the electricity that ran through my veins at the notice of her in the room enough to warrant that? Was it the fact that when I first met her, and she clung to me so violently, she needed me in a way that no one else ever had? She had chosen me to be her guardian that day. And all the silliness in between now and then was trivial. Was I in love like Merrick or Jeffrey? No. But could I see the potential within myself to be?

I got up from my pallet and made my mind up. Even if she refused me, at least we'd both know where we stood. I pushed my sheet curtain aside and made my way through all the pallets and boxes.

I found her speaking with Miguel. She was crying and he patted her back as they stood close. Some strange fire burned through my chest at the sight of them. I cocked my head to the side and felt my eyes narrow in a glare. Miguel looked up and caught my gaze. His eyebrows jumped and he nodded to me. He said something to Ellie and patted her back once more before nodding my way.

She turned. Embarrassed, red eyes met mine. I felt like the worst kind of scum. I made a swift path to her and looked around before grabbing her arm and pulling her into the designated bathing area. Her lips were thin and she let me pull her easily. Her face held this little defiant tilt that told me she was willing to fight if need be, but her willingness to come with me belied that.

"What?" she asked in a hard voice. One I'd never heard before.

Was it true anger or passion?

"Why did you run out? Why are you crying?"

She wrenched her arm away from me. "I don't need to stay where I'm not wanted."

"What makes you think I don't want you?"

She scowled and repeated my earlier words back to me. "I don't understand you. I don't know what you want from me."

"Those are valid questions," I said, but hurriedly added, "It's not all right for me to wonder about you?"

"That didn't sound like wonder," she muttered. "It's sounded like contempt."

"I'm not a human," I told her bluntly and blasted all of my worries at her. "Do you understand that? I'm not human. I'm thousands of years old, stuck here in a body that doesn't belong to me. You're in love with this face, not me."

"Not your face," she whispered and looked up at me. "When you held me in the van, I couldn't see your face. It was *you."*

I didn't know what to say to that, so I just continued on with the truth. "There's a place that Keepers go. The After. The closest human word to describe it is paradise, but it's so much more than that. Merrick and Jeff, they know they'll never see the After and they're fine with it. I'm…not all right with it. If I were to…fall in love with you, it'd make me want to stay." I looked her straight in the eye and said as clearly as I could. "The After is all I've ever wanted and when this is over, I will be going there. It doesn't matter what I feel."

Her chest started to shake with little sobs that I couldn't stand to hear, but she had to see that I wasn't capable of giving her what she wanted, not matter how much this body wanted it. "Don't make the mistake of falling for this body, because the person inside it is gone and soon, I will be, too. I'm sorry-"

She pushed away from me. "Why are you saying all of this? I never asked you to give up your paradise and stay here with me."

"But you did," I countered. "When you kissed me-"

"You kissed me!" she said and glared.

"All right, yes, I kissed you. The way you were looking at me-"

"You kissed me and I get blamed? And that suddenly means that we're going to get married or something?" She laughed humorlessly. "Wow, you're so arrogant."

"It's not arrogance, it's knowledge. I've watched women for years."

"Apparently not the right ones."

"I won't budge on this, Ellie. I like you a lot and I don't want to see you hurt, especially not by me. That's why this has to stop now. As much as I may want… something more."

She reached her hand up. At first I thought she might slap me, but she touched my scruffy cheek. She smiled sadly. "I'm just sorry that you're not the man I thought you were."

"I'm not a man," I couldn't stop myself from saying.

She let her hand slide from my face and turned as she said, "I can see that."

Well, I got my way. She was officially knowledgeable about my status on this earth and she walked away from me with grace.

So why did I feel like someone had kicked me in the guts?

Supper was served up by Marissa and Ann. Rice and beans. It was beginning to be a running joke. Ellie kept her distance and kept quiet, too. I tried not to feel guilty for what I had said, sparing her seemed the best thing for her. But looking at her now…was it? She looked silently miserable and even though it hurt, it also was a eye opener. She was upset about me which made my stupid human heart beat for different reasons other than keeping me alive.

So it seemed that my little chat to talk her out of falling for me was making *me* fall for *her*.

I tried to ignore her by filling my routine with Calvin and Frank. Frank was still slow moving around with Calvin practically his indentured servant. I remembered actual indentured servants. Calvin was a pretty good one, but Frank was a horrible master. I smiled at them as they played cards.

"Uhuh, it's twenty one, not three card poker! Keep up, man!" Calvin complained at Frank dealing.

"Right. Ok, ready to get spanked?" he said as he re-dealt.

"Ha! Bro, they totally don't say 'spanked' anymore."

"Who doesn't?"

"Anybody!" Calvin said and laughed. "At least not the cool peeps."

"No one says 'peeps' anymore, I bet," Frank rebutted sullenly.

"I'll let you have that one 'cause you're cripple. Deal, man."

He flung the card across the small table at him. "I'm not a cripple! It's just my wrist." He looked down and grinned. "Wicked scar, right?"

"It's sick, dude."Calvin leaned back in his chair all cool like. "If there were chicks here, they'd be impressed."

I shook my head as I tried to keep up with them.

"Can I join you?" I asked.

"Sure, Ry. Color the man up, Franky."

I asked quickly, "What does that mean?"

"It means *it don't matter 'cause we got no money anyway*," Frank explained....sort of. "Quit trying to be cool and show your cards, C."

He threw down a king and a nine. "Booyah!" He yelled.

Frank grinned and laid out a king, then slowly revealed a queen. "Take that!"

"Dang, man! I smell a cheater."

"You mean you smell a winner? Don't mind if I do," he said happily and grabbed all the trinkets and string from the center. I looked at Calvin questionably and he explained that all they had were little objects to bet for. Whoever won the hand won whatever had been anted in the pot.

We played a few hands before they started yawning. Frank said he needed a nap, so we left him there to do just that. I went back into the main area to see Merrick pacing. His mind was filled with scenarios of Sherry not coming home. I sighed and went to his side. "She's fine."

"Every time she goes out without me, something happens," he explained loudly. "She's a magnet for trouble, always has been. I should never have let her go."

"It's only..." the quick look at the clock showed it was almost six at night, "oh."

"Yeah, oh. I know Cain's with her, but..."

I looked over to see Lillian doing basically the same thing as Merrick on the other side of the bunker. Daniel was sitting on the floor, his head leaned back against it as he watched her every move with interest. I turned back to Merrick.

I focused on the fish bowl I was in. The answers to my internal fight had to be here somewhere, hidden in silver linings and subliminal messages that people received in times like this. I just needed to pay attention.

I watched Merrick pace. I watched Lillian twist her hair over and over. I watched Daniel as he pined over the girl he couldn't have and didn't really understand why. But all of them would do anything for the one they loved.

I just needed to figure out what was worth it.

Breaking her heart when I left for the one place I'd waited my entire existence to go to, or leaving her to her anger and hoping it was one day replaced with friendship.

Could I just be friends with her? That would have to be answered in time. I guess the real question was, would she always be so beautiful when she looked at me like she wanted to devour me on the spot?

A Need So Great
Chapter 15

Daniel

It was the worst kind of torture to watch Lillian pine over her human male. She was making a thorough job of it, too. I felt a grimace touch my face at remembering how he'd gotten her to marry him. The human tradition was apparently one of importance.

The look on her face as he said those words to her… I turned my face as if doing so would wipe it all from my mind. I turned back and saw that she'd stopped and was leaning on the crates as if exhausted.

We had all eaten long ago, except for Lillian who refused, but Lillian and I both had sat there and waited for something. She was waiting for Cain to return, I was waiting for him to not. So harsh and evil, that thinking, but there it was. She couldn't be mine if he was here. He was the line in between us so the natural process would be to snub out the line with my boot.

That's what I wanted to do.

But right then, as I looked at Lillian's hips and lower back as her shirt rode up, I saw an opportunity to offer her some authoritive guidance. She was rail thin these days, as were a lot of the humans, but from this angle, Lillian looked positively ghostly. And since she seemed to enjoy Cain's efforts to boss her around…

I got up and took cat-like steps to her. She was in a daze and I didn't want to startle her. She saw me then and the reluctant smile that touched her full lips couldn't be coincidence. She had to feel something for me. Had to.

"You need to eat something," I told her gruffly. I realized that I hadn't spoken all day. "You haven't eaten all day."

She smiled in a distracted way. "How do you know that I haven't?"

"I've been watching you," I answered matter-of-factly.

"I know," she whispered and finally looked at me. "You shouldn't."

"I can't seem to stop."

"I used you," she said and straightened her back. "Do you understand that? I knew you'd help me because you had a crush on me."

"I'm assuming that crush means that I have feelings for you?" She didn't answer, but I hadn't expected her to. "Then yes, I knew that and wanted to help you anyway."

"Why?" she said in true confusion as I stepped even closer. I was now in her personal space and could tell by the slight hitching of her breath that she realized that fact, too.

"I thought it was obvious," I said low, my chest rumbling. "Lillian..."

"Don't," she whispered and shook her head. "Ok, let's just get this out in the open. It'll take my mind off Cain anyway." She crossed her arms and let me have it. "I do feel something for you. What? I don't know. It feels like there's some connection there, but it's not a crush for me, or love, or anything along those lines. I just feel...like you should be here. Not for me, not for us, just...be here."

"Like I might serve a purpose?"

She nodded. "Exactly."

"A purpose to your human cause?"

She shrugged. "I have no idea. I can't imagine that that settles well with you. Just helping us and getting nothing in return."

I chuckled without human humor. "Oh, Lillian." I broke her unspoken boundary and touched her cheek lightly. "Just being here with you is worth anything and everything that has or could happen to me. I'll take what I can get."

"Then, please don't touch me anymore," she asked, but didn't swat me away. I took my hand back and she continued. "Friends, right?"

She held out a congenial hand to shake on it. Like it was a binding contract between us. "I can't shake on it."

"Why not?" she asked, but her eyes told me she already knew.

"Because I can't just be friends with you. Even if it's just one sided, even if nothing ever comes of the connection between us," I leaned and spoke into her ear, "you'll always belong to me in my mind."

"Daniel, you can't." She looked up, her face so close to mine. I was assaulted with the memory of what she tasted like. "Why torture yourself? Why can't we just be friends and you accept that I'm with Cain?"

"What if Thomas Edison had listened to all those people tell him it was impossible to make a light bulb? We'd be standing here in the dark."

"Ok, fine, yes, but this is different."

"You say tomato, I say potato." She laughed and covered her lips. "What?"

"Nothing," she said and laughed. "Ok, potato, tomato. I get it. Still, this girl is stuck with potato soup. No tomato soup allowed, all right? Just friends."

I smiled. I refused to answer her. I didn't want to lie and I didn't want to make her worry. Instead I just scooped her some rice into a bowl and handed it over. Our fingers touched, as was my plan, and she jolted her eyes to mine.

I knew how the phrase was supposed to go. Tomato, tom*a*to. But in this case, we were so opposite that changing it seemed appropriate. Cain was a potato, I was a tomato, and Lillian was some version of the two.

I needed to get her across the tomato line. Pronto.

Hot Wired
Chapter 16

Sherry

I heard the screeching and swung around to see the van sliding to a skid. Cain had stopped and was closer to them. I was rooted to my spot with fear as men jumped out of the back and pointed guns at the warehouse. They wasted no time, not wondering if the people there were innocent or not. They just opened fire. I saw the lady who had told us to look at the camera. She was the first to go down and my stomach turned as I watched her fall.

Cain was yelling and waving at the men furiously, but they didn't listen. They ran inside the warehouse and I heard more shots fired before they ran back out with stacked boxes in their arms. They were there to steal the food and had taken out anyone there that may have tried to stop them.

For a split second I wondered why the Lighters weren't there. I figured they would be to protect their precious system and make sure it all went as planned. This seemed more like a government operation instead.

The men jumped into the van and one of them saw Cain as he ran to stop them. He must've thought he wanted a ride instead. Maybe thought a big guy like Cain would help their outfit as they played Robin Hood and stole food. The last thing I saw was Cain trying to fight him off as one of them grabbed Cain's arm and dragged him inside the back doors even as they took off. Then Cain was shoved inside and the doors slammed as they ran passed me.

Cain looked out the back window. I saw him beating on it and pointing to me, but they never stopped. "Wait! Stop!" I yelled, but they never even slowed down.

I gulped when the dust in the air was the only thing left of them. I stood there, empty handed and couldn't think of a single thing to do.

I turned and searched for someone. Anyone. I was alone in the parking lot. I ran back to the Jeep and yanked the door open. No keys. Cain still had them in his pocket. I squeezed my eyes shut tight.

I tried to think of what to do. I had to get out of there. If only I had keys, I could follow Cain. I peeked into the window of the car next to me. No keys. I slid down to the ground along the car side and tried to think of anything that didn't involve freaking out. Glancing up I saw a few thin wires sticking out of the steering wheel.

I didn't know how to hot wire a car, but I was about to try.

I pulled them out of the harness under the steering wheel and tried to make sense of the chaos of colors; red one and white ones and green. I reached under the seat for Merrick's knife that I knew he left there. I used it to slice through the wires and hoped that I could figure it out.

I sat there for at least a half hour, trying all the wires in combinations. I tapped them together, I rubbed them together, I twisted them together. I tried everything and nothing made a spark or noise. I thought back to every movie I'd ever watched where they'd done it so effortlessly and knew it was all a lie.

Hollywood had tricked me into thinking this was something that was actually doable. I fumed, feeling my face heat with anger. I would never make it back to the warehouse if I didn't get this stupid car to run.

There had been a few people to come and go. Some of them came out with boxes of food, others ran screaming back their cars. I tried to ignore them. They sure were ignoring me.

I lay my head down on the steering wheel and closed my eyes. When I opened them, two wires were dangling down further than the rest; a maroonish red one and a dirty white one. I took them in my hands and closed my eyes as I sent up my final prayer that this work. I tapped them together a couple of times and finally…got a spark. So I touched them faster and harder and was shocked to the point of squealing when the Jeep cranked to life.

I slapped the steering wheel in triumph and hopped into the seat. I threw it into reverse and looked back to make sure nothing was in my way…but the one little box of food there took my attention. I sighed. There was no way I could take that puny box home and see the look of despair on everyone faces as they realized it was hopeless. It was going to be hard enough to tell them what had happened to Cain.

Cain.

I laid my head against the steering wheel once again. Oh, God, please… Where did they take him? Maybe he made them stop and throw him out somewhere. I lifted my head as the realization hit me. Of course he did! They ran so no one would catch them, but I was sure they tossed him on his butt somewhere. Probably right down the road and he was booking it back to get to me. I smiled at the thought, but stopped. I looked toward the warehouse. I had to see for myself. I had to see that in there was some food left to grab. And I needed to hurry. I was sure that Enforcers would be there soon.

I backed the Jeep up, pulled it up to the warehouse entrance and put it in park. Leaving it running, because I didn't even know how to turn it off anyway, I got out and rounded the hood. The leg of the lady who had greeted us was sticking out of the large doorway.

I turned, feeling the gag in my throat. I didn't know if I could do this. But then I wondered if someone could be alive. That got me going and I found myself bolting through the door passed the lady and into the warehouse.

If one bloody body was enough to send me reeling, a whole warehouse of them was enough to make me scream. I looked. I didn't want to, but I looked. If there was someone alive, I needed to help them. I couldn't imagine just lying there, waiting for death…

I shook the thought away and made my way down the line. Every person there was lying still. "Hello?" I called hesitantly. My eyes continued to scan the people and found no signs of life. I felt like crying. I felt like bawling my eyes out.

The Lighters hadn't done this to us. *We* did this to us. Humans killed other humans for food.

I picked up the first box I found and looked around for food left behind by the murderers. They had taken all the breads and bags of flour, all the cereals and easy foods. I was beginning to feel the sting of despair once again until I came upon the last table. It was empty, too, and that made me think. There had to be boxes of food somewhere. They only brought out a little at a time to give the people what they needed, but there had to be a stash.

I opened the only door that I could see and gawked at my luck and the mountains of boxes. I knew I needed to hurry so I put my awe aside and opened the first box I found. Cans of fruit were inside. I almost burst into tears right there.

It would only be so long until all the can foods were gone from the world, too. Plants didn't grow so well anymore so there wouldn't be anything left to can. Same with canned tuna and chicken. Soon, they'd all be gone and I had no idea what we'd do then. But for now, I hoisted the massive heavy box of chunked pineapple, sliced pears, fruit cocktail and diced peaches and ran with it to the Jeep. I threw it in the back and ran back for another.

The next box I opened was macaroni and cheese. I grinned thinking of the kid's happiness all wrapped up into one stupid little box of cheesy noodles. I ran with that one, too, and loaded it on top of the others.

After I was finished, only seven boxes would fit in the Jeep and the last one sat in the passenger seat, so when I ran across Cain he'd have to hold that one. And it was full of canned Clam Chowder, the heaviest one. Poor guy.

I slammed the Jeep into gear without looking back and pressed the gas pedal as hard as I could. I was so ready to leave this place. I sped out to the main highway and then adopted a slower speed in case any Enforcers were out and about. And I was sure they were. Or at least I hoped they had some kind of alarm system. But then I thought back. I'd been there for almost an hour… No. There was no alarm system. I idly thought about how long those people would lay there before someone noticed. The next wave of people to come to the food maybe?

The highway was a long stretch of nothing. The grass was nonexistent anymore. Everything was dust and rocks and mud from melted snow. The trees were dead or dying. There was no life left at all. The planet was dying, we were dying. It didn't make any sense. Why would the Lighters destroy the planet that they wanted to inhabit?

Unless they were wiping everything out just to start over.

I made the slow and long ride, feeling the kink in my neck from leaning over the steering wheel for so long to start the car. I almost smiled. I did it. I got the food, hotwired a car and escaped unscathed, all by myself. I wasn't so helpless after all.

And right then, as if the universe wanted to show me how absolutely wrong I was, I saw green lights in my mirror. I could barely see over the boxes, but the lights were there. And I was alone, with a carload of stolen food, fleeing the crime scene where murder had just been committed….at the Need Warehouse.

I chuckled in desperation and disbelief. Could the odds be more stacked against me? "I get it!" I said in hysterics. "I get it, world! You want to put me in my place? I'm there, trust me. I'm being squished on the bottom of the totem pole as we speak!"

"Miss?" I heard muffled through the window. "Exit the vehicle please, with hands raised."

I took a deep breath and did what he asked. If he was going to take me to another enforcement facility, I'd have to just chance it and run. I refused to go back there.

My mind ran with ideas of how to escape when I was looking down the sights of his pistol. He leaned his head to the side and spoke into the radio on his shoulder. "This is unit thirty seven. I'm currently at my last radioed in coordinates. Send back-up, over."

Well…crap. This was it. A bullet in the back, knowing that I did everything I could do to save my family? Or back to the enforcement facility to be tortured and have to wait for rescue, knowing they were risking too much to come and save me?

I turned and ran.

Get A Wriggle On
Chapter 17

Merrick

"I don't know why you're doing that," I heard Jeff say from below me. "It's pointless, isn't it?"

I looked down at him from my perch on the ladder. I turned and went back to nailing the studs with my hammer into the stairs. "It gives me something to do. Though I guess it is kind of pointless." I sighed. "We did so much work at the store and look what happened? All that work for nothing. We just had to leave it there."

"It wasn't for nothing," he argued and crossed his arms. This meant it was 'lecture time'. "Everyone was a little more comfortable because of the hard work we did. We had plenty of room for when new people came. It was worth it in my book. I meant it was pointless to fix the stairs because the wood's rotten. Nails won't help that…" he waved his hand at it, "thing."

I looked at it. No, it wouldn't help. I threw my hammer across the floor, enjoying the solid thud it made against the concrete wall. A few chunks of concrete fell to the floor.

"I know she's gone, and it's not ideal," Jeff continued. "But we knew they might stay out tonight if they needed to. We have no idea what's going on out-"

"That's exactly right. No idea," I barked. "I know all the variables, Jeff, but I don't have to like them. She could be asleep in the Jeep with Cain right now, safe and sound, or she could be in another enforcement facility and we'd never even know until they didn't show up tomorrow night. That's a big window. Do you know how much they could do to her in that amount of time?"

"I know," he placated, but changed his tone when I glared at him. "Ok, I get it. I'm worried, too, if you want to know the truth. And Marissa is upset, too. She's freaking out about everything right now."

I looked at his face. He always had this soft spot for Sherry. I looked around at everyone else. Danny and Celeste were playing cards with Calvin and Frank. I hadn't really talked to him any all day because I didn't want to hear how much he was worried about Sherry. But the fact that his eyes were drifting toward the elevator every five seconds hadn't escaped my notice.

I knew I wasn't the only one that was worried, but she was mine. Mine to keep safe and fret about. The weird sense of déjà vu swept over me as I remembered the last time she was late coming home from a run. Flat tire, Phillip, Marissa…

I rubbed my head in frustration and looked at Jeff. "If she's not here by ten tomorrow morning, I'm going after her. I'm not asking permission, I'm telling you."

"If she's not back by ten, I'll go with you!" he said vehemently. "I told you, I'm worried, too. I think we just need to give her a little bit more credit first."

"Aw, guilt? Really?" I complained.

"Not guilt. I'm just saying."

I looked past him to see Marissa. She held her belly like it was precious, though she wasn't even showing yet. I nodded to her when she slowed cautiously to make sure it was all right to interrupt. "Hey," she said softly.

"Hey," I managed to mutter.

"Pity party for one over here," Jeff said and punched my shoulder. I wanted to punch him for real, but refrained.

"Leave him alone," Marissa scolded him. "What if that was me out there? Wouldn't you be freaked out?"

"Don't even say that!" he argued and pulled her to his lap as he leaned on the stair rail. "It's not the same." He looked at me and frowned. "Sorry. It's just," he turned back to her, "you've got two of you to worry about. No missions for you," he commanded and tapped her on the end of her nose.

"Don't make me break your finger," she sang in a joke…I thought.

"So cute when you're angry," he goaded. She twisted her face in a way that meant she was acting like she wasn't happy about what he said, but she was. He pulled her to him to kiss her chin, and then her cheek, and then her…

"I'm outta here," I groaned.

"Sorry!" he called over his shoulder. "I'll come find you in the morning. Right now," he whispered low into her neck, but I still heard, "I've got some *business* to take care of."

"I bet you do," I muttered, disgruntled. "If you can even wake up in the morning."

"I heard that!" he yelled before picking Marissa up in and taking her to their 'tent' in the corner.

I went in search of Lily, and I found her with Lana. Lana was showing her how to say 'Doll' in sign language. I watched them from back a ways. We still didn't understand what it was Lily was meant to do. She was so normal, it just didn't make sense. But then again, all the Specials were pretty normal.

Lana saw me watching and smiled before waving me over. I sat next to Lily and she showed me what she learned. It was amazing to sit and have conversations without any words spoken at all. Eventually, Lily yawned and I took her to her tent, but thought better of it. I took her to mine with me and chuckled when she'd already fallen asleep from the rocking of my carrying her.

I lay down beside her in our pallet and wrapped my arms around my little girl. She sighed and squirmed to get comfortable before settling against my chest. I was just closing my eyes when Danny opened the sheet.

"Dude, you awake?"

"I am now."

"I'm getting worried, man."

"No more than me. I already told Jeff I was going out to look for her in the morning if she's not back by then."

"But…" He shook his head and rubbed his neck. "But what if something happens to her tonight before we can find her?"

I felt the steel in my voice as I said, "Then God help the ones who hurt her if I find them."

Lily's mumbling woke me. I opened my eyes a bit to find Lily talking in her sleep. She was saying, "The end is swift, the justice equal, the way paved with gifts of the chosen."

It sounded like nothing, but out of a four year old's mouth, it was more than gibberish. I listened closer and she kept repeating the words, over and over. Her voice even took on this little twang that reminded me of…Mrs. Trudy. I gasped a little at the realization that she may not be alone in her head right then.

Then Marissa's scream cut through the silent dark. I ran, leaving Lily in our pallet to her mumbling. I swung the sheet back…and promptly turned as Jeff's backside was all I could see.

Miguel and Ryan followed me. I heard Miguel first, "Ah, mate! Cover up that full moon, why don't ya!"

Jeff seemed to realize that he was naked and covered himself with the blanket. He glared at us before settling his focus back on Marissa. She was mumbling that same thing as Lily. "The end is swift, the justice equal, the way paved with gifts of the chosen."

"What does that mean?" Jeff asked and she sat up.

She looked at each in turn and then to Jeff. "We have to go there."

"Go where, sweetheart?"

"There! To the place where they are! It's the only way to stop them!" She looked at me before whispering, "Lily."

"Yeah, I heard her, too."

"Heard her what?" Jeff asked.

"She was saying the same thing as Marissa."

"Bloody hell," Miguel muttered and yawned. "Ok, so now what? We wage a revenge war? I'm all for that."

"Me, too," Rylee said from behind us. I was too focused on Marissa though.

"That's it?" I asked her. "No more to the message?"

She nodded. "There's more, but you're not going to like it."

"More from who? Mrs. Trudy? What does she have to do with all of this anyway?"

"She says they're disappointed that the Specials haven't been used for their purposes."

"Who's they?" I asked, but I already knew. "How?"

"She's found a new purpose now. She said that…Lily is the key. Lily is all we need."

I gulped down my fear and sudden despair at that. I shook my head a firm, 'No' and then said it out loud for good measure. "No."

"You know she's special," she tried to argue.

"I'm going back to bed," I said and turned to go. I was sick and tired of everyone trying to send my girls away to the enemy. It was bad enough to let Sherry go. Screw them all if they thought for one second I was letting my little blonde angel out of my Keeper sight.

I finished her bowl bath and scrubbed under her nails. She was a filthy little girl who played as hard as she did anything else. She examined her nails and nodded her approval before skipping off. I smiled at her, but the task of the day hit me and I stopped smiling.

I went into the kitchen area and dipped Lily a bowl of oatmeal before finding Marissa. I told her what I was about to do and then asked if she would watch Lily for me. She nodded without a word and then hugged me. I was little embarrassed. She never hugged me, but she sniffled against my shoulder and said, "Find her. Bring her back safe, ok?" She looked up, the sincerity making me ache. "We miss our little mama hen around here."

"I will." I glanced Lily's way. "I won't come back without Sherry."

Loss slammed into my chest. I knew this could be the last time I saw my Lily again. Marissa nodded so I made my way to Lily. I lifted her from the stool and hugged her to me. "Daddy's got to go on a little trip." I pulled back to see her. "I'll try to be home as soon as I can."

"You gonna find Mommy?" she drawled.

"I'm going to try." I cleared my throat. "Hey, do you remember what you dreamed about last night?"

She turned her head and thought, her lips twisted. Then she said, "Zebwas and ponies and horsies. Except in my dweam, they were all pink and puwple!"

I laughed and kissed her cheek. "That sounds like a good one."

"I wish I could live there," she said off handedly. "Even the gwass was pink."

I laughed again and set her down on the stool to finish her breakfast. The dog barked to get her attention and she dipped her finger in oatmeal before letting him lick it off, giggling. I went to the crates and strapped a stake to my hip and the inside of my boot. I lifted to find Danny and Miguel doing the same thing. I started to ask what they were doing, but I knew.

"You don't have to do this," I told them, emotion clogging my throat.

Miguel scoffed. "That little sheila is the reason I'm standing here right now. She's not all piss and wind! It'd be a bastard of a thing if something happened to her. She's done nothing but look after me and cook for my sorry arse. I'm coming with you."

"I'm coming, too," Danny said and held up his hand. "And don't start."

"I'm not," I said gently. "I'm done trying to get you to listen to me." We both grinned as he punched my shoulder.

"I'll come, too," Billings chimed. He rubbed the sling on his arm and scratched under the bandages. "Itches like a mother and I'm bored outta my skull."

"Am I late to the tea party?" Jeff joked as he rounded the corner.

"Not at all," I said and threw him a stake. "How's Marissa?"

"Worried." He shrugged as he sheathed the stake in his belt. "She can't see anything about Sherry so it kind of sucks for her. The one person she wants to see, she can't."

"Ditto," I grumbled. In fact, that gave me a thought.

Baby? I feel a little déjà vu here, but I wanted to tell you we were coming to get you. If you can hear me either hurry so we don't have a wasted trip, or hold tight. If someone hurt you, I'll...make them pay for that dearly. I love you more than life. Please stay with me and be all right.

I looked to Jeff, who had heard my entire plea to Sherry, and nodded my head. "Let's go get my girl."

"Yeah," Danny agreed.

"After you," Jeff said.

"Get a wriggle on!" Miguel barked as we waited by the elevator. We all turned to look at him in confusion. "What?" The doors opened with a ding and he pushed us inside. "It means hurry up. Now come off it, you buggers!"

We all turned before the doors closed. Celeste was biting her lip and waved to Danny. He mouthed something to her and I looked away so I couldn't see what she mouthed back. Marissa was there with Lily on her hip. Even Rylee turned out for the farewell. I waved to my little blonde angel and she waved back before laying her head on Marissa's shoulder.

It was like she understood that no one wanted to do these things, they just had to be done.

"Keep the place clean, why don't ya, ginger?" Miguel goaded. He was rewarded with a finger gesture that would have made Rylee's father angry, but she also smiled while she did it. Progress...of sorts.

And then they were gone. The adrenaline pumped into my veins in rapid form and I welcomed the jitters that came. I was ready for action, whatever it may be.

I just wanted to find my Sherry alive.

Come in Gold Leader
Chapter 18

Cain

"You are so gonna pay if you don't let me out of this van, pronto, buddy."

"We saved your backside back there!" the one driving yelled at me. "And this is how you thank us?"

"I didn't need saving!" I yelled back. I thought about blasting them with my hands, but I'd blow us all up if I did that. "And you left my friend back there." I continued to look at the gun that was pointed at me so I didn't do something to make them stop. "Just let me jump out. You don't even have to slow down."

"Not gonna happen," the armed one said. "Maybe you're one of them green backs."

"Green backs?"

"Enforcers!" He sighed like he had a decision to make. "Now we've got to shoot you. You pretended you didn't know what they were. And we *all* know they work for *them*."

"I do know," I told him calmly, "but never called them green backs before. In the military we called green backs Benjamins."

"Benjamins?" he asked.

"See?" I grinned and crossed my arms. "What kind of idiot doesn't know what a Benjamin is?"

"What the heck is he talking about, Earl?" he leaned over and asked the driver.

Earl balked and yelled, "No real names!" He slapped the steering wheel with his palms. "Dang it! You're supposed to call me Red Leader, remember?"

Oh, boy. What a bunch of idiots. "Let me guess," I ventured and looked back at the one with the gun. "You're Gold Leader?"

"How did he know?" the driver hissed.

I rolled my eyes and glared at the one holding me hostage. The other one was quiet in the corner. Maybe even asleep. I looked them over. They looked like hell warmed over, eaten on a little and then put back in the microwave.

They all had a four week beard going, a head that needed a haircut like, months ago, their clothes must've been attacked by moths in their sleep and don't get me started on the smell…

"So," I drawled and leaned back, throwing my legs forward and crossing them, getting real comfortable. Or at least looking like that's what I was doing. "You're into killing innocent people, huh? Seems like a stupid move when we're all being killed off by the aliens anyway."

"You know about the aliens?" he asked and cocked a suspicious eyebrow.

"Yep, ran into a few of them. They're a little chatty, if you ask me."

"How did you escape?"

"Well," I thought and said, "for one, I didn't use code names from Star Wars. I mean really? It's not like we have technology anymore. Who cares if they hear your name or not?"

"See, Earl! Told you it wouldn't matter," the one with the gun said out of the side of his mouth. He refused to take his eyes off of me. Dang.

"We have a whole bunch of us. We have a bunker where we stay with our families," I said and tried not to think about L.

"What were you doing at the Need warehouse?"

I cocked my head and said sarcastically, "Getting food?"

"Yeah, duh," he agreed. "And that girl you left-"

"That girl *you* left?" I corrected angrily.

"Yeah, her," he continued, un-phased. "She sure was pretty. That your girl?"

"No. My girl's at home, but she was my friend. And now I've got to find a long way back to her whenever you idiots finally run out of gas or stop for another killing spree."

"Them people ain't right no more," the driver commented and then spit out the window. The tobacco missed and dripped down the half way up window. I muttered a "Gross, man" but he kept going. "They all messed up in the heads. Them aliens probed their brains or something."

"I know that," I replied. "I live with one."

"What'd you say?" he said, the fear evident in his voice.

"I said I live with one. And a whole mess of Keepers." I picked under my nails to seem like I didn't care.

"Keepers? Them things they was talking about on the TV?"

"Yeah, them things," I repeated and leaned forward. "How did you watch the TV and not fall under their compulsion?"

"How come you didn't?"

"Don't know," I said and sat back. "I've never been affected by them."

"We ain't either," he said and spit again. "That's how we got together. When I wasn't walking around like a zombie, ol' Zane asked me how come I wasn't like the others. And here we are."

"Fascinating." I crossed my arms again and felt the stake under my jacket. The one in the corner was still asleep and the one with the gun was getting really comfortable. "So how much gas you got, sport?"

"Enough to make it across the state line," he answered easily. "We'll let you out when we have to stop, but I ain't stopping 'til I have to."

The state line… The freaking state line! I couldn't wait that long. It was going to take me an eternity to make it back as it was. Gah, I hoped Sherry was all right.

I watched gun boy. The second he loosened, I was making my move. And I didn't have to wait long. He let the trigger go to scratch his nose and I yanked the stake from my jacket and smashed it into the side of his head. Then I leapt to the back doors. They flew open and I wasted no time. I jumped.

I heard the van's brakes screeching and some yelling, but I just balled myself and prepared for the insane amount of pain I was about to be in. Even with my jacket, when I hit the pavement, my arm dragged a bit before I could make myself roll. I groaned, unable to stop myself, as my arm burned with invisible fire. I finally rolled off the road into the ditch and stayed there.

I tried to breathe normally, but with my arm telling my brain that I was dying, it was a hard feat. "Holy…mother…." I growled. I felt around my upper arm. The jacket had been road-rashed away, and so had a few layers of skin of my whole bicep. It felt raw and slick. "Where's Miguel when you need something hilariously inappropriate to say?"

I heard the van doors close. I thought they might be coming to look for me, but I heard someone yell, "Go, go, go!" And they went.

It was the first time I was ever glad to be abandoned.

"Screw you, Red Leader," I groaned as I stood. It was getting darker by now. I did not want to sleep in the dark. The monsters in the night came out and tried to tear your face off.

I glanced around, holding my useless arm, and tried to see if I could spot a landmark. All I saw was dirt and a dawn sky that held my fate for the night. I'd even lost my stake in the fight with the idiot. Dang.

I took to the highway and started walking. I walked for a good thirty minutes while I tried to think about something other than Lillian freaking out at the bunker and Sherry at the Need warehouse. All alone. Crap! Crap! Crap!

She better be all right. If she's not, Merrick won't have to hurt me. I'll kick my own… Oh, no.

The big blue road sign that I had somehow missed until then was a beacon of unwanted knowledge. "No! No! Man, come on! Are you frigging kidding me?"

That bastard sign said, *Effingham, Illinois : 47 miles*

Translation? *Dude, you're screwed.*

Linebacker
Chapter 19

Sherry

The dirt flew. It was like running on a beach as I trekked down the dunes, trying not to trip as the Enforcer trailed behind me. I wondered if I was outrunning him. He hadn't shot me like I thought he would, which was weird, so I glanced back to see where he was. And that was when he reached me and tackled me to the ground.

He slammed my arms over my head and breathed hard against my face. He was young and built nicely. Not like the pot-bellied Enforcers I'd seen before. "Now, you've gone and made me dirty up my uniform," he said harshly…before laughing.

I squinted my eyes at him. Was he laughing *at* me? Was I so pathetic that the thought that not only getting caught, but being humiliated with laughter was appropriate punishment for my lameness?

He finally stopped laughing and looked at my face. "What's your name?"

"Mary Poppins," I said sarcastically. "And you are?"

"Well, Mary Poppins," he said and chuckled, "I'm Enforcer Chesser. Nice to meet you."

"Forgive me if I don't shake your hand."

He laughed again. "Well, you're just a whole bucket of fun, aren't you?"

"I try."

"Well...what am I'm going to do with you now?"

"Um...let me go?"

He smiled. He had dimples. I'm sure he thought they were charming, but this jerkface was totally barking up the wrong tree. "Now why would I want to do a thing like that?"

"Because it's the right thing to do."

"You've got a point," he said and stood, groaning. He stretched his back. "Can you believe I used to be a linebacker? The good old days." He held his hand out to me as I continued to look at him as if he were a mental patient. "I won't bite." He grinned.

"Aren't linebackers the fat ones?" I asked as I let him help me stand.

"Nah. That's the lineman. Linebackers are lean and mean."

I sneered at him, "I can see that."

"Hey, you didn't have to run," he argued with a smirk.

"Hey, you didn't have to tackle me!" I shouted and checked to make sure I still had my necklace. "Why didn't you just shoot me anyway?"

"I'm not in the habit of shooting beautiful women."

"You can keep your pretty lines for someone who eats that crap up. It's not me." He seemed amused by my rant. "And I'm not going with you to the enforcement facility. I won't go back, so if that's your plan, you may as well shoot me now."

His suddenly serious face worried me. "Won't go back? You've been to a facility before?"

"Yeah. Nice tile floors," I sneered.

"Listen," he said and held his hands up, "I don't mean you any harm. I stopped you so you didn't get stuck out here at night."

"Oh, really?" I poked his chest in my anger at the situation, but he was telling the truth. That didn't stop me, however, from saying, "Why did you radio in for back-up then?"

"I sent them to another location," he answered calmly and smiled. "My last radioed in location was the Need Warehouse on Turner Street."

"You're lying," I said, but I could tell that he wasn't. Why would he do that?

"All truth, scout's honor," he said and flashed the Boy Scout's hand signal. "I got called to the warehouse and figured I'd trail the roads to see if I found anything suspicious. A Jeep full of boxes heading away from the scene is pretty suspicious."

"I didn't do it," I found myself stammering. "I didn't...kill those people."

"I figured that when you got out of the car. I just radioed in to get them off my track, so they wouldn't come out this way. They'll be busy with the warehouse for a while."

I could stand it no longer. "Why are you helping me?"

"No offense, ma'am," he took my arm in his and ran his fingers over the bones in my hand that were prominently more defined over the past few weeks, "but you look like you could use a little help."

I jerked my hand back, embarrassed. It wasn't my fault that my family was practically starving. It was the Lighter's and the Taker's and Piper's. He seemed to understand the look on my face.

"I'm sorry. I shouldn't have said that. Listen…this is going to sound like a serious line…but you need to stay with me tonight." I rolled my eyes at him to let him know that, yes, that was a total line. "I know," he held his hands up, "but it's almost dark and they're on a massive manhunt right now for rebels. They do most of their searching at night because they figure that's when they'll be moving the most." He waited, but I didn't say anything. He went on. "You can come and stay at my house tonight, and in the morning, you can be on your way. I'll even give you an escort to…wherever it is you're staying."

He wasn't lying…again. "Why are you helping me?" I repeated.

"I used to be a cop," he said and crossed his arms over his chest. He stared at the dirt as he spoke. "When all this started happening, I was on board, all the way. I was one of the first ones to join the Enforcers back when. I was under their compulsion pretty bad." I jolted and looked at him. "But I had an accident. A head injury when my old partner and I were on a call for a suspicious vehicle. When I woke up in the hospital, I could remember everything that had happened. I remembered the words they said to get us to follow them, I remembered what had actually happened and what they had made me to believe had happened. I remembered…all the horrible things I'd done." He shook his head. "From then on, I understood everything. And the first time I saw one of those things…the dark guys, I knew something wasn't right and we were no longer alone on our planet."

"So why are you still working for them?"

"Situations such as these." He smiled, showing two rows of perfect teeth. "They never noticed anything was different with me. As long as I don't look at any of them, they don't pay me any attention. And I have others who I've told. Others who know the truth now. We try to help out rebels when we can." He nodded his chin at me with a grin in place. "But you wouldn't know anything about rebels, now would you Miss Poppins?"

"It's Sherry," I muttered.

"Thanks."

"So, what now?"

"Why don't you follow me to my humble dwellings?"

I thought hard. It *was* almost dark. And we had told Merrick and the rest that we might have to spend the night out. They weren't expecting us until morning. That reminded me. "Hey, you didn't see a van, did you? A white van with a few men inside?"

"Not today, but believe it or not, white vans have become pretty popular lately. All the rebels drive them." I grimaced. "Why?"

"My friend was with me," I whispered. I felt a sharp pain in my chest. I hoped he was all right. "The men who…shot everyone. They took him."

"Why?"

"I don't know. He was trying to stop them, I guess."

"Well that explains a lot."

"What?" I asked.

"I was wondering what a little thing like you was doing on a food supply trip. So…how many people you got back where you stay?"

I eyed him. He was just being curious. "Thirty, roundabout."

"Thirty! Whew…" He rubbed his head. "That's a nice little group you've got there. The biggest rebel camp I've found was twelve."

"And what did you do to them when you found them?" I asked and looked him right in the eye.

He grinned. "Gave them a crate of Honey Nut Cheerios."

I laughed. I couldn't help myself. I looked up at his young face and held my hand out to shake. "Sherry..Finch." I grinned. "Nice to meet you."

He shook my hand firmly. "Mark Chesser, but everyone calls me by my last name. It's an Enforcer thing that stuck with me. Nice to meet you, too. Are you ready to come home with me?" His smile grew.

"Sure!" I said brightly. "I can tell you all about my husband over dinner."

He groaned. "Dang, man." He shook his head and made a *That's a shame* noise out of the side of his mouth. "Well, let's go and in the morning, I'll get you back to him."

"Thank you," I said sincerely and we walked back to the cars. I followed him just a few miles up the road to a trailer park. Everything was a bit run down, but I had no room to talk about accommodations.

He got out and came to my door. After opening it, he said, "These places were abandoned. After we learned what was really happening, me and my buddies thought it was a good idea to all stay together." He looked around. "So we found this place and all moved next door to each other."

"I can understand that," I answered and followed him up the stairs. He knocked, so I assumed it wasn't his house. "Hey, McDonald! Open up!"

"I'm coming! Hold your ponies!"

Chesser chuckled and looked back at me briefly. "I will not be held responsible for what comes out of these guy's mouths."

"Deal."

The door opened to reveal another Enforcer, of the pot-bellied variety. "How now, brown cow. What have we here?"

"This is Sherry, a rebel I found on the highway. She's staying with me tonight. And she's married and off limits," Chesser said sternly.

I cringed a little. Should I be worried about this?

The man smiled good naturedly. "Thanks for that, Father. Like I can't make my own decisions or anything."

"Back off," Chesser said and shoved the man as they laughed. I shook my head. If I ever told a girl to back off and shoved her shoulder, we'd have an all out cat fight on our hands. I swore I'd never understand men.

"Come on in, girly!" he said and I tried not to frown at him.

I hadn't been called girly since… I sighed when my stomach rumbled. Of course it had to be at a moment when everyone was quiet. I looked up embarrassed to see if they heard. They did.

"Sorry," I mumbled.

Chesser's eyebrows jumped. "Are you apologizing for being hungry?"

"Now you sound like my husband," I told him and slouched into the little dinette bench seat. A wave of exhaustion hit me. I realized I hadn't eaten one thing all day.

"Hey, here," Chesser said and moved around McDonald to the fridge. He grabbed me a glass of something. I drank it quickly. It was apple juice.

I looked at him. "Do you know how long it's been since I've had apple juice?"

"We only have a couple jugs left ourselves. There's not any of that kind of stuff left at the warehouses anymore. All gone."

That statement sent an unexpected wave of sadness through me. It was one thing while going through boxes of food to speculate that certain things would never be available again, ever, but it was an entirely different thing to hear it straight from the horse's mouth that it was so.

I let my fingers collect the condensation from the side of the glass as they spoke in the kitchen. Something smelled like Hamburger Helper, but my mood had plummeted. Cain was gone, who knew where, and I knew everyone at home was worried about us. I imagined Merrick pacing, Danny bugging Merrick about being worried, Lillian fretting by the elevator for Cain…

I laid my head in my hands and closed my eyes to the dark of my palms.

"Hey, Mary Poppins," I heard. Then a chuckle followed and I lifted my head to see Chesser leaning over me. I'd fallen asleep with my face in my hands. I grimaced at the light above me and then looked down as he set a plate in front of me of the stuff he'd been making and a side of garlic bread.

I took the fork as slowly as I possibly could and took small bites. Even though there was no meat, it tasted like heaven on the end of that fork. I groaned loudly and he chuckled again. "Sorry," I mumbled again.

He sat down across from me and scooted in when McDonald sat beside him. "You keep apologizing," he said and grinned. He took his own heaping bite and watched me eat. "So, what's the deal with your…people?"

"What do you mean?"

"Is everyone else as…hungry?"

I nodded and spilled the beans to him, no pun intended. "Rice and beans is all we have left. And we only manage that twice a day. Sometimes we have oatmeal for breakfast, but not every day."

He pursed his lips. "So all that food in the Jeep…?"

"Is going to save my family," I said with conviction. "At least for a little while."

He nodded. McDonald just kept eating like we weren't there. Then the door banged with a knock and another man entered without waiting for an answer. He, too, was wearing an Enforcer uniform and he went right to the stove to grab a plate of food. He came and made an annoyed noise. I realized he was waiting for me to scoot over, so I did.

He sat beside me and started eating. Chesser smiled at me and nodded his head toward the man. "This here's Smith."

Smith looked at me and nodded. "Mmhmm."

Ok…

"So you're all Enforcement officers?" I asked. Smith looked down at his shirt and back up to my face. He gave me a *Duh* look and went back to eating. "Right, yeah. So you all help people around here?"

"We usually get things in return for our services," McDonald chimed in and smiled at me. He had Hamburger Helper in his teeth. I barely stopped the throw-up.

Chesser cut in with, "What he means is that we usually trade with them. We help them escape, they help us with something if we need it. Nothing like he's trying to make out."

"What?" McDonald said and kept chewing. "Nothing wrong with asking."

"Anyway. You're fine," Chesser assured me. "I'm sure you're willing to help if we needed it, right?"

"Help with what?"

"Just stuff. Like if we need someone to break in somewhere to get info or something."

"What kind of info?" I asked, my curiosity piqued.

"Well, we try to intercept the Enforcers when they bring in rebels to the facility. See, if a group of rebels attack an Enforcer, then it doesn't look suspicious. We can keep right on working as usual, but helping as much as we can under the radar. Keep your friends close, your enemies closer and your soul sucking aliens even closer than that."

I smiled. "I'm sure my family wouldn't mind helping with something like that. And no offense, but you just stop people from reaching the facilities? Anything else?"

"We've been trying to figure out a way to expose the aliens. If people learn the truth, sometimes the compulsion melts off."

I nodded. I knew that.

"See, we had a secret operation going at one of the facilities in Effingham. We had a guy on the inside who told us everything that went on and videotaped it all. Though, those things can't be seen on the tapes." He pinched his lip. "Anyway, we had it all planned out to get all the records and show people that the rebels were being tortured and then killed. There's a big broadcast station near here that we could reach the whole state with. But…some of the rebels came and blew the place up. Our whole inside operation was blown to bits with it."

I stared at him. "That was us," I murmured.

"What?"

"That was us. My family came and saved me from that place. They bombed it when we left."

"That was you!" he yelled. "Ah, I can't believe it. What were you doing there…oh. That was where you were being held," he realized and everyone at the table stopped and looked at me.

"Yes," I answered and ducked my head. I hated to be looked at like that.

"So your family must be pretty well trained to pull off something like that." He cursed and then put his hand flat on the table as he leaned forward a little bit. "I'm so sorry. It sounds stupid to say that by letting things happen, we're working for the greater good, but-"

"It's not stupid. I understand. If my going through that causes us to be able to end all this? I'd do it a thousand times over."

He leaned back. "Maybe, but it still sucks to think about. My friend was in there and he told us the things they made him do…" He shook his head. "I wouldn't have been able to do that to someone innocent just to keep my cover, but we're grateful for him. He helped us a lot and we made a lot of progress for it."

"So, any grand plans now?" I asked to remove their eyes from me and back to their food.

"Well..." Chesser drawled and looked around at them. "We've been thinking about having some sort of mass broadcast. I mean, we all know it won't go further than the state line, but at least we can get this one thing done, right? If we got the whole state to work with us, the aliens wouldn't stand a chance. I'm not sure what we can do...it's just a thought."

Lily was the first thing to pop into my head. Something Mrs. Trudy had said about Lily being the key. That she was all we needed. Something was working in my brain, trying to process it all. I felt like I was on the precipice of something that could great.

"You're a million miles away," Chesser commented.

"I'm thinking about my daughter. Lily," I said and couldn't help, but smile.

He smiled, too. "You got a little girl?"

"She's four. I actually feel a little guilty. I got to eat more than she did tonight." I wiped my mouth and looked down at my empty plate.

"Hey, it's ok," he tried to soothe. Little did he know there was no soothing a Mamma who was trying to protect her baby. "In the morning, we'll get you back to them, ok?" I nodded. "Say, why didn't your husband do the shopping?"

"He's a..." I bit my lip. They could be trusted, but to them, Keepers would still be aliens. Would he refuse to help me if he knew? "Remember that I said that we had Keepers who lived with us?"

McDonald and the other guy perked up.

"Yeah."

"I...I'm married to one." His jaw slacked. I rushed on. "The Keepers are the Lighter's opposites."

"Lighters?"

"That's what the aliens are called. Keepers are the ones who've fought the Lighters from the beginning. They're kind of like...angels. They came here when the Lighters did, to help us stop them."

"And you're married to an alien?" McDonald asked, his lip curled.

"Yep." I crossed my arms on the table. "I know it seems strange, but there are just like you and me. Except they can fight the Lighters like nobody's business."

"Then why aren't they out there fighting Lighters instead of playing house with you?"

I sighed. This was going to be hard. "Have you noticed any people that have shown signs of...abilities or powers?" They stared blankly. I felt defeated and tired of explaining. "The Keeper's job is to watch after his charge. My brother is one of these charges and they have tasks they need to complete. The Keepers watch after them until they can figure out what it is. They can't leave their charge until the task has been completed."

They continued to stare. I turned to stare out the window. There was no back yard. I was staring at the wide plank fence and the highway beyond that. I really wished I was home.

Thankfully, they didn't ask me any more questions and soon, Chesser asked me if I was ready for bed. I followed him to the next trailer and walked into his bachelor pad. It wasn't dirty; there was just nothing in it. The one couch and a TV on top of a box was the only thing in the living room at all.

"Uh…I'll take the couch. You can have my bed."

"No," I interrupted. "I don't want to take-"

"When was the last time you slept in a bed?" he asked and looked at me from under his lashes.

"A long time," I admitted.

"You're taking the bed," he insisted. "I'll take the couch, it's fine. My shift starts at eight, so we'll get an early start."

I nodded and said, "Thank you, Chesser."

"I know you have a family to go home to and all, but it feels…kind of wrong to let you go back there when I know you guys have it rough."

"We all have it a little rough right now." I smiled. "We'll be fine. We always have been."

He tipped his head once. "Goodnight."

"Night."

I went straight down the hall to the impossibly small bedroom and landed right on the mattress. I was exhausted and I didn't even take my shoes off. They hung off the end of the bed and I smelled the man whose bed I was in as I drifted to sleep thinking about Merrick and Lily. Wishing I was home, but taking this small comfort for now.

"I don't need to be the king of the world, as long as I'm the hero of this little girl! Heaven isn't too far away! Closer to it every day. No matter what your friends say…"

I jolted and for a second wondered how Warrant had made their way into my bedroom. Then I growled at the alarm and slapped the 'Shut Up' button. Chesser made his way in and rubbed as his head and neck. "Wakey, wakey."

"So I heard," I grumbled, but straightened. "Thanks. I slept like a dead person."

"Good. I'm gonna shower and then I'll be ready in about ten. All right?"

"Sure."

"There's coffee in the pot."

"Coffee?" I said, but it came out like this dreamy sigh. I said 'coffee' like one would say 'Ryan Gosling'. I cleared my throat as he laughed at me. "Thanks."

"No problem," he said, still laughing as he made his way to the hall and that tiny bathroom I passed last night. "Make yourself at home," he called out before shutting the door.

I practically ran to the kitchen. I took the cup in my hands that he had apparently left out for me and poured the brown brew slowly. It smelled better than chocolate. He even had creamer! It was powdered which was normally yuck worthy, but today, I just didn't care. I threw in some sugar and took my first sip of coffee in forever.

It slid, hot and delicious, down my throat. I sighed and licked my lips. They were a little cracked under my tongue. I turned to peer at myself in the mirror of the microwave door. I almost gasped at what I saw.

Haggard did not even describe how I looked. I hadn't seen myself in weeks. There were no mirrors in the warehouse. We didn't need them anyway, but this was…a situation. We were all getting thin, I knew. We tried not to bring it up or talk about it, but things had gotten dire. I looked at my arms and hands. I *really* looked at them. Not only was I thin, but I was almost grey. It was like my skin held no tone, no color, no…life.

I remembered Merrick's beard as I left, not as full as the other's, but a beard nonetheless, and his shirt was so stained from the lack of soap. He had gotten thinner, too.

I sipped my coffee and tried to think about getting to them, not about the things wrong with us.

I heard rain hitting the roof softly, then at more volume. By the time Chesser got out of the shower, the coffee was gone and the rain was coming down in droves. He was already wearing his uniform and looked ready to go. He said as much and I told him where to go. It would take a little while to get out there and I just hoped that I beat the search party that I knew Merrick was planning.

He followed me as we made our long trek down that highway. I felt kind of bad that he had to drive all the way out there just to see me home, but he said that he was just patrol anyway. That's all they did was drive around looking for anything suspicious and answer calls.

So I led the way back to our warehouse in the rain and hoped that I happen to pass Cain on the way. But I didn't pass Cain on the way and the rain had finally stopped. When I saw the top of the warehouse in the distance I literally squealed to myself in the Jeep. As soon as I pulled in, with the mud flying, I saw them loading the van. They all turned to look at who it was and when I saw Merrick, I slammed on the brakes. I yanked open my door and took off.

He dropped the bag he'd been holding and blurred to me, picking me up and holding me against him. I dropped a kiss to his mouth and he kissed me back with the passion of seven suns. One minute I was standing in the parking lot, the next we were in a sauna in Cuba!

Oh, God, thank you, thank you, thank you, thank you....

That continued in my mind and I fought my tears before pulling back a bit. He laid his forehead to mine in true Merrick fashion and breathed his happy sigh against my face.

I heard from behind me, "I'm assuming this is the husband."

I turned to introduce Chesser, but everyone was surrounding him with their guns and stakes."He's not a Lighter! Don't stake him!" I pulled Miguel's arm.

"Worse in my book, love! He's an Enforcer!" He glanced to Billings. "Sorry, mate."

"No offense taken," Billings said easily.

"He's helping me," I insisted. "He made sure I got home safely."

"Or he's just leading the rest of them right to us," Miguel proclaimed with a twitch of his hand on his stake.

"I can tell if he's lying, remember?"

That made him pause. "Yeah. I forgot." He looked at me. "You're sure?"

"I'm sure."

He lowered the stake, but didn't holster it. That was as good as I was getting with Miguel. The rest of them lowered their weapons, too. Chesser turned slowly to Billings, who was at his back. "Enforcer Billings?"

"Yeah," he answered, "what's it to you?"

"You went through my mentor class. You don't remember?"

Billings squinted at him. "Eh."

Chesser waved in dismissal. "Whatever." He turned to me. "I got you home and now I've got to get back."

"You could stay, but I know you won't," I offered.

"There's too much good I could be doing out there. But thanks. We'll cross paths again. You know where I am if you need me."

I crossed to him in the mud and hugged him. "Thank you. For everything."

"No problem," he whispered and set me back. "I have a good feeling about this."

"About what?"

"About us running into each other. I think…I think the war's about to take a turn."

I thought of Lily and Ellie and their new gifts. "I think you're right."

He waved and started toward his car. Danny and Miguel both yelled, "You're letting him go?"

"He's an Enforcer! We could use him if nothing else," Miguel argued.

"I'll explain everything later, I promise, but he needs to be out there. He's doing good for us."

Miguel sighed and twirled the stake in his hand. Then he pouted. "So we don't get to stake anyone?"

I laughed. "Why are you so blood thirsty!" I hugged him around his middle. "Thanks for coming to get me though. Even if it was just the parking lot."

"Anytime," he said and squeezed me. "All right, let's get back into this box of bricks before you make me wail like a woman." He stood straighter. "Wait, where's Cain?"

I felt my throat tighten. "There was an incident." Merrick's hand tightened around mine. "I'll tell you about it when we get inside. He's alive…I think. Someone…they took him. The rebels took him."

Everyone was silent for a moment before Danny asked, "So what did that Enforcer guy do to help you?" I noticed him for the first time and felt ashamed. I hugged him to me.

"He just told me all the good things they're doing on the roads and at the facilities. There are a few of them that know the truth and try to help the rebels."

"Ah," Miguel drawled, "so he's a *real* figjam." He scoffed as he took the first ladder rung and started climbing. "I know his type!" He yelled down. "Good riddance!"

I shook my head and watched as the rest of them made their way up the ladder. Jeff winked at me. I mouthed a 'Thank you' to him. I felt bad that they always got dragged into my drama.

I felt Merrick's arm go around me from behind, his face on my shoulder. I rubbed his cheek with my thumb and turned my face to him as much as I could. "I'm sorry I worried you."

"Nah, you didn't. We were just getting some fresh air," he joked.

I turned full on then and tried to smile up at him. "Such a bad liar. I'm so sorry."

"It wasn't your fault."

"They took him," I heard my voice scratch. "They took him and all I could do was stand there."

He held my face firmly. "Cain can take care of himself. Let's go talk and see what happened, then we'll see if we need to go after his sorry behind."

He was trying to act like it wasn't bothering him, but it was. Cain was his best friend. I felt like pond scum. He pulled my face up and kissed me gently, once, twice, three times and I lost count. "Thank you for coming back to me," he whispered, his anguish evident.

"Thank you for coming after me."

"Anytime, sweetheart. Anytime."

I took the first ladder rung, but stopped. "Oh! I almost forgot."

I ran back to the Jeep and Merrick followed. I threw open the back hatch and pulled the first unmarked box out. "What is this stuff? It's not all…" I opened the lid and showed him the gleaming cans of fruit just waiting to be devoured by our family.

He looked at me in an awe filled, stunned expression. "Miguel!" he yelled to stop him from going inside. Miguel peered from the roof and Merrick waved him down. "How did you do this?"

"I used every opportunity to my advantage," I said and tried not to frown.

"You forgot to turn off the car," he said off handedly, not taking his eyes from the food, and turned to do so. But stopped. "You..." That look was back. "You hotwired the car?"

"I had to," I answered.

"Oh, my…" He wrapped me up in another embrace and spoke against my hair. "I'm so sorry for ever doubting you." He leaned back and smiled. "Wow, you're incredible."

"I try," I said coyly. He rested his forehead to mine. "I love you," I said.

"That never gets old," he replied and chuckled. "Gah, I love you."

"I know."

It's So Hard To Say Goodbye
Chapter 20

Daniel

Fate had the whole bunker empty of anyone of importance and rank. They all left to find Sherry and Cain, who had not come home at their time to. And my stupid human conscience was taking a beating for it. I had hoped that Cain wouldn't return, but I hadn't figured Sherry into that equation.

The thought of Cain not returning yesterday had given me almost a happiness. But today, watching Lillian pace with actual tears in her eyes, made me feel an ache inside. Not a good ache.

And Sherry had been nothing but hospitable and caring for me.

It felt strange to feel so…ashamed.

Marissa and Lily were doing some sort of math problems. A form of human education, I assumed. I listened in and found myself laughing at little Lily's answers and the way she worded things. Her little blonde headed bobbed and jiggled as she laughed and spoke. I had stayed away from her since she saved me. I didn't really understand why. But the fact that I had watched her take the life of my brother and give it to her Keeper father could have something to do with it.

It wasn't that I was afraid of her, it was more like I didn't feel worthy to be near her. She held a power in her innocent hands that beguiled us all. And to be so close to that made me feel as if I was spoiling it.

To be honest, I had stayed away from everyone. No one had come right out and said they blamed me, but the Graphter had said all of this was my fault. That my changing sides had messed up the balance and so, he was created. I couldn't tell if people were angry with me or not. No one spoke to me before all this and no one had started since then. Things were same, which didn't help me in my conclusions. But I could imagine they couldn't be happy with the developments.

Marissa saw me looking and tilted her head to the side as if figuring out something. Then she waved to me in a way that suggested I join them. Was I going to be in trouble for watching them?

I got up from my perch on the floor and walked in their direction. Lily smiled at me and I formed a smile to match hers. "Hello, young Lily."

"Hi, Daniel. Wanna know what four plus four is?"

"Of course."

"It's eight. Maybe you should come do some school with me."

"I would love that one day," I answered truthfully. Anything this child asked of me was instantly something I had no intention of refusing.

"Uncle Cain and Mommy are late," she said and pursed her lips a little.

"I heard that." I also noticed that Marissa had said not a word to me. She just watched and I let her. "Can I ask you a question?"

"Sure!"

"My brother…I mean, the Lighter that you…took and used to save your father. What happened to him?"

"He went home."

I jolted. "You sent him home?"

"Mhhmm. He can't come back. He wasn't too happy about dat," she said and gave me a look. "He said I was a little fool, but I don't know what dat means."

Marissa chuckled and covered her mouth, but I didn't laugh. "I'm sorry he said that."

"It's ok. Do you want to go home, too?"

I was taken aback by her comment. Did I? What was waiting there for me if I did? Nothing. I shook my head a 'No'. "I just wanted to know if there were others like me out there; other Lighters who might have switched sides like me."

"No, Daniel. You are the only one." She said it so clearly that it seemed out of place. Marissa stared at me. It was unnerving. I felt like it was two against one, but I didn't even know what the wager was.

Marissa's eyes fluttered a little and she gasped, the smallest intake of breath, and finally spoke. "Daniel, do you feel like…you have something you're supposed to be doing?"

"You mean like taking out the trash?"

She smiled a little. "No. I mean like in the grand scheme of things. Do you feel like you serve a purpose that no one else can serve."

I thought about it. "I am so jumbled on the inside I have no idea what I feel."

She nodded. "Do you want to have purpose?"

I didn't know why, but I nodded emphatically. She reached across the counter and whispered, "Don't fight it."

When she touched my cold hand I got this sense of importance. It washed over me in warmth and color and I closed my eyes to it. There was a part of me that wanted to pull back, to reject whatever this gift was she was giving me, but I held still. When she finished, she removed her hand and waited for me to say something. I looked at her and knew that what she had given me hadn't been a gift at all in the real sense, but I saw the only way to ever see Lillian smile again in the task she gave me. That was a gift in itself.

I looked over at Lillian. My Lillian who didn't want me, but wanted me here. Little did she know she couldn't have it both ways. I focused back on Marissa. Her eyes were watering a little and she smiled through them. "I'm so sorry. I wish I'd gotten to know you better." She held my hand like I mattered, like I was human. "It may not help you to know this, but I saw beyond and…what's waiting for you…isn't hell, Daniel."

"Thank you. I'm not afraid. I always knew death would find me eventually. If I can die to save my Lillian's heart, then so be it."

"You're not just saving Lillian, you're winning this war for us. Everyone will know what you did. I'll make sure of it."

I nodded and heard Marissa telling Lily that her Momma was almost there as I walked away. I needed to leave now. The vision Marissa had shown me, the purpose she had dispensed to me with her Muse's Wrath, was so clear, unlike any dream.

I walked with purpose to Lillian. I knew it may be wrong and she may not understand, but I had to do this one last thing. I slowed upon seeing her. If there was a God up there, he had made one beautiful creature. She looked up and wiped her cheeks. "Hey," she tried to say brightly.

"Hi. How are you holding up?"

"I'm not really."

"Lillian…Cain will come back, I promise you that. But it won't be today."

"What?" she said, puzzled. "What do you mean?"

"It's just…intuition. But I promise you you'll have your Cain back."

She looked up at me, all innocence and beauty and a radiance that I never knew existed before her. She wouldn't understand. When she figured out what my purpose was, she wouldn't understand it for what it was. She would be angry, but what she didn't know was that I would take anything anyone ever handed to me to bear to have had been able to be with her again. I still didn't understand why this new soul in my chest had latched onto her so strongly, but I didn't want her to be angry.

I wanted her to think on this later and know that I knew the end was coming for me. That I was at peace with it. That her happiness, though it didn't include me, was more important than anything else to me and I would have given anything to know that a smile would remain on her face.

I reached my arms out for her to come into. My cold arms that held no life, but now held purpose. She walked into them carefully and let me hug her. She assumed, I'm sure, that I was offering comfort. But this selfish heart just wanted to feel her against me one more time. I rubbed my chin in her hair and even in our dire situations, she still smelled delicious. I whispered into her hair, "Can I ask one favor?"

"Sure," she said simply.

"It may seem crazy, but I…need this, Lillian."

She pulled back and looked at me. "What's the matter?"

"Nothing, I just want to ask you for something, and I want you to say yes."

She stared into my eyes as if she sensed my next words, she stiffened a little. "Daniel…"

"Please," I begged in a whisper against her forehead. "Give me this one last thing...before I let you go."

I knew she'd misunderstand my words. I knew she'd take it as I was letting her and Cain be in peace together and giving up my plight for her. She didn't know this was my goodbye. She considered it for a long time, her eyes indicating that she wasn't the sort to cheat or lie. I begged her with my eyes, I pleaded with her and waited.

Then her lips parted and I took my chance.

With my arms still around her waist, I lowered my mouth to hers. The cavern of her mouth was warmer than anything I'd ever felt and it warmed my whole body. Her little hands pressed against my chest, a barrier she was trying to set, but that was all right. I moved us to the wall at her back so I could feel every inch of her pressed against me, boots to forehead.

Oh, God in heaven that I hoped was up there, she was worth it. This little moment was worth everything it took to get here. I was the only one who could do the task set out for me and this small gift made it worth it. For the first time in my existence, I felt like I was worthy.

I crushed her to me and almost died right there on the spot when she whimpered and pushed my chest a little harder.

Pulling away she said in protest, "Daniel."

I wasn't ready to let go yet and pressed her mouth to mine once more. I lifted one hand to her cheek and caressed her skin there and on her neck. The jasmine she had worn the day that we met was long gone, but the memory was so fresh that I could almost smell it.

I began to slow, my heart breaking to do so. I took one more deep taste of her tongue, then her top lip, then the corner of her mouth. I stayed there, unable to leave and let my fingers skim her skin. I tried not to let her harsh breaths excite me further. I knew what this was and wasn't under any notions that she had changed her mind about who she chose.

"Daniel," she sighed her chastisement, and I almost groaned.

"Lillian."

"Look, I'm sorry," she said and pulled back to look at me. A trail where a tear had slid down her cheek was evident. I looked at it in the greatest awe. Then I moved my eyes back to hers. "I'm sorry that I couldn't love you. I'm sorry that I used you. I'm sorry that I made you feel something and come here just to be so out of place, but you just can't do that anymore."

"I'm not out of place, and don't ever be sorry for that." I touched the marvelous wetness on her cheek. "I'll be forever grateful that you saved me that day."

She looked stunned. "Why does it feel like you're saying goodbye?"

I didn't answer, I just stared at her, taking my fill. She took her hands and placed them on my cheeks. She pulled my face down and looked into my eyes. "They should have always been silver. That's who you are. But you can't kiss me, Daniel."

"I know it doesn't matter now," I whispered, letting my forehead touch hers, "but if I could imagine what love felt like, it would be this."

"Daniel-"

"I'm finished, I promise." I smiled and leaned up to kiss her forehead. "Thank you. I'm going to go clean up a bit. A bowl bath," I said and she laughed a little awkwardly and nodded.

I left her there with no idea that she'd never see me again. Even though my chest hurt, I felt lighter than I'd ever felt, no pun intended.

I felt free and that freedom gave me wings as I went into my tent, packed a few clothes and then snuck my way past everyone. Sherry had returned and there was a fuss being made as boxes were brought in and reunions being done. No one was paying attention, except for Marissa.

She waved to me as the elevator doors closed and mouthed to me, 'Good luck'. I nodded to her and hoped she was right. Though I didn't need luck to do what I was setting out to do.

I needed a car.

Home Sweet Warehouse
Chapter 21

Sherry

It was the longest meeting we'd ever had.

And it was an uncomfortable one because there were no chairs or couches. Lily sat in my lap and Merrick let us lean against him as we sat between his legs. Home, that's where I was. I told them all about the whole event as everyone munched on their can of fruit. I told them about the Need Warehouse and the little bit of food we'd gotten, then the shooting, them taking Cain, me getting the food and then getting caught by the Enforcer whose house I'd also slept at.

Everyone was entranced as I told them about their plan to break into the broadcast station and see if we could break the compulsion of the people. I saw something in everyone's eyes that hadn't been there when I left them here.

Hope.

A big shining light of it. I wanted to cry. Finally we were getting things back on track to take back our world instead of constantly fighting forward a step only to be pushed back two.

Jeff, per his usual self, had squeezed the life out of me when we got inside. "The next time you make a food run, I prefer applesauce," he goaded and laughed when I poked his ribs. He rubbed my head like I was a toddler and gave the next person their turn with me. Celeste had practically bowled me over with her massive boobs. It was sick, really. Everyone had gotten thinner, including her, but her boobs stayed the same size. So it reality, it looked like she went up a cup size. And that massive cup size had singed my cheek with the friction. I had pushed her away, with nothing but love for her, and listened to her as she pouted about my having slept in a real bed for a night. She called me 'Diva' for the rest of the day.

Josh, aka Simon, was pissed. Not at me, but he said he hadn't felt his conscience buzz that we were in trouble. He talked furiously with the other Keepers, trying to make sense of it. I didn't know what to tell him. He tried to leave, but strangely, it was Racine who talked sense into him. She said that if we all organized something together instead of him running off half-cocked, we'd have a better chance of finding him. He went to his tent and jerked back his curtain. That was the equivalent of a slammed door I guess.

And Lillian. I broke down at just the sight of her and she knew something was up with Cain. She came to me and hugged me. I had half expected her to slap me for losing her man, but she hugged me to her and listened as I told her first what happened. Then I promised her we'd go after him. I looked to Merrick for confirmation and he nodded. "Of course we're going after him," he almost bellowed in his vehemence, but saw Lillian's state and tried to joke. "He owes me five bucks."

It worked and she laughed at little reluctantly through her tears.

So there we sat, all talking and trying to figure out a way to communicate with people on the outside. We needed to organize somehow with the other rebels, but for all we knew they were hardly any rebels left! The daily news made out like they were running rampant, but that may not have been the truth.

The fascination with Chesser and the other Enforcers was expected. Billings was all up in arms about Cain. He wanted to lead the search party and couldn't help but ask a million questions about Chesser. He said he remembered how hard it was for him to believe us when he first got there and was skeptical that Chesser was telling the truth.

I explained that knowing the truth was what I did.

When we decided to be done for the night, Marissa and Lana offered to cook since I'd been through an 'ordeal'. I told them cooking the food, the actual food that had nothing to do with rice and beans, was all I could think to make me happier at that point. So that's what I did. With the crates as my countertop, I got busy.

No one cared that we'd all just had fruit, everyone was just grateful for something real and scarfed down the supper. I smiled. I was feeling like the new Trudy again.

So, Marissa and I finished the dishes. She seemed quiet, but lied and told me nothing was wrong with her. I let her lie and didn't press, but I did press about the baby. She said the baby was fine. She said the baby was going to be a Muse like her, she just knew it, because her gift seemed to be amplified lately. And she sometimes got visions for herself, which never happened before. She could only guess it was because of the baby getting visions for her. She said it was a girl, she had no doubt, and that Jeff was completely over his shocked stage. He was in full-on Daddy mode and was the sweetest and happiest she'd ever seen him.

I'd seen that with my own eyes. He was bouncy and laughy. It was a good sight to see.

So, later on, the men were plotting *Operation Rescue Cain* when Marissa finally revealed why she had been upset earlier. Daniel was gone. He went after Cain himself. She said she saw in a vision that he was to go after him, so she talked to him about it earlier and he'd gone to do just that.

Lillian was upset to say the least. She stood and her face held more than shock as she looked at Marissa, it held betrayal as well. Marissa tried to explain it further to her, but she wouldn't listen. She walked away from the group to her little tent and I knew that she was being torn in two.

I'd seen her face when Daniel had shown up at the bunker that day, but she had still chosen Cain. There wasn't any contest, but it still hurt. Marissa understood and waved off Jeff's concern. "She has every right to be upset, Jeff. Poor thing. Daniel knew she wouldn't understand."

"It's weird, right? For him to go after Cain?" Jeff asked. "Is anyone else worried that Cain could be in trouble by this?"

"No," Marissa assured, "you're such a guy! Daniel's in love with her. So he went to find Cain so Lillian would be happy."

"What?" he asked in a high voice. "How in the worlds does that make sense?"

"Ugh," she groaned and laughed as she snuggled into his lap. "Just be glad I love you."

They laughed, but I turned to Merrick and told him I was going to go visit Lillian. "Just…don't be gone too long," he begged and kissed my temple.

I smiled and bit my lip as I agreed.

I found her on her pallet with Bones laying on her stomach, her head under the pillow and her covers thrown over her. I patted her arm and she must've known I'd be the one to follow her in because she said, "Sherry. Please make him be ok."

"Daniel's had centuries of training-"

She sat up. "I'm talking about Cain. And now I have to worry about Daniel, too." She sniffled. "Why would he…" She covered her mouth. "Oh, my gosh. That's why he…kissed me earlier. He was leaving and he knew it."

"He kissed you?" I asked.

She gave me a wry smile. "This is a little déjà vu, huh?"

"A little."

"He kissed me…and I thought he was letting me go, that he was going to stop trying to be with me, but he was saying goodbye." She looked at me, her lip quivering. "Why do I feel so guilty that I couldn't love him back? Cain was here first and I love him. I do, I love him *so* much. I wouldn't change anything about that. So why do I feel guilty?"

I lay down beside her and linked my arm with hers. "Oh, Lillian. Trying to make order of the chaos that is love is like trying to figure out why chocolate ice cream makes your toes curl."

She chuckled and lay down beside me. "Ok, point taken."

We lay in companionable silence for a while. I wondered if she'd fallen asleep. Then she said, "I know Marissa said that Daniel would find Cain…and he'll be ok. You believe her, don't you? Cain will be ok and he'll come home to me?"

"I know it's true. You can't lie to me. It's just a matter of *when* he'll be here."

"Ok." She let a breath go and paused as if thinking. "It's hard to just believe that and not worry. Not…think the worst." She started to choke up.

"Think of something else."

She sniffed. "You know…I really miss brownies."

I burst out laughing, Lillian eventually joining me reluctantly. Even the dog barked along with us as if he were just as happy.

I felt myself being lifted. My head hung over a very warm arm and the rest of me was pressed to a warm chest that shook with laughter when I lifted my hand to his face. "Hey," he whispered to me as he moved our sheet to the side. "Sorry. I couldn't let Lillian keep you all night."

He laid me down and then lay beside me. "That's ok. I didn't mean to fall asleep."

"That's ok," he echoed. "You've had quite an ordeal," he joked. I'd been poking fun of people for saying that to me all day.

"Yes. Quite." I laughed.

"So, was she all right?"

"Oh, you know. Love lost, love scorned, love come back again. We should start a soap opera. *The Bunker Diaries of the Apocalypse!*"

He laughed. "Too bad there's no one to watch it."

"Yeah, too bad. So," I started, "are you leaving in the morning to search for Cain?"

"Actually…no. Daniel's already gone after him and Marissa assured me that in her vision, he finds Cain and Cain makes it home safely. So we thought it would better suit our time to try and figure out this broadcasting deal. Maybe go and take a look at the station, see what we can find."

I nodded and yawned. "Yeah."

He pulled me to spoon with his front to my back. "Go back to sleep. We'll talk in the morning."

"You don't wanna…" I asked and wiggled against him with a grin.

He chuckled. "That's not all my brain thinks about. Sometimes, I just want to hold you and know that you're safe," he squeezed me to him, "right here."

"Ok," I agreed. It was sad how tired I was and willing to give up.

He kissed the back of my neck and spoke into my ear in a soft growl, "But in the morning, all bets are off, sweetheart."

I smiled and let his warmth carry me to sleep.

After waking up to being deliciously wrapped around my husband as he promised, I had left him there, exhausted, naked and asleep in our blankets. I couldn't help but grin as I went to find Lily and get her some breakfast.

But she was already there with Calvin and Frank, munching down on some kind of granola bar that must've been in the boxes I brought.

Marissa and Jeff were reading a book and feeding each other peach slices. Danny and Celeste were playing the slap-hands game and laughing. Ryan and Ellie were studiously avoiding each other, and Miguel and Rylee were watching each other openly over a crate marked 'Guns'.

I was slightly alarmed by that, but got my breakfast and made Merrick a bowl. Just in time, too, it seemed. I felt his hands on my waist from behind me. I turned into him to thank him for…this morning, when we all stopped.

The squeal from the elevator was loud above all the other noise. Merrick shoved me behind him and motioned for Jeff to toss him a stake. Everyone got ready for a fight and waited.

The doors stopped with a thud that sounded wrong. It never made that noise when we rode it. I squeezed Merrick's arm as the doors creaked open to reveal Chesser. Chesser and a whole butt-load of people.

"Chesser?" I said and moved around Merrick. I looked at the posse gathered behind him. There were at least twenty. They looked scared, dirty and hungry.

"Hey," he smiled easily, "I assumed you took strays, otherwise…this will be awkward."

"Of course, we just…" I looked around. "I mean, it's nothing fancy."

Merrick and Jeff came to flank me. "Brother," Jeff said a man stepped forward. He was scraggily to say the last, but still managed to hug Jeff.

"Brother," the man said and then looked at Merrick. They repeated the process and then a woman came forward. Then another. At the end of introductions, there were five Keepers and only one Special. The rest were just rebels.

I pulled Chesser to the side a little to let them talk Keeper talk.

"What do you want us to do with them?"

"Just add them to the cause. Are you working on how to help us with the broadcast?"

"Yeah," I replied and smiled small. "Everybody's a little revved up about it."

"Good!" he shouted and laughed. "We'll need all hands on deck for this thing."

"I know." I nodded my head to the kitchen. "You hungry?"

"And steal the precious food you worked so hard to steal?" He grinned. "Nah, I'm good. But thanks."

"So, where did you find them?"

"They got stopped crossing the river. I was supposed to transport them to the nearest facility, but…" He shrugged. "I know things are tight here, but I didn't know where else to take them. And I'm hoping that we can get everything organized soon for the broadcast."

I nodded. "We're fine. They can stay. We'll wait to hear word from you."

"Alrighty." He touched my arm and nodded before walking to the elevator. He explained to the newbies that he was leaving them there with us, but he would see them soon. And then he was gone and the newbies and us were just staring at each other.

"Who wants some breakfast?" I ventured.

They all jumped at the chance for that and I proceeded to make a huge pot of oatmeal and even had sugar and cinnamon to add to it this time. It reminded me so much of how we used to be at the store. It reminded me of Trudy.

More rebels added to the cause. Now we just had to figure out how to get word out. We had to figure out a way to make this work.

Collision
Chapter 22

Ryan

Ellie was steering clear of the crowd that moseyed around, occupying every empty corner and cranny. To say that I hadn't noticed was a lie because I'd been watching her.

I thought to say the words out loud gave them power. We'd always been taught that. So I thought to say those awful things to her would make the power behind them ring true. I *did* want to go to the After. But did I actually think I was ever going to get there? I had no idea. Either way, I shouldn't have said those things to her.

I'd never tasted the kind of venom I used on her that day and it still stung to think about it. She hadn't spoken to me since. And now, I watched one of the men as he watched her. She was beautiful, plain as day to see. I felt like the biggest kind of fool for feeling like I had some claim on her.

She caught me looking, but I didn't look away. And when the man approached her and asked her name, I still didn't look away. Calvin came and stood beside me. He propped his foot up behind him on the wall and crossed his arms, mirroring my pose. "What are we staking out?" He grinned. "Or should I say *who*?"

I frowned. "Nothing and nobody."

"So the fact that your eyes are glued to Ellie have absolutely no basis on our study?" he said seriously. I had a feeling he was making fun of me.

"Calvin," I sighed.

"Ry! Come on, man! I'm a kid stuck in a bunker! There's nothing here to do. Please, let me live vicariously through you!"

"What does that mean?"

"It means to go tell Mister Grabby to keep his paws off your woman!" He nodded his head toward Ellie and the man was invading her personal space and then some. She was trying to be polite to him, but my brain didn't think and my heart didn't beat as I made swift steps to her.

"Excuse me," I told the man and moved him slightly to reach Ellie's hand. I gripped it gently and the thought hadn't occurred to me until then that she might snatch her hand away and tell me to scram. But she didn't.

She followed me to the elevator doors, which seemed like the only semi-private area. I could hear her clearly as she said, "Thanks."

"You're welcome."

She started to walk off, but I couldn't let her. I grabbed her elbow gently and when she refused to turn to look at me, I felt my heart break a little. I had done this. I had slammed the wedge down between us just like I wanted. So why did I feel so horrible in my guts about it?

"Ellie," I whispered.

"I'm not a yo-yo, Ryan. You can't just jerk me up and down." She turned to face me and her cheeks were flushed. "You either want me or you don't, and you made it pretty clear that you didn't."

"I want you, I just don't know how to give up something so I can keep something else," I said dejected. I let it all hang on my face like a mask. I let her arm go and leaned against the wall. I had no idea what I was doing anymore. My fingers worked their way into my hair…the body's hair, I reminded myself. Not mine.

I was raw and raging with no end in sight of relief. I'd never been so confused.

I had expected Ellie to leave when she was released by me, but I felt her hand on my chest. I opened my eyes to find her in front of me, looking sympathetic and confused herself.

"My whole family is gone," she said and bit the side of her lip. "They all died and…I wish they could come back more than anything." She gave me a pointed look. "That would be my heaven, but that won't happen. But, if we're being honest, if I could go back and have them live, I would. That would mean I would never have met you."

Her meaning bowled me over. I felt sliced down the middle for this girl. "I would want that, for you to have your family back, even if it meant we'd never have met. Their loss is greater than anything you'd ever gain from me."

She steeled herself. "And the loss of your After place is greater than anything you'd ever gain from me."

I felt my chest rush with breath. "I'm not so sure that's true anymore."

"But that's the point, Ryan. Some things can't be changed, some things can. Whether or not you can go there doesn't matter right *now*. I'll never get my family back and that won't change." A tear that had been begging to fall slid gracefully down her cheek. "There might not be a tomorrow for any one of us. You have to hold on to right now, you have to live like tomorrow isn't coming. And right now." She stepped closer. She didn't wipe her tears away and I'd never seen her so open and raw before. "Right now I'm standing in front of you, right *in front of you*, and I'm not asking you to give up anything for me. If the time comes, I'll gladly let you go to the After because I know what it means for you and I'll be happy for you, but right now…I want you to put your arms around me and pretend that there *is* no tomorrow."

I yanked her to me. I couldn't even be sorry for my rough treatment of her, but she wasn't complaining as she put her arms around my waist. I reveled in the feel of her. She was a tiny thing and her head fit right under my chin.

She had managed to take something so confusing and heartbreaking in my mind and break it down to a simple fact: That we are all here for the same thing right now, to survive, and you have to take your happiness where you could find it.

"I'm…" I tried, but it just seemed so unconvincing. "I'm so sorry, Ellie."

"No, I'm sorry," she replied and leaned her head back a little.

"No," I insisted, "I thought I was doing you a favor, but I wasn't. I hurt you and I…"

"I forgot that you haven't been a man for very long." She smiled and rubbed my chest with her fingers. "I expected you to be something that you're just…not. I threw it in your face that you weren't the man I thought you were, but I realized that I'm happy about that." She laughed. "Human guys are overrated."

I felt my mouth pull wide in a grin. I lifted my hand to rub her cheek bone. Such softness over something so hard. Used to protect the face, but also made her look beautiful. The human body was a fascinating thing. And this human body under me was gorgeous. "We'll just see where it goes. No expectations. Just day to day."

"That sounds perfect, Ry."

I startled at that. "Have you been talking to Calvin?"

"I may have," she said coyly. "He's such a smart kid."

I thought I heard a hint of something in there. "Did he give you some advice?"

"He said to stop being such a *girl* and forgive you. That you were a good guy, and he was right."

"I'll have to thank him," I said in a low voice. "I'm sorry."

"No more being sorry." She smiled, her eyes crinkling in the corners showing me she meant every word. She reached up and put her hands on my cheeks before pressing her lips to mine softly. My eyes closed on their own accord and I felt a shudder ripple through me at her sweetness. She pulled back and said, "Wanna share a can of pineapple with me?"

"I've never had pineapple," I said, dazed.

"Well that won't do, Keeper."

She dragged me to the designated crate for the kitchen, hopped onto the crate, opened the can and popped the first piece into my mouth. It was so sweet and juicy I groaned. She licked her fingers and said, "I guess that means you like it."

I jumped up to sit beside her on the crate. I looked down and saw the words 'Ammunition' upside on the side of it. I chuckled to myself. I was sitting on a crate of bullets, arms and legs pressed to a girl's who was feeding me pineapple and licking her lips that she's just kissed me with. My charge was running from his friend and play fighting, my brothers were all absorbed in their woman or their talks. For now, my earth family was safe.

It was sounding a lot more like Heaven every minute.

And So, We Meet Again
Chapter 23

Cain

My arm, or I as was beginning to call it, the lifeless throbbing bastard, was dead weight in my jacket that I tied around my neck to support it. The thing was hurting so badly from all the missing meat and dirt rubbed into the sore that I contemplated trying to fall down and go to sleep.

But I couldn’t. I knew that the bad guys were out and about so I had to be on my game. It was getting dark again and I hadn't seen a soul all day. The van had left me long ago, hours maybe, and I had trudged through the dirt, staying off the road. My shoes were full of sand and I could literally have collapsed, but I didn't.

I hadn't eaten anything all day yesterday and my stomach had been growling at me.

More hours passed. Even in the military, with all the exercises and training we did, I'd never been this exhausted before. It did me no good to be awake. With the blood I'd lost and no food in my system and lack of sleep, if I was attacked, it wasn't like I could have fought them off.

Things went from bleak to bleaker as headlights rounded the hill. I debated for mere seconds on whether to take my chances that they might help me. At the last second before they could see me, I followed my gut and ducked down. The movement jammed by arm into my leg and I cursed as I lay in the dirt and groaned as silently as I could. They passed by and I raised my head to see. Good call because they were frigging Enforcers. I let my head fall with a thud to the sand at my close call. I couldn't get up, just couldn't.

I thought about Lillian. I wasn't one to dwell in a bad situation, but I wondered if I'd ever see her again. I imagined her fretting over me, wrapping my arm and humming me to sleep with one of her daddy's hymnals, like a good wife. I smiled. I must've been delirious because I could actually hear her humming in my ear.

If terror falls upon your bed and sleep no longer comes,
Remember all the words I said. Be still, be still and know.
When you go through the valley and shadow comes down from the hill,
If morning never comes to be, be still, be still, be still.
If you forget the way to go, and lose where you came from.
If no one is standing beside you, be still, and know I am.
Be still and know that I'm with you, be still and know I am.

I woke with a boot on my neck, and the sun was down again. I glared up at the Lighter whose long block ponytail hung over his shoulder. A ponytail? That alone made me want to hurt him. Pansy.

But he had the upper hand on this one. My body was still exhausted beyond belief and he was pressing the breath out of my windpipe. I croaked, all bravado, "You should've killed me when you had the chance, Lighter boy." He smirked. "Now you're in trouble."

"What a big mouth on the boy who's under my boot." He laughed and smiled menacingly. He pressed harder and I hissed. "What was that?"

I punched his calf with my palm and his foot slid off my neck. He laughed even more as I sat up and he circled me.

"Why didn't you just kill me while I was sleeping?"

"There would be no fun that way," he said like it was obvious. "I knew you were a rebel, out here all alone. I wanted you to wake up," he clucked his tongue, "but from the looks of things, you're in no condition to put up much of a fight. Shame."

I stood trying not to wobble. "See, this is why nobody likes you. That's just rude."

He smirked. "Are you going to pull the *all talk and no action* routine?"

"Nah. Let's go," I beckoned. If I was going out, I was going out with my fist busting a Lighter's jaw.

He circled me before blurring to my right and slamming his fist into my back. I groaned, but stood my ground. And learned. He tried that move again and that landed him a punch in the gut. I tried to blast him with my hands, but I was just too beat and he evaded it every time. We went round and round before I had to admit to myself that he was just toying with me. He knew I had no fight in me and could have ended it at any time, but he didn't. I wondered why.

"Ah, they're here," he finally said.

"Who's that?" I asked with dread.

"My brothers." I turned to see headlights and huffed out angry breaths.

"Oh, come on. Don't you Lighters fly and soar and other fairy crap?"

"But then your ignorant humans would know something was different, now wouldn't they?" He smiled evilly to the ones approaching us. There were three of them, all different, but all the same.

"You know you all look the same?" I goaded.

"Shut your mouth, foul human!" one of the newer ones yelled.

I laughed. "Foul human!" I laughed some more. "Dude, too many evil movies for you."

He backhanded me in a blur that I didn't see coming. I spit the blood off to the side and tried to keep my cool.

"We are done playing with this one," one of them said. "End it or bring him in for questioning."

I remembered Sherry's *questioning* they'd performed on her. That wasn't happening. "You can just kill me now. I won't be talking to you about anything. Unless you've got the latest news on Gossip Girl. Man, I miss that show."

He frowned and cocked his head in confusion. "Enough!" the other one barked. "Finish it. We've got other work to do."

"Allow me," the one in the back said. He stepped forward and his steps shook the ground. That Graphter thing. Crap.

I always imagined how I'd die, all bad ace and chin raised in defiance, maybe give them the finger. It didn't quite work that way. I accepted it though. I'd put up a good fight, but this was it so I'd bow out with grace. I closed my eyes and thought of my L.

My eyelids turned red with another approaching light. I opened them to see another car. They were pointed our way, just sitting there. That looked like the… Gremlin! How the heck had they found me? And why the heck were they just sitting there?

The car's engine revved. Then whoever was driving pressed the gas and rushed us. I leapt out of the way in a *just in time* manner and managed to be missed. The Lighters and that other…thing…moved, too, and gawked at us as the Gremlin slid into the sand next to me. The passenger door opened. I scrambled up and into the seat without even looking and slammed the door shut as he smashed the gas and turned a one eighty. The Graphter looked peeved and when he lifted his hands I knew what was coming. "Punch it!" I yelled and squeezed my eyes shut tight just as the Graphter clapped his hands.

The windshield shattered at the boom.

We kept going, knocking one of the smug Lighters over in the process of our sliding. I figured they'd give chase, but we weren't big enough fish I guessed. I turned back to the front, shielding my eyes from the wind coming at us from the now wide gaping windshield. "Dude, that was…what the hell?"

It was Daniel.

He looked at me and then back at the road. "I've been driving all day and night looking for you."

"What for?" I asked, flabbergasted. "Why are you here? Where's everyone else?"

"I came alone. I told no one."

"Ooooh," I dragged out, "so you snuck out to find me and off the competition, huh?"

He gave me strange look. I could see him in the lights from the dash as he sped down the highway. "I can only assume you are referring to Lillian, and I can guarantee you that won't be happening."

I chuckled without a trace a humor. "Giving up?"

"Yes," he said quickly.

"Why? I thought you said you loved her." I had no idea why I was arguing with him once he said he'd given up, but it just came out.

"I do," he said sternly and flashed a look that held contempt and regret, one in the same. "But she is in love with you."

I almost smiled. "I know."

"I kissed her," he confessed and I balled up my fist.

"Again?" I asked, thinking he was talking about the first time.

"Yes." I almost choked him right there. "When I…said goodbye," he clarified. I imagined the two of them, Lillian's strange affection for him, him bidding her goodbye forever… "I wanted to be upfront with you. She…" he shook his head, "she doesn't love me. She worries about you constantly, her eyes are searching for you even when you're not there." He looked at me. "She looks right past me when she's looking at me. She can't help it."

What was I supposed to say to that? So I said, "I still owe you a beat down for what you did. Don't think I've forgotten."

"I haven't forgotten," he said calmly and kept driving. I eyed him, biting on my lip ring and cracking my knuckles.

"So what are we doing? Going home? Did Sherry make it home all right?"

"She did," he answered. "And no, we're not going there. We have a task."

"What task?"

"We're headed to the state line."

"What for?" I asked angrily. I wanted to go home and see my wife. I wanted to see her and I wanted to ask her why she let Lighter boy put his lips on her again. She wouldn't lie to me, or cheat on me, I knew she wouldn't. And I knew she loved me, I just couldn't understand this strange…thing…with Daniel.

He finally answered, but it was so low I barely heard it. "We're going there for me to die."

I didn't take his bait. I wanted out of that car, but it was a necessary prison. I held my aching arm to my chest and tried not to groan at the pain that suddenly hit me from being still. The adrenaline had said *bye-bye* and the pain was settling in. I felt a shudder rack me and felt like cursing. This stupid arm was going to make me go into shock or something. I hadn't been able to clean it. A day and a night…it was probably already getting infected.

Daniel must've heard my complaining. "You're injured."

"Thank you, Captain Obvious."

He frowned. "You need a doctor."

"Nah," I said, but knew that was a lie. I needed to clean this thing. "I'm good."

"I think I should bring you to a human facility that attends to medical needs."

"No hospitals. Last time didn't go so well for us," I told him, remembering Marissa and I with Billings.

"You may not have a choice. What good would it have done for me to have come to save you if you die from infection?"

"Point well made, Lighter boy," I groaned. I hated that he was right. "Maybe we'll just stop in for a quick visit."

"I have your back. No need to worry," he assured and I swore, if he patted me on the back like some 'Good ol' Chap' I was going to go ballistic on him. But he didn't, he just kept right on driving. I leaned my seat back, throwing my good arm over my face and let him navigate.

I wasn't sure what his angle was, but he wasn't getting any unnecessary chatter from me.

He told me that he had stopped by the store bunker and the place had been trashed. All the food and supplies were gone. Even Piper, who'd been left in the back room, was gone. I didn't know what to make of that.

A while later I felt him slowing down. He was eyeing a small clinic. He pulled in and put the car in park. "How did you learn to drive anyhow?"

He looked at me as if that were a strange question. "I learned from the humans, of course."

"Ok," I said and raised my eyebrows in sarcasm. "Well, I'll be back, champ."

"I am coming with you," he insisted and in a stupid move, put his hand on my good arm.

I glared at him. "You're gonna need a hospital for your own arm if you don't let go."

He lifted his hand. "I am sorry, but I *am* coming with you. I will make sure you make it safely back to your Lillian."

I shook my head. "Whatever, man." I leaned over and opened the door. It creaked loudly in the empty parking lot. He got out, too, and we made our way to the automatic doors.

I hadn't thought about the mess I would look like to her; my bloody jacket wrapped around my neck, holding up my bloody arm. I was dirty, head to toe and who knew what else. The woman gasped and covered her mouth with her hands in a true *Oh, no!* face. She ran around the counter and took my good arm immediately.

"What happened to you?"

"Boys being boys," I drawled.

She didn't laugh. She dragged me back to one of the rooms and plopped me on the table. She was short and a little plump, but had the sweetest little face. "Let me take a look at what you've done to yourself," she scolded. "What were you doing? Camping with a bear?"

Daniel had followed us in and he watched her hands move with interest. "Uh…" I tried. "It was more like sandhill bogging. Got in the way. Whatya gonna do?" I tried the smile, but she wasn't having it.

She frowned, her hand on her hip. "My… Well, I guess I'll get the doctor to take a look at you. You're going to need some antibiotics and a fresh bandage," she peeled the jacket away and grimaced, "and this has to be cleaned. There's dirt and sand scrubbed almost down to the bone," she scolded again.

"Can't a guy get some sympathy around here?" I joked. I pouted my bottom lip out and saw her eyes glance at my lip ring. "I'm an injured man."

She smiled, but it was out of tolerance. "Well you're just a scoundrel, aren't you?"

"If I say 'yes' can I have a lollipop?"

She outright laughed at that and I grinned inside. I still had it.

"Oh, shush, you." She went to peek out the door and then opened it wide to let the doctor in. It was then that I steeled myself. He was about to scrub this sand out of my wound. The wound that had already started to heal.

Things were about to get ugly.

Next thing I knew, we were talking about what happened, he was taking a little look see, then Doctor Sly had stuck me with a needle in the arm and I was going down fast. He leaned over and smiled smugly. "See you in a bit," he taunted. I wanted to punch him, but the sneaky sleep he'd given me was quick.

So my brain dreamed of Lillian and our honeymoon, our first night together. Gah…I remember gripping her hips, bones very obvious, but sexy and right in my hands. I remember all the noises she made, all the times she grabbed the back of my neck and begged me not to stop…

But she kissed Daniel. Or he kissed her. That was something I'd have to deal with later. She wasn't a cheater. After what I went through with my fiancé', Lillian wouldn't do that. But letting him kiss her…

A sharp pain growled its release through my throat and my arm was on fire. I looked to see the flames, but it was a bottle of clear liquid, not flames that I saw. I looked at the Doc's face. He was all business. "I'm awake," I told him and he poured more of that demon liquid on my arm. "I'm awake and can totally feel that!"

"I know," he said calmly. "That's how I wake my patients up." He laughed at his own joke.

"Dude. Comedy school, pronto."

"Are you saying my jokes aren't funny?" he asked even as he still laughed. I didn't answer him, I just groaned like a sissy and tried not to curse like a sailor. "My patients usually don't mind. All done. I put you under because it was not going to be fun to clean that arm." He pointed to the nice clean bandage and sling. "Here's some ointment and bandages. Keep it dry and clean."

"Gotcha, Doc. Thanks."

"So…where are you from? Not from around here, huh?"

"Why do you say that?" I said with caution. Doc was acting weird.

"Well…we're an animal clinic." I jerked my gaze to Daniel. He looked confused. "The *people* hospital is about three miles on the other side of town." He grinned in a teasing way. "I didn't turn you away 'cause you were in bad shape and we weren't busy, but my patients used to come in on four legs."

"Nice going, Daniel," I said and glanced at him before settling back on the Doc. "Thanks. Sorry and yes, we're just passing through."

"Not a problem. I'm surprised the front door was unlocked. We usually lock it. Now we just run blood tests and do analysis for the Enforcement centers since animals are no longer around. We also stock pile meds for the hospitals since they've had so many break-ins. Well, uh, there's a motel that takes cash next door," he offered.

I eyed him. Man, if only Sherry were here, she could decipher this guy. "Ok, thanks."

"I'll let you guys get back to…passing through." He smiled and gave the nurse the papers. "Felicia will handle this for you at the desk."

I nodded, but had no intentions of staying and filling out some papers. And I didn't have a dime on me, so that didn't matter either. We followed her out and I was amazed at how much better my arm felt. It hurt, oh yes, but the pain was more of a good pain now. It was no longer life sucking, it was manageable.

When she turned to go back to the front desk, we turned right and kept right on going. Swiftly we got back to the car and I wondered how I missed it. Right there in big letters on the sign it said "Meyer Clinic - K9s are our specialty". I glared at Daniel as he put us in drive once more.

"I know, I know," he said. "But you're bandaged and better now, so I think anything other than that is irrelevant."

I huffed and stared out the window. We passed the motel the Doc had told us about. "We'll need to stop somewhere to sleep eventually."

"Not there," he said. "He may have been nice enough for a human, but I got a strange feeling about it."

"Nice enough for a human?" I scoffed. "Really?"

"Humans have never been anything but hostile to me."

"You took over our freaking planet!" I yelled, the jolting of my voice squeezing a pinch through my arm.

"Yes, I know. And I'm not saying humans weren't founded in their actions to me, but they remain the same."

"Sometimes you can't just spout things even if they are true. Some things need a little bit of explanation," I told him.

"I will try to remember that," he said wryly, like it didn't matter.

"Did you say you were going to die earlier?" He stayed silent. "I could've sworn I heard you say you were heading to die."

"My death is my burden."

"Fine." I yawned into my good hand. "I'll look out my window and pretend that I never asked."

"You'll know everything soon enough," he grumbled. I ignored him and we rode on.

Tag-along
Chapter 24

Merrick

"Hey, gorgeous," I told her as I watched her from the corner. It was night time again. She was changing her clothes and looking at her stomach. It was so thin and I knew she was getting self-conscious about it. But it wasn't her fault. Everyone was struggling with that part.

"Thanks," she said half-heartedly and then tried to change the subject. "I'm glad you shaved. You look like you again."

"I'm being completely serious." I put my arms around her from behind. "I never loved you for your looks anyway, but you're still beautiful."

"I know, but…" she sighed, "it wasn't like I had a lot to lose anyways."

I turned her to me and took her fingers in mine. I pushed her back to the wall, lifting her easily and wrapping her legs around my waist. I pressed her hand to the wall by her head and took her mouth roughly. She gasped into my mouth, which was tinder to my fire. I used my free hand to run strokes from her cheek, to her neck, to her chest, to her stomach, to her hip, to her behind. I growled as she tightened her legs on me and I tried to find places in her mouth I had yet to discover.

My lips tingled, making my whole body tingle. Did she really think that I didn't love every piece of her, no matter how thin or fragile? In honesty it made me love her more. My caring little martyr who took care of everyone else so thoroughly and left crumbs of everything for herself.

I felt her fingers in my hair, tugging and claiming. What I wouldn't have given for a closet sized room right then so I could claim her properly. I let my lips lower to her chin and then her neck. Her lips parted and her eyes closed. I kissed as low as her shirt collar would allow me and then yanked the whole thing off in one smooth motion.

Yeah, we were in the 'bowl bath' area, but apparently, I had no dignity any longer because I was going to have my wife, right there.

"Bloody hell!" I heard and quickly covered her with my body. Miguel was barely containing his laughter as he turned away. "What kinda bloke bogs into the wife in the wide open, huh?"

"Get out, Aussie."

He looked back and grinned. "Well, look at you. Grinning like a shot fox."

I threw the first thing I could grab; a metal mixing bowl. He laughed, ducking it easily and kept right on laughing as he made his way back to the others.

I looked at Sherry, expecting red cheeks and flustered breaths, but she was laughing. We laughed together, sharing breath, before she finally said, "This wasn't exactly discreet, Merrick."

"I was trying to prove a point," I said huskily.

"What was that?" she said, her breaths soft and panting.

I whispered against her mouth, "That I want my beautiful wife anywhere, everywhere, always, in *all* ways."

She chuckled. "We're never going to get dressed if you keep that up."

"Ok," I agreed easily and she laughed again.

She kissed my lips and held my face. "Thank you."

"I love you, wife."

"I know you do, husband. Now put me down." She grinned.

I did what she commanded of me. I would always gladly do that.

After getting ourselves situated, I took her hand and towed her to the new commons room. We had decided this morning that a stake out of the radio station was needed. Sherry and I along with Ryan and Ellie would go. I'd bring Sherry, for obvious reasons, because she could tell me when someone was lying, and Ellie, because she could hide my Keeper senses from the Lighters. They wouldn't be able to tell what I was. Jeff and Marissa were coming, too, to drive and watch out for things while we were inside.

Celeste and Danny were on Lily duty. As I watched Lily braid Celeste's hair on one side and Danny on the other, preening like a little girl as he did it, making Lily giggle, I knew they didn't mind.

Sherry and I both ate a small can of fruit with the others in our group that were going. Marissa was plowing through a can and then gladly accepted the rest of Jeff's. He grabbed something else from the box and ate it quickly.

I hadn't even thought about the ramifications to the baby in Marissa's belly. It was one thing for *us* to be hungry, but Marissa was another.

We finished and everyone was dressed as properly as we could be. We looked normal again which wasn't a luxury we were rewarded often anymore. Miguel ran to catch up with us and smiled in a jaguar kind of way. "Hey, why don't I tag along?"

"Me, too!" Billings chimed and slung his arm around Miguel's shoulder. I guess those two were on better terms. "If I don't get outta this bunker, I'm going to start eating my own flesh or something. I'm going crazy here, man. Besides," he said and cleared his throat, "maybe we could look for Cain a little while we're out."

"Well…you can come, I guess. We're not doing much today, just seeing what to make of this broadcast station that Chesser was making such a big deal about."

"Broadcast station?" Lillian asked. We turned to look at her and I tried not to grimace at the redness of her eyes. "Cain and I have been there."

"When?"

"When he took me to that club," she said, her voice choked a little. "The club is next to the station."

"A club…" Miguel mused. "We could hit the boozer while we're there," he said and wiggled his eyebrows.

"Have fun," she said and ran a hand through her disheveled hair before turning away.

Miguel told her to wait up. He went to her and wrapped his arms around her in a soothing manner. It was at that time that Rylee strolled up, all dressed and ready to go. She had her hair up and even had a little make-up on. Rylee looked up and an expression of devastation smacked into her.

She looked at Miguel as if he were betraying her. When he looked up, he saw the look on her face and his mouth fell open with an explanation, but no words came. It got awkward real fast.

"Rylee," he said and Lillian raised her head. She looked between the two and I could've sworn she rolled her eyes before detaching herself from Miguel and walking away. He kept his eyes on Rylee who crossed her arms, always the tough cookie.

"Are we going or not?" she spouted to me.

"Sure," I said uneasily. We'd never been to town like this together without going for food or necessities. I knew Ellie could keep us hidden from their senses, but it still felt strange to be walking into their turf so easily.

We got into the elevator and rode to the roof. It was dark now, but even though it posed more risk of getting caught on the road, it posed less risk of getting caught at the station. I went first and waited at the bottom of the ladder for Sherry. I gripped her tiny waist and brought her to me. I left her feet dangling in the air and she giggled before smacking my arm.

She gripped my fingers in hers as we made our way to the van. Everyone else followed behind us, but I refused to look at them. Marissa sat up front with Jeff and the rest of us sat scattered on the van floor. Sherry crawled into my lap and leaned against my chest. Ryan and Ellie were sitting side by side with their hands clasped. I smiled at him. I guess he got all his crap worked out. He'd been a basket case lately and I couldn't help but hear his inner turmoil.

I understood. I did.

I gripped Sherry tighter. But I understood *this*, too.

Rylee and Miguel glared at each other from opposite ends of the van so nothing had changed there. Jeff must've felt the tension when he turned onto the highway, because he flicked on the CD player. Some song I had never heard before and frankly, never wanted to again was playing.

The words said something about a tear in his beer and he was crying for her, dear. I grimaced and tried to tune it out.

"So," Ryan started and I was grateful to him for taking some initiative. "What exactly are we going to find at the station?"

I explained, "We're looking for something to justify what Chesser said about being able to organize a statewide broadcast. That way we can break the Lighter's compulsion on everyone. It would only be the state, but it's a start."

"I see," he said and I saw in his mind that he knew, he was just trying to get some conversation flowing.

"If we could get the compulsion broken," Miguel continued, "then people would fight back. We wouldn't be alone anymore in trying to take them out. And once the compulsion is broken, they can't be under it again right?" I nodded.

Rylee spoke loud and clear, "Maybe we could find a way to link the state stations and take this thing continental. And then Global."

"Maybe," I mused. "Let's just call that *the plan*." I smiled at her and she softened a little until she looked over at Miguel.

"Pretty smart, ginger."

"Die, pig.'"

He laughed. "You're never going to give me a fighting chance, are you, love?"

"Nope," she spouted sweetly and smiled. "Besides, since Cain's gone, you can just move in on Lillian."

"That's not what I'm doing," he answered calmly. "Don't you just need a hug sometimes?"

"No," she said and gulped. "I don't. I can take care of myself."

"That's not what I asked," he told her softly.

"Whatever," she eventually said. "I don't need anything from you. Or anybody."

"Maybe not," he ventured. "Maybe not."

Billings just rolled his eyes and groaned as he scratched at the bandage on his arm.

The club was jumping, as they say. There were cars and people everywhere and I knew we'd made the right decision to come at nighttime. No one was going to be paying attention to us and what we were doing.

We parked the van on the outskirts of the parking lot and Jeff put it in park. We all sat, as if waiting for a clue that it was time to go.

"All right," I drawled. "Whoever's going, let's go. Jeff," I put my hand on his shoulder, "we'll be back soon."

"Guard you, brother."

"And you, brother." He clasped my fist in a grip. I heard him and Ryan doing the same behind me before I opened the door slowly. I felt Sherry at my back and knew she was eager and anxious about this. She always wanted to help in any way she could, but I almost felt like we were using her.

We heard hear the music from the club out where we were. The van's windows rattled a little from it. I got out and helped Sherry down with a hand. Ryan and Ellie came, then Miguel and Rylee. He tried to help her, but she snubbed his hand and went to the front of us. "How about you guys go stake out the station and I'll going into the club and see what's bouncing in there."

"No," I said and immediately changed my tone at seeing her face. "We need to stay together if we can. This is a delicate situation, Rylee."

She laughed and shook her head. "No offense, Keeper, but I am anything but delicate."

She turned to go toward the club. "Rylee!" I hissed as loud as I dared, but she didn't even look back.

Miguel ran and turned to say, "I'll get her. You do what we came to do. Don't worry!" And then he turned back to catch up. She had already weaseled her way in the door.

I cursed and banged my fist on the van window. "I knew it was bad to bring those two."

"Just go," Jeff said, leaning protectively over Marissa. I guessed she had changed his mind about letting her come on missions. "We'll keep an eye out. She's just being dramatic, I'm sure they're fine. You don't need them to do the station mission anyway."

I growled and huffed before feeling Sherry's palm on my cheek. "Hey," she said softly. "Let's not freak out. We'll go and see the station and then if they still aren't out, then we'll freak and see what we need to do. Ok?"

I sighed and pulled her close. "Ok." I kissed her forehead and then took her hand. I nodded my head for them to follow us and we lead the way.

It was beautifully strange the normal and simplistic way we walked across the parking lot amongst all the other people from the town. I never thought we'd have a moment like this.

She must've gotten the same feeling as me because she looked up at me and smiled this gorgeously happy smile. "Don't you feel utterly normal right now?"

"It does feel weird," I agreed and laughed. I put my arm over shoulder and kissed her temple. "Weird in the best way."

And it was hard to not look around constantly for an enemy. Ellie, I knew, was keeping us safe from detection. I looked back at her for a second. She was still pretty shy with everyone except Ryan, but right then, she looked…giggly. She smiled and bobbed her head to the music we could hear from the club and bumped Ryan's shoulder as she did so, trying to goad him into playing. He bumped back and they both laughed.

When we reached the end of the lot and the back of the cars I casually kept going as if I knew right where I was headed. Ryan and Ellie followed and we reached the back door to the station. I looked up and followed the long line of the tower way into the sky. This had to work.

I remembered what Marissa had said about Lily being the key… No. This had to work.

The door was locked, of course, so I used my strength to take the door knob off. They'd know someone had messed with it, but that couldn't be helped. I towed Sherry up the stairs to the main hall. I had absolutely no idea which way to go, so we split up. Well, we split from Ryan and Ellie who took the left and we took the right. I wasn't about to let Sherry from my sight, and Billings followed us.

"Let's just try not to touch anything if we can," Ryan explained in a whisper. "I don't want them to think we're onto them."

I nodded. "Fifteen minutes and we need to get out."

He nodded, too, and then they were gone.

The building was dark except for security lights that paved the hallways. Just enough light for us to see. I wasn't sure what we were looking for. Some security panel or control room, I guessed.

"There," Sherry said and pointed to a door with a wide window. There was a wall of screens and a control board inside. I tried the knob and when it turned easily, we went inside.

"Ohh, looky, looky," Billings stated happily. "Gadgets."

"You know what these things do?" I asked.

"Course!" he scoffed. "If you can run a DVR, you can figure this stuff out."

I had no idea what he was talking about, but watched as he sat in the chair and began pressing a few buttons. There was a loud whirring, ringing sound and then every screen on the wall lit up…

And Cain's face was staring back at us.

He grinned and said, "Remind me to give Marissa a big kiss right on the lips when I get back."

Sherry gasped belatedly, shocked, and then hissed. "Cain! What…where are you? Are you ok?"

"We're at the state line. We've got a map here." His head moved off screen a little. Daniel was beside him and said something before Cain's face appeared again. "There's only three stations that span the state that'll run all the broadcasts. If we got all the stations going and online together, we could make a broadcast, easy."

"But there's no internet or cell service," Sherry argued. Ryan and Ellie came in behind us and gawked at the screens; twenty pictures of Cain's mug. "How will we get the stations to link with each other?"

"The stations are run on frequencies to each other, but they're also run by landlines for back-up. All we have to do is turn back on the connection of those cables to each station. They turned them off to keep word from spreading."

I frowned. "But what about the third station?"

"We're headed there now." He looked at his watch. "We've already accessed this station's panel and turned it back online. You do that there and we'll be at the other station by tomorrow night." He leaned closer. "Be back at the radio station tomorrow night with something to broadcast."

"But it's almost midnight?" Sherry argued. "Hardly anyone would see what we broadcasted at midnight anyway."

"We'll set up a transmission to play at a certain time. That way, we won't even have to be there when it's broadcasted. By the time they realize what's going on, it'll be too late to stop it."

I grinned. "It's good to see you, man."

"Sherry baby, I'm so glad you're ok. It's really good to see you guys," he spouted with a huffed breath. "How's Lillian?"

"Holding up," I said. "She's knows you're ok, but knowing and seeing are two different things."

He frowned. "Yeah, they are." He glared over at Daniel. "Let's hurry this thing up, huh? See you tomorrow night."

"We'll be here."

The screen clicked off and we all stood in silence. Everything seemed to be falling into place. Billings searched the wall for the 'core', he said. They needed a hard line that had nothing to do with wireless or radio frequency signals. He bent down and shoved his face under a table. When he said, "Aha," we knew he'd found something.

"Got it. The control panel is in the floor. All right, everything is back online." He pulled himself up. "Now if we just come back tomorrow, it should just be a manner of uploading the video and setting the program to a certain time. Easy, peasy."

"Let's hope," Ryan said and looked around.

"We have to go see Chesser," Sherry said. "Tonight."

Ryan and I both nodded at each other before he said, "Why don't we get out of here before we press our luck."

"Done," I said and dragged Sherry along. I was sure she was tired of me by now, with all my dragging and never letting her go, but when I looked back at her, she was smiling.

Miraculously, I was able to get the knob to screw tight again and it looked untouched. Once we reached the parking lot, I called out to Jeff.

All done. Any problems?

Just one. Your boy never came back and neither did the man-eater.

I growled. *Crap, Miguel. All right, we're going in after him.*

We'll wait here. Be careful. It sounds...rowdy in there.

I knew what he meant by the time we reached the door. The bouncer worried me for a split second before he opened the door and swept his hand for us to enter. Wasn't much of a bouncer.

I turned to them. "I hate to say this again, but we need to split up."

"Agreed," Ryan said loudly so everyone could hear over the music. "We'll take the back."

"I'll take the middle!" Billings yelled and went straight for the bar.

I shook my head at him.

I'll guess we start here.

She nodded and looked around. I'd never been in a bar or club before. Danny was too young to get in when I watched them and Sherry would never have gone to places like this, so I had never seen one either.

It was packed beyond packed and everyone was in their own little worlds. I noticed we were the only ones standing around that weren't making out, getting drunk, or dancing.

We should do something other than stand here. Let's go…mingle or something.

She laughed and nodded as she tugged on my fingers. She took us to the loft of the club so we could look out and see everyone and everything at once. I felt underdressed. But the ones who were dressed in party clothes were barely dressed themselves. I glanced away from all the obvious cleavage to study my wife. She looked around the room with a steady sweep.

"I've never heard this song," she said offhandedly, "but I like it." She swayed her hips and rubbed her back against my front. I suddenly got the appeal of the club scene.

"I like it, too…now." I kissed the back of her neck and waved the waitress away that asked if we wanted something to drink. She giggled and continued to move. She wasn't really dancing, just moving enough to stay with the beat. I continued trying to look around the club, and so did she, but she kept at her dangerous little dance.

"I don't see them anywhere," I whispered into her ear, and in an act that was so human I almost laughed, I tugged on her earlobe with my teeth. I told her, "I really wish we had time to play."

She giggled and wiggled against me. "Me, too. Though," she turned to me, putting her back to the club and the railing, and put her arms around my neck, "if we were going to play, Finch, I'd rather be home in our pallet, not in some dingy club." She kissed my chin before leaning back and letting go. I tried to keep her there, but she laughed and walked backwards as she pulled me along.

"Mmm," I groaned and yanked us both to a stop. I pulled her to me, chest to chest, and noticed how smug she looked. "I'd give anything to be able to live a normal life with you. We could do anything. Can you imagine going to a movie or bowling with me?"

She turned her head to think. "I'd just kick your butt."

I swung us around and pressed her to the wall there making her laugh harder. "You don't seem scared."

"Should I be?" she replied coyly and bit her lip. I realized then how much better at this game she was than me.

She had the upper hand and I was feverish.

I took her mouth gently. She seemed happy with the fact that I had caved. She let me in and I devoured her tongue with my own. It was so dark in that corner and a million things I wanted to do to her flooded my mind. But hearing Jeff's question about how things were coming along made me stop.

S*till looking.*

So to correct the lie I'd just told him, I chuckled in a *'you're in trouble'* way and said, "You're so going to get it later."

"I hope so," she whispered, her fingers walking my chest up to my neck. She kissed my chin again and I kissed her lips once more. She smiled up at me and then glanced behind me. She gasped. "There's Miguel!"

I peeked back just in time to see Miguel's shirt back turn the corner. I marveled at good timing. If we had been still at the railing, we'd never had seen him. The wall was in the way.

I pulled her as we made our way back down the stairs. Ellie and Ryan must've seen him at the same time we had, because they met us half way. I searched for Billings and found him still at the bar. My eyes widened. He was about to be pummeled and didn't even know it.

Cruisin' For A Bruisin'
Chapter 25

Sherry

Billings was chatting up a blonde with boobs the size of Texas. Each.

But when he reached out to touch her cheek, he didn't see her enormous boyfriend that was staring him down at his back. The woman did. They must've had a fight because she was taunting him over Billing's shoulder.

And poor Billings was under the expression that he was about to score big. I did the first thing I could think of. I turned to Merrick. "Please, please, trust me. Stay here."

I took off. I felt him try to grab at my hand, but I kept going. I went right up to Billings. The woman and her man looked between Billings and me. It was obvious I had something to say. That was when Billing noticed the other man. He sat up straighter as he understood the direction the situation had turned in.

That was when I slapped him across the face.

He looked shocked. I tried not to do it hard, just enough to be believable. "What the hell?" he bellowed.

"How could you?" I accused. "I go to the bathroom and you try to chat up the first beautiful girl you see?"

"Uh…." he gulped, "well, you know me."

"Oh, I sure do. And you are in serious trouble, mister!" I grabbed his arm and pushed past the big guy. "Excuse us."

The guy never said a word to us and as soon as we were out of ear shot I said, "You can thank me later."

"For slapping me!" he hissed. "You had to slap me?"

"Better than having your butt handed to you. We were here to find Miguel anyway, not smooze at the bar."

"Oh, yeah?" He grinned. "Here to find Miguel, huh?" He touched my neck. "And Merrick sucking on your neck was how you looked for him, right?"

I covered my neck, my blush creeping up. "Shut. Up."

He laughed. "Man, that guy has some serious mack."

"Oh, my gosh. You're not even speaking English anymore!" I laughed back.

"Hey," Merrick said as he reached us. "Um…so, you slapped him."

"He deserved it," I argued. I grabbed Billing's arm and then laid my hand on my forehead. "How could he betray me with that bimbo?"

Billings laughed and rubbed his cheek. "She got me good, boss." He nodded his chin to Merrick. "You better be good to this one."

"I plan to," he muttered and took my hand. He smiled and shook his head like he didn't know what to do with me. "Let's hope Miguel's still through here. Ryan and Ellie went to find him."

We turned the hall near the bathrooms and peeked down the massive line. A sign said *Exit* with an arrow pointing the way out and Merrick guided us that way. Ryan was there. "I didn't see him."

"He's got to be here somewhere," Merrick said.

"Maybe they went out the door?" I supplied. "Let's just go see." I pulled my shirt away from my body. "I'm dying in here, anyway."

As soon as Ryan slung open the door, we all stopped.

I'd seen people suck face before, but these two were trying to embed themselves. And they were completely oblivious to us or anything. So the group of Lighters and Enforcers that had just turned the corner hadn't been noticed.

Well, we'd gone this long without seeing any. We should be glad I guess. At least we learned something to help with the broadcast. Now whether we'd live to carry it out or not was another story. They kept coming and didn't stop. Not even a second glance as they walked between us, and Miguel and Rylee.

I let my breath go as soon as they turned the corner and heard Ellie do the same. I looked at her and she was green as Ryan held her to him. She hadn't expected her ability to work? Miguel noticed us then and growled at us, "Bugger off."

"Time to go, man," Billings told him and grabbed the back of his shirt. "Crap just got real."

"What?" Rylee said. "What happened?" she asked and wiped her bottom lip.

"Did you not see the Lighters who just walked right past you?" Billings scolded them. "Within punching range!"

"I was…busy," Miguel said and smiled smugly. He put his arm on the small of Rylee's back to direct her through the cars and she let him. Once we reached the van, he helped her inside. "Up you go."

She snatched her hand back and gave him a look. "Just because we made out doesn't mean that you can boss me around."

"I wouldn't dream of it, love," he replied good naturedly and grinned as he got inside.

We all followed suit and once we were loaded, Jeff asked us how it went.

Ryan cleared his throat. "Well, I got to use my first public bathroom. That was interesting."

"I made out with the Aussie," Rylee stated matter-of-factly.

"I made *up* with the ginger," Miguel said and grinned back at her.

Jeff stared at us.

"I got slapped in the face," Billings offered.

"By me," I supplied.

"And we got to talk to Cain at the station on the big screen," Merrick said happily.

Jeff still stared while Marissa giggled into her hand. "So it went good then," he stated. "Great."

He turned in his seat and pulled onto the highway. Our laughter that we fought eventually came out.

Once I gave Jeff directions for how to get to Chesser's house, we crept our way along the highway to the trailer park. I told him which one, but Merrick wasn't letting me go alone. So, we both got out and told the others to wait for us to signal the 'ok'. I climbed his rickety stairs and knocked on the door. I heard movement inside and then a scuffle. At first I thought he might have a visitor of the female persuasion that we were interrupting, but then the door was yanked open and a gun shoved in Merrick's face. It wasn't Chesser, it was that other guy, whose names escaped me.

"Hi," I said softly from behind Merrick's brick house of a back. "Remember me? I thought I was at Chesser's house."

"This is Chesser's," he drawled. "What are you doing back here?"

"We need to talk to him. It's important."

The man was shoved aside and Chesser smiled at us. "My favorite rebels!" I laughed in relief and loosened my grip on Merrick's arm. "Come on in."

Merrick kept a firm hand on mine and said, "I can understand why you're a little trigger happy." Merrick gave the man with the gun a long look.

Chesser lowered the man's barrel with his hand. "Whoa, slick." He laughed. "Let's settle down a little. You remember Sherry?"

"Sure," the man said dead-pan. "Who's this guy?"

"Her husband, Merrick. It's ok." He lowered the gun slowly and gave us one final look before moving to the couch and plopping himself down. Chesser turned to me and with a raised eyebrow said, "What are you doing here?"

"We decided to follow up on your broadcast idea." He looked confused so I kept going. "We came to stake out the place and-"

"You went to the station?" he yelled.

"Yeah," I dragged out. "What's your deal?"

"I can't believe you just *went* there. Like it was something normal, like going to the store to get toothpaste. You *broke into* the radio station!"

I scoffed. "What? You gonna arrest us?"

"No," he said and shook his head. He looked at me strangely. "So what did you find?"

"The answer," I said with pride. "We found the way to broadcast through the whole state. The broadcast goes out tomorrow night."

His mouth opened and he looked between us.

"Dang." He grinned. "You've got cojones, girl."

I burst out laughing at that. I forgot about the others in the van so I went to the porch and waved them to us. They came up cautiously, looking around as if Lighters were going to jump out of the bushes. I introduced everyone and we got right down to business. We told him everything we'd learned and what we were planning to do. Then he said, "Ok, that all sounds great. And I think you need to be the one to record the video."

"Sure," I said. "I can hold a camera like nobody's business."

"No," he laughed, "I mean be *on* the video." I stilled. "Your face is sweet and you're just so non-threatening. We need someone like you on the video that people will pay attention to and believe."

I gulped. "But what will I say?"

He stood. "You'll say what you would tell someone if they were sitting in this room and asking you why they should stop following the Lighters and start being human beings again."

I nodded, but I had no idea what to say. He pulled a small handheld video camera from the top of the refrigerator. He pulled a chair out and pushed me into it. I gripped the undersides with my fingers.

This was stupid. It was just a camera; there was no reason for me to be so crazy about it. Then I felt *his* hands on my shoulders. I leaned my head back to look at my Merrick. He smiled. He was beautiful even upside down. I smiled, too, and steeled myself that this was what I needed to do.

The little red light came on and Chesser pointed his finger at me in a *You're On* motion. I cleared my throat delicately and started the best way that I knew how.

"I know you don't know me…and I don't know you, but we share something in common; this planet. Or at least we did. Now we all share it with beings that don't belong here, and have tricked you all into thinking that they want to help you. The moon disappearing was the first sign. The weather being all messed up, the cell and television service going haywire, the animals…it's because of them. Think real hard and remember what it was like when they first started showing up. Remember our friends and family dying. Remember the way everything in our world is worse, not better, because of them. I've met these beings and their leader, who is no longer alive. They want you to believe these lies so they can keep controlling you. Just think for yourselves. These things can't be killed the usual way, you have to stake them with something all the way through. They are not human. Things are going to get bad and then worse, but we're here. There are so many of us out there who are waiting for you to join us. We'll fight side by side and take them all out. They call us rebels? We call ourselves human. We are the revolution. Join us and take back what was yours in the first place."

I stopped talking and waited. Merrick's hands rubbed a small caress on my neck and shoulders. I finally looked up. Chesser was nodding. "That was…good."

"Really?" I said softly, fear rearing its ugly head.

"Really." He pulled the tape out of the recorder and handed it to me. "You keep it, just in case. But we'll meet you at the radio station tomorrow night and get that baby loaded up and ready to go." He took a deep breath. "I can't believe we're doing this. I've thought about it for so long." He looked me straight in the eye before looking around and doing the same to everyone else. "You know what this means right? This will be war. There will be panic, there will be riots and fights and …we'll have to be ready to fight at any opportunity."

"I'm ready," I said and gripped Merrick's hand on my shoulder. "We're all ready."

Once back 'home', we ate some supper and went to bed. I lay next to Merrick, but once again I felt restless and uneasy, like I needed something. I turned a little to see Merrick and he was awake, too. I pulled his hands and towed him to Lily's tent. We lay down on either side of her and she sighed as if her world was complete.

If only that were true.

Merrick rubbed my cheek with his thumb and looked at me over Lily's head. "You did good tonight."

I decided to be honest. "I'm scared to death."

"I know."

"I'm scared that…"

"I know," he sighed. "I'm scared that I can't protect you like I want to."

"I'll be fine with you right there with me."

"I want you here with Lily, not with me. If things go badly tomorrow… What if there's an ambush? What if the transmission doesn't work? What if we get caught and never stood a chance?"

"Then we'll be together and I'll know I was with the love of my life at the end."

I felt my eyes water just as Lily stirred. She looked pleased that we were with her. "Hey, Mommy."

"Hey, baby," I said and sniffled. "Go back to sleep."

"I can't. What's dat song you sang to me about the angels? The one about Daddy."

I smiled at Merrick over her head and sang in a whisper, because that was all that my crying would allow.

Sleepyhead, close your eyes, I am right here beside you.

I'll protect you from harm. You will always be in my arms.

Guardian angels are near, so sleep on with no fear.

Guardian angels are near, so sleep on with no fear.

I looked at her sweet face, her eyes closed, her little world so simple and small. I hoped this wasn't the last time that I got to hold her, but it might be. I needed her to remember us this way. All three of us, together, loving each other, peaceful and happy.

Merrick's thumb rubbed my cheek once more, robbing my attention. "I love you, baby," his said, a slight crack at the end that I tried not to notice.

"I love you, too," I whispered.

"You're the strongest woman I know. And the most determined." He nodded as if trying to convince himself. "I'll keep you safe. We'll be all right."

I nodded, too. "We have to be."

I kissed Lily's hair and fell asleep with the feel of Merrick's thumb sweeping my cheek. Strangely, Merrick being scared made me feel better, not worse. It meant that he was being real with me.

Things were about to take a turn, either for their side or ours.

Deep In My Bones
Chapter 26

Ryan

The human book was titled *Last of the Mohicans*. I had swiped it before we left the bunker and had begun to read it slowly at night when everyone else slept and my mind refused to shut off. It opened with a quote from Shakespeare, who I'd heard of, but not read.

"Mine ear is opened, and my heart prepared
The worst is worldly loss thou canst unfold
Say, is my kingdom lost?"

My kingdom lost… That thought hung in the air as I pondered what I'd read so far of the book. It was all war and sacrifice and hardship, wills taken and given. It honestly wasn't making me feel better to read about these things.

I had just closed the book in my lap when Ellie came out of the back around the corner. She rubbed her eyes and then her hair in a frazzled manner. It was adorable and cute and…sexy. Man, it was sexy. She hadn't even noticed me yet, but when she did, she grinned in a way that let me know she was truly happy to see me.

"What are you doing up?" she asked, her voice husky from sleep.

Unlike every other couple in the bunker, we weren't sleeping together, in any way. She had her tent, I had mine. I had yet to sleep with someone lying on me or next to me. In truth, the way my human body flounced around at night, I couldn't imagine it being a nice experience.

"I have problems going to sleep," I told her and tossed the book aside. "What are you doing awake?"

"After everything that happened today…and everything that's going to happen tomorrow…"

I nodded. She didn't need to explain more. "Yeah," I agreed. "Are you all right?"

"I'm ok," she assured, swaying back and forth as she stood. It was like a subconscious act for her. Her bottom lip started to tremble a little.

"Really?" I asked incredulously. "Ellie?"

"I'm fine," she said again and pulled her hair back with her hands. "I just hope that I can help in some way. That my ability doesn't fail or…hurt anyone."

"Your ability is amazing, Ellie, don't doubt yourself." She just watched the floor. "Come here."

She wasted no time in coming and crawling into my lap. She faced me, her legs on either side of me as I sat on that hard concrete floor. I held her face gently and tried to get her to see her as I saw her. It must've been all right for me to touch her that way because she looked at me as if she had a million questions and I possessed all the answers.

"You have this gift that was given to you for a reason, Ellie. It'll work because that's what you were made to do."

She took a deep breath. "Ok."

"Do you want to…" I felt too bold. I needed to start trusting my own responses to things. I steeled myself and smiled a little. "Do you want to come lie down me?"

She nodded and looked relieved. "I don't want to be by myself."

"You don't ever have to be," I said softly and took my boldness one step further.

I moved forward to kiss the corner of the mouth. She corrected my course, as if it had been a mistake that I missed, and kissed me again right where I wanted her. It was sweet and a little desperate. This girl needed me tonight. We had no idea what the rest of our days were going to look like.

I helped us up and then took her to my tent. She snuggled right up against me, trusting, eager, willing. A small part of me that I had yet to explore of my human self felt a little smug. I smiled in the dark as I stared at the black ceiling. To feel *chosen* felt amazing. I had no idea what she saw in me, but for the first time, I was really happy that she did.

"Dude, Ryan!" I heard someone hiss and turned my head to find Calvin holding the flap of my tent open. He hissed again in an overly loud whisper. "You bagged Ellie! Finally!"

"Get out of here!" I whispered back. "And I didn't bag anyone…whatever that means."

"If you don't even know what it means, then how do you know you didn't do it?" he asked, his eyebrows jumping in suggestive manner.

"Calvin-" I started, but then Frank poked his head in as well.

"Shyeah!" he said excitedly. "Way to go, Ryan, my man."

"Get out, the both of you, before I jerk a knot in your behinds!"

"You don't even know what that means, do you?" Calvin taunted.

I jerked up and made like I was going to get up. They both took off like little cowards, hooting and carrying on as they ran. I groaned a little and then heard and felt Ellie's giggle. I looked down at her face on my shoulder and felt my breath stop. I'd heard it so many times over my many, many years; that expression men said to a woman about being beautiful in the morning. It was absolutely true.

"What are you laughing at, beautiful?" I heard myself say and my eyes went a little wide.

She smiled brightly. "You, defending my honor."

"It didn't need defending," I reminded her. "I was a gentleman."

"True, but they didn't know that." She was still smiling.

"So…tell me something about you." Her smile faltered. "You don't have to. I just wanted to know about you, your family, your life before all this."

Her eyes moved to my neck and stayed there. "I was a teacher. I was engaged. I had a big family. All of that was taken from me the day *they* showed up." I felt myself frown. "We were headed towards my engagement party. I was running late because I'd forgotten the wine that I knew my mom liked. She was a sweet lady, but she was a picky lady." She smiled, though her eyes began to fill. "One of those things was in the road and my family swerved to miss it. They all died…all at once. Except me. I've been alone ever since."

"Where's your Keeper?"

She gulped. "Never came," she whispered. "When I got here and heard all of your stories about the Specials and Keepers and about how you all came to save them, it made me wonder why my own Keeper never came for me. I thought maybe it was because he couldn't sense me, so he couldn't find me."

"No," I told her. "He or she watched you. He would have known where you were."

"Then why?" she said and I could see that this truly upset her.

"There's nothing that can keep a Keeper from their charge. Something must have happened to him on the way to you. An accident. He didn't abandon you, I promise."

She nodded. "That's good. I thought I was defective or something."

"You are anything but defective," I told her and kissed her forehead. It was getting easier by the minute to touch her and not feel like I was making her suffer some violation.

"Thank you," she said, "for letting me stay in here last night. I was a little unhinged."

"You're welcome," I whispered.

"I usually read before bed, to unwind, but last night it just wasn't working."

"I was reading last night, too."

She blinked in surprise. "You were?"

"Yeah. I …borrowed a copy of Last of the Mohicans from Mrs. Trudy's collection."

"Last of the Mohicans!" she laughed. "Well, that's a cheery little novel. No wonder you couldn't sleep."

"What do you read?"

She grinned. "Stay right here." She got up swiftly and made a quick escape from my tent. When she returned, she was carrying a small book that was beaten and bruised. She smiled. "I *borrowed* a book from Mrs. Trudy, too." She showed me the cover. E.E. Cummings.

"What's it about?"

She sat by me and opened the book to a piece of receipt paper she was using as a bookmark. She flipped the pages and then turned to me. She moved my knee over so she could scoot between my legs and nestled into my chest with her back. She pointed with her finger as she read the lines.

I carry your heart with me (I carry it in my heart)
I am never without it
(anywhere I go you go, my dear; and whatever is done
by only me is your doing, my darling)
I fear no fate (for you are my fate, my sweet) I want no world
(for beautiful you are my world, my true)
and it's you are whatever a moon has always meant

and whatever a sun will always sing is you
here is the deepest secret nobody knows
(here is the root of the root and the bud of the bud
and the sky of the sky of a tree called life; which grows
higher than the soul can hope or mind can hide)
and this is the wonder that's keeping the stars apart
I carry your heart (I carry it in my heart)

I was…stunned. "What was that?"

"It's E.E. Cummings. Poetry," she said softly and turned to me a little. My rough chin touched her cheek. She didn't seem bothered. "I like to read things that give me hope of one day being normal again."

I rubbed her arms with my hands. "Will you read me another one?"

She smiled up at me in her profile. "Of course."

i like my body when it is with your body.
It is so quite new a thing.
Muscles better and nerves more.
i like your body. i like what it does,
i like its hows. i like to feel the spine
of your body and its bones, and the trembling
-firm-smoothness and which i will
again and again and again
kiss, i like kissing this and that of you,
i like, slowly stroking the, shocking fuzz
of your electric fur, and what-is-it comes
over parting flesh ... And eyes big love-crumbs,
and possibly i like the thrill
of under me you so quite new.

Her breath hitched a little at the end and she wouldn't turn to look at me. I had no words… It was beautiful and sexual and described exactly the confusion and awe I felt for Ellie. I let my hands float down her arms once more, skimming and teasing. She shivered and pressed herself further into me.

"I didn't read that one on purpose," she promised. "I just picked one."

"That was a good one," I told her. "It was perfect. Thank you." I wrapped my arms around her and kissed the side of her neck. She made a little noise of appreciation that had me pausing. It was a beautiful sound. "Can you read more?"

"You like poetry?"

"I'm not sure, but I like when you read it to me."

There were a few precious hours until we had to meet Chesser back at the broadcast station. If leaning my back against the wall with Ellie in my lap was my punishment for the day, I would take it with a smile.

We sat there, just like that, all day. She read to me and I listened and tuned out the sounds of the bunker, all except her smooth voice. When the book was done, she didn't leave me, however. I moved down a little and we napped.

It was a perfectly normal and human thing to do.

Later when they came and got us to tell us it was time to go, I mourned my missed time with her. If we came out of all this alive, I planned to never take that time for granted again.

Things Are About To Get Real
Chapter 26

Sherry

In the time it took to make our way to the elevator and up to the roof, I'd fought down vomit three times. This was it. They didn't know it, but the whole state, and if I wanted to give my ego a little notch up, the world, was counting on us to make tonight happen without a hitch.

Jeff had finally stepped back into his leadership role. We knew it was an adjustment to find out you're becoming a father, so he deserved a little slack. But I was glad to have him back. His *rally the troops* speeches were epic. And this one was no different. Everyone understood the significance of tonight.

Pastor's prayer this time had been short and sweet. "Lord, help us today as some of us head out into the lion's den." He had glanced at Rylee and looked sad. "We know that we need this. The end result is what matters now. Keep them safe, God. Keep them light footed and nimble handed."

And everyone seemed extra lovey with each other. Ryan and Ellie hadn't said anything, but were doing this little half snuggle thing. Jeff and Marissa couldn't keep their hands off each other. Rylee and Miguel stood close, not touching, but their glowers carried enough heat to light a birthday cake. Poor Billings was all alone.

I held Merrick's hand tightly and tried not to think about my goodbye with Lily. Lana had finally taken her to the back room, Bones trailing behind and looking up at her with worried eyes, but she usually never cried when we left.

Tonight, she cried.

And Lillian. She had been so eager for us to come home last night, certain we'd found Cain. She was becoming less and less faithful to Marissa's vision. When we had come in late, the bunker was as spotless as it could be. She had made everyone's…pallets. All the crates were stacked neatly against the walls. She said she just needed something to do. She also said that if Daniel hadn't found Cain by the next night, she was going after him herself. There was no point in arguing about it with her. I would have done the same thing. At least she was trying to be productive.

All that didn't set a good mood or tone for the trip for me. But we pressed on and as I climbed the ladder down, I thought about the events that were about to take place. Last night, everyone had been quiet and reflective.

It was a process, it seemed, to get ready for what could possibly be the last day of the Apocalypse. Just now, as Jeff spoke to everyone, even the ones staying behind, he had said, "It's either them or us. No more hiding and coexisting. No more being the underdogs in a fight that should have ended long ago. Today, we take the first step towards ending this thing. Tonight, we're more than just family. Tonight, we're soldiers."

I couldn't have agreed more. I *felt* like a soldier. Or at least like a kid sneaking through the window. I felt like I could get caught any moment and that provided a rush in my veins. A rush I needed.

"Hey, slowpoke," I heard and almost missed the last step. I turned to glare at whoever it was, but it was Jeff. So I glared up at his dark, handsome face causing him to laugh. "Whoa, nelly. I just wanted to make sure you were…all right with this tonight." He glanced at Marissa who stroked her belly anxiously. "Not everyone is taking the news of a war so easily."

"I can understand."

Merrick came and put an arm around me on my hip. "We don't have a choice," he said with conviction. "We have to be all right with it. It's now or never."

Jeff nodded. I put my arm through his and then my other arm through Merrick's. They both smiled down at me like I was something precious. It used to unnerve me, but now I got it. They were precious, too, to me.

"Ok," Jeff huffed and turned in the driver's seat. "What if they figured it out and this is an ambush?"

Billings laughed. "What if this Chesser fellow is just after the twenty thousand dollars and we're falling right into his plan?"

"Why would he wait 'til now and not have just taken me the first night?" I asked, bristling in defense of the man who sheltered and fed me for the night.

"This way he gets more people doesn't he?"

I waved him off and turned to Jeff. "If it's an ambush….it is. We talked about this. This is it; we can't just sit by and be outcasts and hunted anymore. Even if this doesn't work, we'll have to choose something else another day. We have to stop them. End of story."

Merrick's arms around me tightened. He kissed my temple in that *I don't want to agree with you, but you're right* way of his.

"Same as last time?" Jeff asked, but included a huff of exasperation. "We wait and lookout for you guys, you go and upload the tape?"

"Yep," Merrick said. "We get the easy job," he goaded and punched Jeff's arm. But then they locked arms and silently told the other what couldn't be said out loud.

Jeff hugged me to him. "You could stay. Let the big boys deal with this," he offered.

I looked at Merrick. The hopefulness in his eyes that I would do just that was almost heartbreaking. "No," I said and switched my gaze back to Jeff. "No, I need to be there. What if something happens and they need to know who to trust? I won't be there to see who's lying."

"Fair enough," he said, but it sounded like he no longer believed it. He leaned closer and spoke in my ear. "Please be careful."

"Of course," I told him. "Save me a bear hug for when I come back."

He laughed. "Oh, you'll get a bear hug."

Marissa's eyes were already watering as I hugged her. I didn't say anything. I would cry if I did. So, I stepped out with Merrick and waited for the others. Ryan and Ellie, Miguel and Rylee, and Billings piled out behind me; our usual band of misfits for this kind of thing lately.

Once again the club was raging, but we ignored it this time. I noticed some new graffiti on the side of the club near the alley. It said, 'THE END IS HERE'.

I felt my hands shaking with excitement and anxiousness. This was it, literal steps to take back our fate and put destiny back in our hands. Even the freaking wall agreed with me.

Merrick's grip on my hand startled me. I hadn't even felt him touch me. He gave me the look. The *I have something to say that you might not like* look. "Baby, please stay by me. If anything goes wrong…it's my job to play hero."

"Merrick-" I started to argue, but he stopped me.

"No, I mean it," he said, his voice harder. "By. Me. I don't want to worry about you the whole time. I know this is kind of your baby or whatever, and that's fine, but if trouble goes down, you stick to my back, you got me?"

I took a deep breath, ready to plead my case, the whole bit. But he pulled me to a stop, right there in the middle of the parking lot. Everyone behind us stopped, too, and waited for...something. Merrick began and from his tone, both anxiety ridden and agonizing, I knew I should listen carefully.

"You listen to me," he said low. "I won't even take you in there if you're going to make me regret it." His face crumpled and I knew the exact next words out of his mouth as he took my face in his hands. "I was certain something horrible had happened to you and Cain. I thought you weren't coming home. I *know* you know what that's like." I flinched at the memory of watching him die. He had me there. "Don't make me go through that twice. It's not a man versus woman thing. It's an *I love you so much and I was built to protect you* thing."

"You're not my Keeper," I said softly and smiled, knowing what was coming next, but begging him to say it.

"Yes, I am," he provided and smiled, his thumbs caressing my whole cheek. "I was your Keeper the moment I first saw those brown eyes, looking at my charge like he was a disease and a blessing all at once." I barked out a laugh. "You two have been my life, my whole life. I've never felt the way I feel for you two and no matter what my brothers or sisters say, I know without a shadow of doubt that I was meant for this. To come here, protect you, send the Lighters straight to Hell and then love you and Lily for the rest of our lives. I plan to do all of those things."

I wanted to wipe the tear that clung to my eyelid, but his hands were in the way. Instead I just stared up at *my* Keeper and watched him watch me. The world faded into darkness and it was just him. He let his smile make my breathing cease to exist. His lips were beautiful magnets and I reached up on my toes to reach them. He kissed me reverently. It had been forever it seemed since we'd been able to *be together*. But this kiss reflected none of the frustration from that. He sucked on my top lip gently and let out heads rest against each other. "Sherry, you're everything there is for me. I love your spirit, I do, but you have to let me take the lead on this one. Please let me protect you."

What could I say to that, but, "Ok."

He pressed closer into the place where my breath was his and his breath was mine. "Promise me," he whispered.

He spoke right to my bones when he said things like that.

"I promise," I told him and accepted my reward. He titled my head a bit and slammed his mouth to mine, and I accepted every bit of him. My fingers wrapped in his shirt front, his buttons in between my fingers. His hands didn't move from my face. He just held me there, captive in his loving grasp, a willing prisoner.

"Hey, mates," I heard and clung to one last kiss before breaking away. "That was a beauty, a real corker it was, but we've got things to do, eh?"

"You're right," Merrick agreed and grinned down at me. He growled, "This time when I say we'll finish it later, I mean it. Even if I have to embarrass myself to make it happen."

I blushed. I freaking blushed! I pressed my lips together to stop the smile. He ran his finger across the pink there making me blush harder. He groaned. "Oh, my… Wife, you're killing me. Do you have any idea how hot that is? After everything we've…done, I can still make you blush?"

I grinned, but Miguel with his big mouth interrupted. Again.

"All well and good. Let's skip the details on that one, love." We both turned and glared at him at the same time. "Glower all you want," he taunted, "as long as you're walking while you're doing it."

"Oh, Miguel," I goaded and let Merrick's grip on my hand lead me. "You've lost your romantic touch."

His gaze swung to Rylee. "I highly doubt that, love."

She just looked at us and then back to the destination. And then she smiled. My eyes could have bugged right out of my head.

"Miguel's right, you know," Billings spouted. "You two are sickening sweet."

"That's not an insult, Billings."

He shrugged and smiled. "I didn't say it was."

Merrick led the way to the back door we'd went through last time. The knob opened easily, still broken. "I wonder if anyone has been here at all," he mused and pulled me up the stairs.

Once inside, we went straight to the control room. Billings got to working on how to program a broadcast, and Merrick and I found where the old school tapes went. We plugged it all in and when the little wheels started turning, I sighed in relief. Billings said he'd found a way to program the timer. The tape would play at ten the next morning over every radio and TV station in the state.

We had to hope that Cain and Daniel had made it to the next station.

A noise at the door startled us all. Merrick pulled me behind him as Miguel jumped toward the noise. He backed up, hands raised, as Chesser and a few others came in with guns in their hands.

But that wasn't the bad part. The worst part were the real Enforcers and a Lighter behind them with guns in their hands, too. This wasn't a stick up by Chesser.

This was an ambush by the enemy.

A Long and Dusty Road
Chapter 27

Cain

"I just can't believe you've been on this planet for a year plus some and not heard of Johnny Cash before."

My point was valid. Daniel didn't think so, as he groaned again and pretended not to hear me, but it was just weird.

"Your human ideals, such as music, are wasted on my kind. There's no-"

"Don't knock it 'til you try it." I got an idea. I searched the glove-box and sure enough, there was an old cassette tape in there. I pulled it out and almost peed myself. "Holy crap, there's a Beastie Boys tape in here!"

I popped it into the player and when I heard, *'Now here's a little story I got to tell about three bad brothers you know so well!'* I said, "Yeah! Paul Revere!"

"Paul Revere was an American Silversmith, am I right?" Daniel pondered.

I laughed. "He was. He was also a Beastie Boys song."

He wrinkled his nose. "This is music?"

"Some of it. You don't like it?"

"It's painful to listen to."

I pointed out his window. "Stop the car and get out."

"I'm assuming you're using your usual wit and sarcasm, so I won't be pulling over."

"If we had radio signals we could listen to that, instead of just sitting here and pretending things aren't awkward because we hate each other."

"I don't hate you," he said and thought. "I just dislike immensely."

I felt the headrest hit the back of my head as I laughed. "Dude, you don't hold the punches, do you? Well, the feeling is mutual, Lighter boy."

He shook his head a little, but kept driving. I wanted to ask him about Lillian. I wanted to know how she was doing. I hoped she wasn't worried about me. But worse, I hoped she wasn't worried about *him*. No, I refused to bring Lillian up to him again. He was probably thinking about her already anyway. That thought had me itching to punch him.

He said he'd kissed her, but she hadn't kissed him back. I know it. She wouldn't do that to me.

I pushed all that aside and thought about the task at hand. The mission of the day. The Gremlin was a horrible excuse for a war vehicle, but it was all we had. I chuckled. We looked so pitiful driving down the road with no windshield. Two guys who obviously had no love for each other.

The last city sign pulled my attention to the road. The map we snagged from the other station showed we were close. I really hoped this worked and I wasn't wasting all this time with Daniel when I could be home instead.

He had been very tight-lipped about how he knew what we were doing or where we were going and all the details. He seemed confident though. I suspected that maybe Marissa had had a vision. Maybe that was why he was being so quiet about the details. Maybe we were going to die. It had to be done, but we weren't going to make it. Or maybe I wasn't. Was that why he was letting all my cracks on him go? Because I was going to die and he was giving me a final kindness before taking my girl from me after death?

I groaned and covered my eyes with my palms.

My stomach growled, too.

"There's food in the backpack in the backseat, remember?" Daniel reminded me.

I yanked the bag forward and glared at him as I looked at what he brought. "Beans? Really?"

"It was the only thing to take and be undetected."

"Ah, so no one knew you left," I guessed. "Well, it makes more sense now."

"We're here," he said and pointed in the sky to the radio tower. "Eat your beans fast."

I opened the can with my pocketknife and scooped my fingers inside. I chewed and spoke at the same time. "You're not having anything?"

"I won't need anything," he said cryptically. "You know," he started and took a while before he spoke again to finish, "we weren't always this way."

"What way?"

"The Lighters. We used to be a normal, functioning society. But some of us got greedy and wanted more. Earth has always been their target and we've come here many times, but always failed until now. This is as close as they've ever gotten to taking you over. They're cocky and they're ill equipped to handle a planet of this magnitude and complexity. They won't survive, even if they did push humans to extinction." He looked over at me. "If we can pull this off, and you can fight the war that needs to be fought, you'll have your planet back. Just don't give up, or all of this," he points at us, "was for nothing. Your humans will need you to help lead and guide them."

I rubbed my thumb over my bottom lip. "I've got no plans to lay down and die. You know something I don’t?"

"No," he said too quickly.

"Uhuh. Fine. You don't have to worry about us, slick."

"What is with you and the nicknames?" he growled.

"It's a military thing, I guess. No, scratch that, it's a human thing."

He chuckled humorlessly. "Which I'm not a part of. You know," he said and gave me a death glare, "if I didn't have something to do here and it wouldn't upset Lillian so much, I'll dump your human behind out here and go back to the bunker. I could live your life and be perfectly happy for the rest of mine."

"Let's go, bucko," I goaded. "Anytime."

"I take back what I said. I *do* hate you," he said in a voice that resembled the Lighter I knew he was. "With everything in me."

"Whoa," I laughed. "What brought all this hostility on all of a sudden?"

"You don't deserve what you have. You're always joking and so smug. Lillian is a fool. A beautiful fool that kisses like an angel, but a fool."

"Shut your mouth about Lillian." Was he trying to pick a fight with me? "You can crack on me all you want, but don't talk about her."

"Sadly, there isn't time to debate further. We're here," he said and pulled into the rickety station parking lot. He stepped out and slammed the door. I just rolled my eyes at him. He was so strange.

The parking lot was empty in the middle of the night, so we didn't need to worry about running into anyone. The door lock was easily picked and we entered. The equipment was pretty ancient. It wasn't like anyone would want to steal it anyway, but it suited our purpose. I found the control panel while Daniel watched and looked around like he was waiting for something.

"Dude, what is with you?" I asked before groaning as my hand slipped and banged into the panel door.

"Nothing. I'm just wondering if I should rethink my part in this plan."

"What plan?"

"This one. It's close to over." The cryptic message hung in the air.

"Well, I'm not going to pretend to know what you mean, but-"

We both turned our heads towards the door as it banged open. Daniel slammed the control booth door shut, but it was made of half glass, so that wouldn't stop them for long.

"Hurry!" he hissed to me and kept going as he watched the Lighter come toward the door. "Fix this. Make sure you get this up and running and you'll have a good start to saving your people."

"What are you-"

"Tonight, after you're done, you need to get in the car and drive back to Effingham as fast as you can. They'll need you there."

"For what?"

"For war," he said low and then rammed into the door the same time the Lighter did. They fought and threw each other around as I tried to find the right switch to flip. The labels were so old, it was hard to read.

"Hurry, Cain!" I heard behind me. I didn't say anything. It was moot. What did he think I was doing in here? Painting my nails? I saw one marked 'Online Con…..' That looked like the one to me, but before I could touch it, I was yanked back by my hair and thrown across the room. My back slammed into a hard edge, knocking the breath from me.

Daniel charged him again, but the Lighter threw him back. Then the Lighter picked up a chair, slung it back and over his head to smash into the control panel. Everything stopped for me. That was it, our one chance, and it was gone now. I was raging mad. I picked up the first thing I could grab and ran to the Lighter, slicing it into his back.

He went up in a blaze of lightning, not knowing what hit him. I wondered how he knew to come here. And how he knew to smash the equipment. Someone was on to us, which meant what we had been going to do would have worked. They wouldn't have been so scared otherwise.

But none of that mattered as I jumped and ran as the ceiling began to come down from the destroyed building. Lightning would do that. I pushed Daniel back and we bolted through the doors just in time to survive the avalanche of debris. I cursed and slammed my fist into the concrete. "Now, we'll never get it going and have no way to let them know that we failed!" I lay down on my back, banging my head once on the hard surface. "They're walking into an ambush and we can't even warn them."

"Come with me," Daniel groaned and stood. "There's something we can do."

"What? What can we possibly do now?"

"There has to be something!" he yelled. "Maybe the equipment survived," he ventured. He obviously knew nothing about it.

Wait… There had to be a back-up somewhere. They always had back-ups or main control panels for places like this. We just had to find it. I could see under the wooden steps as we lay out there. There was no basement, it was a crawl space. "Where's the radio line map?"

Daniel pulled it from his pocket. "I don't know what you'll get from it now."

I snatched it from him and laid it out flat. It showed where all the hard lines went directly into the building. Aha! There was a control box under the building. A failsafe in case of fire or building repairs. This way the lines were safe no matter what happened. And we had to get to them.

I got up and ran to the edge and looked under the building. There was a ton of water under there, from all the melted snow that hadn't evaporated away yet, I guessed. I could see the electrical box where all the lines ran to and knew there were switches inside it that controlled everything, the online connection being the main thing we needed.

I started to go in, but Daniel jerked me back and pointed at the ground. There was a spark as the wires from the above floor hung and touched the water. Great. "I'll just go around them," I told him and tried to go again, but he grabbed my shoulder.

"No," he said slowly and gulped as he looked at everything. "You'd never make it. Once you flip that switch, all the wires will be live, not just that one."

I winced. Crap he was right. "Well, it has to be done," I told him and nodded. It *had* to be done. The fact that I might not make it didn't matter. We had to give them a fighting chance to send that broadcast. It was the only way we'd have a real chance at winning the war. "I'll go." I looked over at him and nodded. "I know I probably won't make it, but I have to go." I looked back at the mine field I was about to enter.

"No, you can't. Lillian will be upset."

I smiled. "Lillian will be alive and have a chance to live a normal life. If I didn't do this and selfishly just went home without even trying, I'd never forgive myself. Tell her…" I tried to think of something poetic, something beautiful that would convey everything I wanted her to know, but nothing of the sort came, just, "Tell her that I loved her with my last breath."

He sighed and I took that as all the agreement as I was going to get from him. I nodded to him and tried not to think about the possibilities he must have had running through his head right then. "Take care of her, all right." I said it as a command, not a request.

I didn't wait for an answer. I lowered myself to crawl through, but he stopped me once more. I jerked up, irritated. "What?" I barked.

"I know you love her and that's the only reason I'm doing this. This doesn't change my hate for you, this is for Lillian."

"What is?"

And before I could react, he cold-cocked me right in the jaw. I went down and blinked just in time to see him crawling through. That bastard! I sat up and yelled something at him, but was so anxious about him making it to the box, I couldn't even remember what I said.

He barely skated past the live wire and the support beam without being fried. He reached the box and lay on his back as he looked it over. He yelled, "There's so many lines connecting to the box. They aren't marked."

I cursed again. "What color are they?"

"Most are white, but one's red."

I thought hard. "Red would be my guess."

He looked over at me. He was lying in a large puddle that couldn't be avoided to reach the box. I had a bad feeling, but it got worse when he smiled. "In another life, we might've been friends."

"Maybe," I mused. "If you weren't trying to steal my girl, you wouldn't be so bad."

"I'm not sorry I kissed her."

"I didn't expect you to be."

"But I am sorry that my time is over." I frowned. "I would have loved to have gotten to be a real human."

"Come on, man. Stop talking like you're not crawling outta there."

"I'm not. This is the vision I saw." He took a deep breath, laying his head back for a few seconds before lifting it back up. "Tell Lillian she doesn't have to be sorry that she couldn't love me. I know she'll be in good hands."

"What… I don't know what-"

"Goodbye, Cain." And then he flipped the red wire switch.

Everything sparked and lit up. I gasped as I fell back and watched as the water sizzled for long minutes. Then it quieted and I could see through the haze. Daniel was lying there, motionless. How had he known that was going to happen? He…saved me by punching my jaw.

I wanted to go and see if he was alive, but saw the smoke coming off his boot. I knew he was gone, but I still called out his name anyway. When he didn't answer, I got up and ran to the Gremlin.

I sat in my seat in a slump, letting my head rest against the steering wheel. That just happened. Daniel, the Lighter who hated my guts, saved me. He could have let me go and I'd have died instead. He knew he was going to die and…he still did it.

And he told me that I had to make it back as quickly as possible to help…with the war. Then something was going down soon.

I sat up, cranked the car, jerked the car into gear and pressed the gas as hard as it would go.

His sacrifice wouldn't go unnoticed. I'd tell everyone about the Lighter who risked his life to save the humans. The Lighter who won us this war.

This Is Our Town
Chapter 28

Merrick

"I didn't bring them here," Chesser said pleadingly and then winced when one of the Enforcers bumped him in the head with the butt of his gun.

"Shut it."

"Well, what have we here?" the Lighter in front spouted and smiled halfway.

Sherry's hands on my back tensed. She peeked around my shoulder and before I could say anything she told him, "We were trying to see if you have anything to steal. You're kinda starving us, you know."

I felt my eyes bulge. What was she doing?

"Oh, it's obvious you're a bunch of thieves. Hungry thieves at that," he said and chuckled. "All skin and bones covering that pretty body of yours."

I tightened in anticipation of slamming my fist into his face. Sherry's arm squeezed mine. She was trying to tell me something, but I wasn't getting the message.

"Well, I guess we can leave now. Nothing was stolen, so no harm no foul, right?" she ventured and smiled.

"Not exactly, pretty one." He grinned evilly. "You broke our door; public property." I was so glad that Ellie was with us. This whole conversation would be going differently if he knew two Keepers and a…whatever Ellie was, was right there.

"We don't have any money," Sherry told him.

"Let's go," he ordered and ticked his head to the door. "Breaking and entering gets you a night in our nice county jail, run by Enforcers of course."

I kept Sherry right behind me the whole time as they herded us out. It was then that I realized what Sherry had been trying to do. They were taking us outside and completely oblivious to the video tape we had planted. Even if…we didn't make it, at least the tape would play tomorrow morning.

We followed them outside to a van they had waiting for us. I wasn't going to any enforcement facility and neither was Sherry. I'd die first. They opened the door and I saw Miguel getting ready to start swinging. But then one of the Lighters to the front of the van jerked and turned to his co-workers. Marissa slipped back from the front of the van just as the man jammed the butt of his rifle into the other man's face. Blood gushed as the man went down. Then the Marissa-compelled gunman went for another one, but he didn't get him before the Lighter took his head in his hands and broke his neck. He fell to the ground along with his comrade.

He turned and Miguel was ready. I pushed Sherry back a little and met Miguel just as he tried to stake him. The Lighter was ready for Miguel though, but he wasn't ready for me. He backhanded Miguel, but I got my stake deep in his gut. I flinched back from the lightning and knew we needed to get out of there soon. Ryan quickly put the other Enforcer in the sleeper hold and threw him to the ground indignantly.

All right, we really needed to get out of there. The others would have seen the Lightning and known what it meant. Marissa and Jeff came around the van and he barked basically the same thing. I turned to grab Sherry, but she was gone. I did a quick circle to find her and saw her little head bouncing as she walked between the cars. I blurred to her and started to ask what she was doing, but she picked up a can of black spray paint under the graffiti at the side of the club.

She smiled softly at me and then walked down the wall to the street. I followed closely behind and watched as she gazed up at the town sign, 'Welcome To Effingham, Illinois'.

I felt the others at my back and turned to Miguel. He had a curious look on his face. Sherry turned to me. "Lift me, babe."

I didn't ask why, I just did it. I hoisted her up easily to sit on my right shoulder and watched as she shook the can and sprayed it, her arm moving and swinging with the motion. I couldn't see what she wrote, but when she stopped, I lowered her back to my side and we all looked at it with a reverence I felt pulsing through us all. She had written over some of the words.

The sign now read, "Welcome To Our Town".

"Looks good," Chesser said and crossed his arms. "Sounds like a country song."

Everyone laughed behind us. I looked down at her and she looked up at me. We both smiled at the same time. "Let's go home," she said. "Let's go wait and see if all this was worth it."

So I picked her hand up in mine and we all walked back to the van.

"You'll need to come home with us. You know that right?" I looked at each of Chesser's men. "You're all welcome."

"Well," he said and sucked air through his teeth. "I'm not sure we could go home again, so I guess we've got no choice but to take you up on your offer."

The others agreed vigorously.

As soon as we were pulling out of one side of the parking lot, another van was pulling in on the other. I had no doubts it was the Lighters and Enforcers and we had dodged a major bullet. But the ride home was uneventful and as soon as we pulled in, it was apparent our night of anxiety had been for a good cause. We did it and now, just needed to wait to see if the tape played or not.

"I just don't get it, I guess," one of Chesser's men said.

"Get what?" Chesser asked him and looked around at the dilapidated warehouse.

"I just don't get this compulsion thing." We parked the van under the tree and made our way to the ladder.

"What don't you get?" Marissa asked and went up the ladder ahead of Jeff. We all lumbered up to the roof before he spoke again.

"How can the Lighters compel us? And how come this tape thing is going to work?"

"One compulsion overrides the other," she explained and punched the elevator button. "They compelled those people. Sherry's tape, in a sense, will override the compulsion and they can think for themselves again. Sherry can't do compulsion, but…." She shook her head. "For some reason, when someone is told the truth about the Lighters, the compulsion wears off."

"I see." He rubbed his chin and looked around the elevator. "Then how come I was never under the compulsion to begin with?"

The elevator dinged and the doors opened. Marissa shrugged and sighed as she went through. "Don't know, but it's so good to be home!" she exclaimed. That was when I saw Lily bolting through the crowd toward us. I pushed the jabber mouth out of the way and lifted her sweet smelling self into my arms. Sherry was at my side and hugged her, too.

"What have you been eating?" I asked and laughed at the fruit pulp stuck on her lip.

"Peaches," she spouted.

"That's why you smell so sweet," I told her. "Did you and Lana have fun?"

"Not reawwy," she admitted and whispered the rest. "She wouldn't let me eat anything but peaches while you were gone."

Sherry chuckled and covered her mouth with her fingers. "What did you expect her to do, bug? Feed you everything there was just because we were gone?"

"Um, yeah! Isn't dat what babysitters do!" she crossed her little arms and pouted in the cutest way. I hugged her to me before seeing Chesser over Sherry's shoulder. I hoisted Lily to my chest and turned to him. "As you can see it's not much. We sleep on pallets. It's concrete. It sucks," I admitted, but he laughed.

"No worries. I just feel bad that we couldn't bring anything with us," he said and looked around. "Things just went from bad to worse tonight. They caught us as we were going in. Sorry."

We'd all been so quiet, reflective, on the way home that we hadn't talked much. We had no idea what had happened.

"No worries, mate," Miguel grinned his wolfish grin and slapped Chesser on the back. "We got lots of chores for you to do to earn your keep."

Chesser grinned back good naturedly. "I bet you do."

Miguel laughed and came to me and Lily. "Come on, little love." He winked at me. "Daddy and mommy have lots of…talking to do tonight."

Sherry laughed into my arm to hide her blush, but I just couldn't do anything but be grateful to that Aussie. "Thanks, man."

"You got it." He held out his free hand to Rylee. "You coming, sheila?

She looked at us all in turn and then straightened her back. She took Lily from Miguel and hoisted her to her hip. "Come on, little girl. Let me teach you the importance of pepper spray."

Miguel just laughed, turned and gave me a very suggestive thumbs up, and then trotted after the girls. I switched my gaze to Chesser, who seemed pretty amused by things. I pointed at the crate near us. "Sleeping bags are there. Bathroom, and I use that term loosely, is back there." I smiled. "Goodnight."

I took Sherry straight to Danny. I knew he'd have some horrible timing later when he realized we were home and I didn't want any interruptions. He, Calvin, Frank and Celeste were playing some gambling game against the wall with dice.

"Hey, we're home," I wasted no time. He wrapped Sherry in a hug before doing me the same. "Ok, goodnight."

"Whoa, wait," he argued. "What happened? No details?"

"No details tonight. We're…tired."

"Ah," he said, but then grimaced. "Ew, gross!"

"Danny, leave them alone!" Celeste chastised.

He shooed me. "Just go violate my sister and don't *ever* talk or hint at it again."

"What does violate mean?" Calvin asked as Sherry and I sprinted away laughing. Nothing mattered tonight except her and her skin and her breaths. Nothing.

I grabbed Sherry's hand and towed her to our 'tent'. Having no walls sucked, especially on nights like this when I wanted to spend hours devouring her, but we just had to make do.

I pushed the curtain to the side and pulled my wife to me. She was smiling in the dark and I couldn't help but smile, too. I pressed my mouth to her cheek so she could feel it and know that I was happy.

I hoisted her up and her short, but luscious legs wrapped around my waist. The one back wall held us both up and I let her feel everything. All my tremors of excitement and all my rough skin on her softness. I cupped her face. "I'm so proud of you."

"For what? Not jumping you in the hallway?" she joked and giggled. That giggle sent tingles everywhere.

"No…well, yes, but no. I'm proud of you for what you did. You saved the day back there."

She shrugged. "I just figured it might make them not think about what we were *really* doing there. And it worked."

"Yeah, it worked." I nuzzled her neck. "Like I said, you saved the day."

She sighed in a breathless way. "Merrick." I groaned at that. "Will you stop trying to make my ego swell and kiss me instead?"

"If this works," I continued, pretending I hadn't heard her plea, "things are probably going to get bad in town…well, everywhere. This is just the first step, but we haven't even seen the worst of it yet I don't think."

"I know," she sighed in defeat and sagged.

"All I'm saying is that things have to get worse before they get better. We did the right thing, though it may not seem like it soon. One day, everything will settle down. One day, Lily will play with Calvin in a real yard. One day, I'll ravage you in a real bed."

She laughed softly. "Right now, I'd do with a ravaging in a pallet."

"For now, this'll do," I heard myself growl before kissing under her chin. Her fingers knotted themselves into my hair and tugged.

"Ah, Merrick," she groaned, hitching up the heat in the room a notch. "Your lips are my favorite thing about you."

"Really?" I teased and leaned back. "Your favorite?"

She grinned before putting her hand behind my neck and pulling my mouth to hers. The taste of her was *my* favorite thing. She was like sweetness that stayed with you long after the cookie was gone. She was every tart and sweet thing I've ever loved rolled into one dessert that lasted forever. So I took my fill of her mouth for long minutes before moving on.

Her fingers let me know she was done with this part of the game and moved on to removing my shirt. I leaned back, keeping her pressed against me and up against the wall. We'd grown so good at this dance. One finishing the acts the other one started. Becoming bored wasn't a problem. Every time I unwrapped her, it was like the first time. Her smiles were always a little different, a little sweeter one day, then a little more sassy the next.

She the most delicious little puzzle and I couldn't wait to piece her together and then make her come apart.

She kissed the tattoo behind my ear, the one that defined me as a Keeper and damned me to the outside world as a traitor. Her hand whisked down the tattoo on my chest. The bull. I think it had grown on her as much as it had me.

I disposed of her shirt and let my palm drift down her torso, from neck to belly. Then I was done. No more games, no more playing. We took care of the rest of the binding clothes. Skin to skin was the best feeling in the world, and for once she was the one who had to tell me to be quiet.

Once the world stopped spinning we lay there, breathing a crazy rhythm that brought back memories of flushed skin and lips and arms.

She rolled over and threw herself over my chest, her hair on my neck. I rubbed circles in her back, loving the way she sighed, so content. The smug feeling was welcome inside knowing that I was the one who could make her that way.

"What are you smiling about?" she asked, though she was facing away from me.

"How do you know I'm smiling?"

"Because I can feel it," she said and smiled. She was right, I could feel hers, too.

"I'm smiling because the most beautiful creature in the universe lets me-"

"Keep it PG, Keeper," she laughed.

"Now who's the perv?" I joked and laughed when she elbowed my ribs. "I was going to say the most beautiful creature lets me try to make her happy."

"You don't try," she whispered. "You do make me happy."

I let my fingers tangle in her hair. "And you make me happy." I pulled on her arm. "Come here."

She came willingly and settled her chin on my chest as she looked up at me. I rubbed her arms and began slowly and with the deep breath that I needed, "When the war comes, and it will, I won't stop you from being a part of it if that's what you want."

Her jaw dropped as much as it could with her chin resting on me. "What? Why?"

"You want me to change my mind?"

"No…" she shook her head, "I'm just confused."

"You've shown me over and over that you're capable. You're amazing and as much as it pains me to say, and frankly, pisses me off, I know that you're here with us for a reason other than to just be with me." Her smile was tentative. "So…if it comes down to it and we have to fight, I'll stand by your side the whole way."

She reached up and caressed my cheek and the stubble on my chin. "I love you, Merrick. And I appreciate that."

I gulped and nodded. "I love you, baby."

"I know," she said and hoisted herself to sit on my stomach. "Whatever happens, Merrick, it was worth it. All of this was worth it."

I sat up to meet her. Even with her straddling me on my lap, her head was still lower than mine. I lifted her chin with my fingers and waited. Her face as she waited for me to devour her in the dark was priceless. I leaned forward and nipped her chin. She gasped the smallest amount, but it was still adorable.

She wrapped her arms around my neck and I knew what was coming. I kissed her with intent. We had all night and if this was truly our last night on Earth, I was about to make it count.

The Day The World Ended
Chapter 29

Sherry

We all gathered around. It was time. Morning had come and we'd all sogged through breakfast and paced and waited. Miguel clicked on the TV as we all stood or sat in huddles. Everyone was present and eager.

This was it. It was almost the time we marked for the broadcast. We would see if everything was for nothing.

Lillian sat beside me and told me she was going to look for Cain, but when I told her what had happened and what we were waiting for, she sat down just as eager to watch our little nine inch TV.

Right then was the normal broadcast that they played on a loop. They mentioned the reward, the rebels, the Keepers as they always did. The time we set came and Miguel pointed at the clock to tell everyone to wait. The minute ticked by slowly, a watched pot that refused to boil, and then it passed. I felt so deflated, I could barely breathe. Lily was in my lap and I was in Merrick's, and if it hadn't been for his presence pressing behind me, I'd have fallen over with disappointment.

I felt his arms encircled us both and he whispered, "It's ok," but before he could finish the picture changed and there I was, clearing my throat and beginning with, "You don't know me…"

The silence of the room was everywhere, as loud as a roar, as everyone waited. When the tape kept playing, Miguel let out a "Whoop!" and that started the cheers. No one even heard what the rest of the tape said, but it didn't matter. The point was that *they* heard it. All those people glued to the TV at every opportunity so the Lighters could keep poisoning them with their compulsion. Merrick squeezed me and kissed my hair and neck. Lily jumped up and down, though she didn't really understand what it was for. But hey, it was a party, right?

Miguel came and stole me from Merrick's lap and hugged me with my feet in the air. "You brilliant girl!"

"They made me do it," I defended.

"No one could have done it but you." He let me down and looked me in the eye. "You deserved to be the one set these people free. They'll thank you one day."

"Aahhh," I groaned. "They do all know what I look like now, don't they?" I hadn't thought of that. I peeked back at Merrick who was coming to the same conclusion I was.

I was now a target.

Then the last sentence played, "We are the revolution. Join us and take back what was yours in-"

They cut me off. So they finally found it and stopped it, but it was way too late. The news had gotten out, the word received, the message out to the masses. I could have kissed someone! So I did.

Merrick's warm arm held me captive and I relished it. I knew he now had a new thing to worry about, but this was our small victory, our rebellion, and we needed to take them as they came. Jeff soon joined our hug and the whooping and hollering continued for a long while.

Calvin and Frank stopped their victory jig long enough to talk to me. Calvin said, "Sherry, you were great! How does it feel to be a celebrity?"

"I'm not a-"

"Shyeah, you are!" Frank cut in. "Everyone is going to know about that hot chick who stopped the Lighters!"

"Dude!" Calvin hissed.

"What? She's hot. What?" he yelled when Calvin punched his shoulder.

"Don't talk about her like that!" I wanted to giggle. Even Calvin was in for the *Sherry Protection Detail*. I smiled at them both.

"It's all right. Thanks, Frank…I think. And thanks, Calvin." I slung my arms over their shoulders. "What do you say you help me make some lunch?"

"That's chick's work," Frank complained.

"Oh, really?" I scoffed. "Just for that, you can do the dishes, too."

"Oh, come on! I take it back!"

"Too late," I drawled and dragged them to the kitchen with me. "Open these cans and then I'll show you what to do next."

"You and your big mouth!" Calvin hissed. "I swear, you're not gonna make it in the real world."

"Uhuh!"

I tuned them out and started the noodles. Things were looking up and the bunker was alive with excitement and happiness.

Though I knew it wasn't going to last, I was surprised by how quickly things went downhill.

The TV had been left on and the fuzzy screen played for hours before their regular program finally turned back on. But it wasn't the regular program. One of the reporters was in the streets and zooming the camera right and then left to show all the chaos.

People weren't looting like Miguel had expected, but they *were* fighting. You could see the people fighting each other, but you could also see a few cornering an invisible body. Finally, *finally*, people were realizing that things were different about the Lighters. They didn't know how to fight him properly, but there were so many of them that the Lighter eventually went down I guessed, though the Lighter was invisible to their cameras, because they stopped fighting him and moved on.

Once again we sat stunned and I realized then why Merrick had told me that no matter what happened, that it was worth it. Things had to get worse before they got better. I tried to remember that as I ached for all those people who had just learned the awful truth.

Merrick and Jeff stood at the same time. We knew it was time to go. We couldn't let those people just run around like chickens with their heads cut off. We'd said the rebels would be there for them and we needed to be.

Everyone that was going started getting ready to go. Some of us needed to stay. I wondered about that.

But as everyone was running around we began to hear this loud noise. It sounded like footsteps. Big ones. Kay and Max were in the kitchen with me when the first one struck and both looked at each other. I waved my hand at them. "No. No Keeper talk. What's going on?"

"Don't know," Max said and turned his ear toward the ceiling. "A helicopter maybe?"

"That's a big helicopter," Kay mused. "It's moving too slow to be that."

Merrick blurred in and looked around. "What was that?"

"That's what we're trying to figure out," Max told him.

Miguel walked in ready for a fight, all tensed and muscles rolling.

"What's the matter?" Merrick asked.

"That's the Graphter," Miguel said and Key gasped. Max nodded and Merrick's eyes got wide. "I'd remember that big boy from anywhere."

"Then they're here," Merrick said solemnly. He looked at me for just a second before kissing the corner of my mouth. He whispered, "Remember what I said." Then he yelled, "They're here! Let's go, people!"

Everyone scrambled around to arm themselves. Pap was handing out the few rifles we had, while everyone else took the guns from the crates. Guns were useless against their kind, but it felt like you were actually doing something to have a weapon in your hands. Miguel was loading every limb of his with straps and stakes and Rylee was helping him, strapping some to the holster for his back. He looked like Van Helsing by the time they were done.

Merrick was loading up his weapons, too. He kept looking up at me, trying to see what my decision was going to be. Lily shook in my arms as she watched everything happen around us. I shook my head at him. I wasn't going…this time. He looked relieved and came to us. He hugged us both and smiled at Lily. "Mommy's going to stay with you this time, but I've got to go."

She pouted, but nodded. "I know. Mommy has to stay anyway."

I frowned. "Why's that, bug?"

"To stay with me, of course!"

I smiled. "Ok. Glad we got that straight." I looked up to Merrick. "You better go," I commented, noting that half the others were already loading up in the elevator.

"I know." He leaned forward and captured my lips, holding my chin. "I love you."

"Love you," I tried not to croak, but did.

"Take care of Mommy, Lily."

"Ok. Bye, Daddy," she spouted easily. "See you soon."

"See you soon," he repeated and walked backwards to the elevator. He mouthed 'Always' to me and I tried to smile for him. He hopped on with the others. Danny came and gave us both swift kisses on the cheek before he, too, was gone. So were Miguel, Jeff, and Ryan. We watched as the men in our lives left for war.

Lily was calm and serene. It was a little eerie. She helped me with the dishes.

Dishes. That seemed so stupid and mundane after what had happened and what they were doing out there now. I felt torn in every way. But then Lily looked up at me from out of nowhere. "Mrs. Trudy says it's time to go now."

I felt all the breath leave me in a rush. "What?"

"Mommy, let's go!" she urged and pulled me toward the elevator.

"What's going on, Lily?" I said harder so she'd stop.

"Ellie's already out there! Now it's my turn. We have to go."

"Lily, stop," I told her and grabbed her upper arms. "Tell me what you're talking about."

"I'm the key," she said softly. "Mrs. Trudy told me. I have to go out there and be with Daddy."

"No," I said and shook my head. "No, Lily."

"Mommy-"

"You're not going out there!" I huffed. "I stayed behind to keep you safe, so why would I-"

She touched my cheek with her little hand and there she was. Mrs. Trudy was there and she was smiling the smile I remembered. I felt a tear escape me. All those dreams…all those visions… "It was real?" I asked.

"Honey child, I can't leave the kitchen until the casserole's done." She smirked. "This casserole is almost cooked."

"You mean-"

"This is going to work? I sure do. But you have to have some faith. Faith that's the hardest kind to have."

"And what's that?" I asked, but knew.

"The kind where you take your little girl up topside and let her finish her task."

"No," I told her, just like I told Lily. "No."

"It's time for the Specials to do what they were made to do."

My lips parted, but no words came. I couldn't…could I?

"She's only four," I argued.

"And you were only four the first time you saved Danny's life, remember?"

I thought back to what she was talking about. "He fell in the pool and I grabbed a hold of his diaper. Not the same thing."

"It is exactly the same thing," she said haughtily back. "You were where you were supposed to be when you were supposed to be. So is Lily. So is Calvin. So is Danny."

I thought about Calvin and Danny outside right now. It didn't seem right, but…it also did. I was torn again and it was beginning to hurt in my chest from all the ripping. "But…"

She hugged me hard. It was her and she was real. She smelled the same, that scent carrying me to a better time and place. "It's time, mamma. It's time you let her finish this thing for us. What we've done and who we've lost," she gave me a pointed look at she leaned back, "won't be in vain." I felt my lips purse to hold in my scream. I wanted to scream for everything that had been done to me and mine. And now they were taking my little girl from me?

She wiped my tear away and smiled through her own. "Sometimes, we have to let go when that's the last thing we want to do."

Then she was gone and I was left looking at my little girl and knowing I was about to take her up the elevator. Merrick would never forgive me for what I was about to do.

I took her fingers in mine and I walked toward the elevator. She hummed as I pressed the button. It was something soft, something sweet. It didn't fit and the eerie feeling I had from before came back tenfold.

I was taking my daughter to the Lighters because my dead friend had told me to. I shook my head. Not only would Merrick never forgive me, but neither would Danny nor Miguel nor Calvin. But I had to.

I had to trust my gut as I always had. Because that whole time that Mrs. Trudy and Lily had been trying to convince me, I hadn't heard one lie come out of their mouths.

Crashing
Chapter 30

Merrick

When we emerged from the elevator, we knew we were in for a big fight. All the Specials and gifted ones had come along with all the Keepers and all the guys who could hold a stake.

We ascended to the roof and looked out. My breaths accelerated into overdrive. I knew they'd come for us eventually. The Lighters weren't known for their mercy or forgiveness, but this was swift punishment. As we looked out at the line of evil coming our way, I knew we'd never make it. Markers lined the sky, Lighters blurred, and Graphters…there were at least five of them.

Miguel hissed and grabbed his scarred leg as he glared up at the Markers so close.

I took a deep breath and started the descent of the ladder. I led with my head high. We had to do this. At least my girls were safe inside and hopefully, the Lighters wouldn't go poking around for more once they were through with us.

The Graphters steps were shaking the building as we made our way down. I looked down the line of my people and then the other way. Everyone was solemn. It must have hit them like it hit me. This was the end, but we were going out swinging as Cain always would say. Too bad my friend wasn't here to see this; all of our family so brave and ready for whatever came their way.

All that was missing was war paint.

Danny stood beside me. He bumped my shoulder with his. I looked at him and he smiled tightly and nodded. "Thanks, man."

"What for, Special?"

"For coming and making my sister so happy, Keeper." He gripped my shoulder. "You're a good *man*." He emphasized the man and I got a little choked up. I gripped his shoulder, too.

"Danny…you're a good man, too. I've always thought so."

He nodded. "Let's do this."

I glanced down the line again. Miguel and Rylee were gripping each other's hand. Celeste and Danny were doing the same thing. Marissa was crying soundlessly and Jeff was worried about the baby as he pulled her close and kissed her temple. When I thought I'd given everybody enough time to say their goodbyes, I started toward the fray.

They were just past the trees and were just as ready for us and we were for them. I could take it no longer. I looked over at Miguel, my partner in butt-kicking. He shrugged and said, "I've been waiting to have another blue with these buggers. Look," he pointed to his pants, "I've even got on my fighting daks."

I laughed, even if this situation. I shook my head. "You know I never know what you're saying."

"I know." He grinned. "Let's give this mongrel mob what for, eh?"

"That I understand." He hugged me halfway and pounded my back. "Good to know you, man."

"Pig's arse!" he argued. "Don't act like we ain't coming back. It'll all be apples, mate."

I patted him on the back, too. We turned to the war and ran. Miguel's battle cry was a starting point for them all and we ran and yelled. They thought we were an easy target, but we weren't going out without a fight, no matter how bleak.

Some time later, we had compelled them, staked them, been slammed into trees, been slammed into each other, Marissa had them staking themselves and each other, Calvin was flaming them as Ryan protected his back, Rylee was using the balloon bombs and Miguel was stabbing them with his iron rod while shooting at the Markers in the sky. The explosives we had had been dispatched and every bullet fired.

But it wasn't enough.

We'd taken a beating. Everyone was spent and wounded somewhere. I'd been shot in the foot by a Lighter who'd stolen Danny's gun. Danny got a tire iron into the Lighter's back for it, but it made it almost impossible to keep going. Though I tried, it wasn't just me that was barely hanging on.

They corralled us, a bloody beaten mess, into a tight circle and what was left of them stood around us. All the Graphters had survived and there was enough of the others left to make me know what fate was coming.

One Graphter in particular seemed to be the silent leader of the rest. He walked back and forth and repeated the process several times before he spoke. "I can imagine you know why we're here."

"I'm so hot you can't stay away?" Miguel goaded. That earned him a kick in the gut. Rylee glared at the thing and helped Miguel sit up.

"Your little stunt with the video tape." He laughed as if he were aggravated. "We worked really hard to make sure everything was right and all lined up. And in one fell swoop, you destroyed all the compulsion to an entire state and started a riot that will only destroy the people and the town. You shot yourselves in the foot, it would seem." He grinned at me, his black teeth shining. "No pun intended, Keeper."

I huffed. "None taken, Graphter. You can keep your jokes. I'm not really in the mood."

"But this is what you wanted!" he yelled and smiled. "You wanted the world to be free of compulsion! You wanted us to know the rebels meant business. You wanted us to know this was *your town*. Well, we know and here we are to congratulate you on a job…piss poorly done. You get an 'A' for effort, but an 'F' for execution."

"Get on with it," Jeff growled. "We don't need to banter with you. Just do whatever it is that you're going to do."

"Well, we're going to kill you," he stated matter-of-factly. "But we have a few things to discuss first. One being this." He yanked Lillian up. My mouth fell open. She'd snuck out somehow. I hadn't even known she was out here with us. I saw Simon beside her and knew he'd been helping her. He would feel responsible to her for Cain. "For two, I've met our traitor, Daniel, now you can meet yours."

Piper walked up from the back of the pack. She shaved her head mostly, leaving only a little black stubble. She smiled at us. I didn't even question the hows or whys. It just didn't matter anymore.

"We found her where you had deserted her in your hideout. We offered her a place if she helped us look for you. She was so close to this place several times," he mused and looked around. "But she's been very instrumental in our pursuits. She followed you home last night and came to tell us. But then you pulled your little stunt, so we were….delayed in coming for our visit. And we won't be killing your women." He grinned at Lillian and she looked as if she might slap him. "We'll be keeping them for our…pleasure."

Then she did slap him. It was the slap heard round the dustbowl. He stared in shock and then his face melted into anger. He let her arm go and lifted his arms as if to smite her in some way, but then a Lighter was blown back and toppled into him, sending him flying with him. A boom resounded to our side.

Cain was huffing his breaths like he'd ran. And I guessed he had. He ran on the other side of our group and engulfed Lillian, even as the Graphter got up and came his way for more. She gripped onto him and we waited.

His steps shook us and his anger was a tangible thing. It filled our lungs and let us know he was done with his banter. Cain raised his hand again, but stopped. "Dang. Forgot you're some kind of freak that can't be blown to bits."

"True. I'm immune to your abilities. But you aren't immune to mine." He clapped his hands and we all covered our ears and groaned. Cain had been the closest. When he pulled his hands back, a small trail of blood was making its way from his ear down his neck.

The Graphter then pulled Chesser up from the ground. He held him up by his neck, his feet dangling under him, and said, "I also have other gifts you have yet to see. Until now."

Then he pressed his hand to Chesser's chest and we watched as his skin became ashen. Impossible! The Graphter was absorbing him!

"Stop him!" I heard from behind us and twirled around in a blur to see for myself that Sherry had changed her mind about coming. And, oh…no! No! She had Lily with her. She yelled again, "Stop him! Chesser's going to be the new Taker!"

It hit me then. I wasn't sure how I knew, but Lily and Mrs. Trudy were involved somehow. I turned back to see The Graphter lowering Chesser's feet back to the ground. They were fighting...internally. Chesser would lose all his color and look sick, and then the Graphter would shake and fight for control again as Chesser's cheeks turned pink with life.

Finally, I saw Chesser was winning. "Merrick!" Sherry yelled and silently pleaded with me to believe her. I did. Chesser was winning over the beast and he would become the new Taker without even realizing what he was doing. I yanked the crow bar from Miguel's hand then staked the Lighter who tried to stop me. The lightning that blasted from him shook the others, who were watching the Graphter display with interest, out of their funk. I avoided them barely and then stuck the bar through the Graphter's back and out toward Chesser through his chest.

Chesser turned to us and I could see it was too late. He was the Taker.

I shook my head at what I had to do, but Lily ran past me and went to stand in front of Chesser. He grinned down at her. "Hello, little girl."

"You don't remember me, do you?" she asked.

I bolted forward to stop her, to get her away from him, when Sherry grabbed my arm. Anyone else would have gotten the shove-off, but she was crying and begged me in a whisper, "I know this is crazy, just please let her do this."

I wanted to be angry at her. What the hell was she doing? I turned back to Lily just as Chesser, the Taker, was answering her.

"I don't remember you, no. Should I?"

"Not really," Lily said and smiled.

"I am kind of hungry," he drawled and stepped a little closer. He crouched down to be at her level and I almost lost it. Sherry gripped me tighter, her sobs getting a little louder. "Know where I can get some souls to eat around here?"

"You are a bad man. You used to be a good man who carwed about his people, but now you only care about yowself!"

He chuckled. "You humans are so full of passion and pity. It's why you taste so good." He reached for her and my heart stopped, but before I could even think about moving, Lily grabbed his face in her hands.

"I see you in there, Chesser." She moved closer, only an inch away from the man who wanted to end her life. "Come back, Chesser."

The Taker jolted and looked around wide eyed. "Help me!" he yelled to the Lighters, but they just watched in an awe that startled me. It was as if they wanted him to die. "Help me, you fools!"

No one moved a muscle, we just watched, horrified and hopeful, as his skin began to ashen. And then real ashes appeared on his body. He looked like he was falling apart. At first I thought Lily was becoming the evil thing, but the wind blew and we saw the ashes float away from Chesser's skin and drift into nothing as the wind carried it away.

Lily let his face go and he just stayed there like that, wide eyed. Lily turned to look at the other Lighters and they all fell to the ground. The Markers burned up and fell the long way to the ground. Black Marker bones and lifeless bodies littered the area. All except for Piper, who knelt in the dirt and looked lifeless and dead inside.

We all waited for something to indicate what was going on. Lily turned to us. "They went home. For good dis time. The Taker was a bad man to them, too."

I rushed her. "What did you do?"

"I did what Mrs. Twudy told me to. She said to tell the Taker to go to…" she looked around and whispered, "H..E…double hockey sticks."

I wanted to laugh, but my body wouldn't. "You sent him away."

"He was mad," she said. "He didn't want to go, but he was a bad man, Daddy. Mrs. Twudy said to make him go away and the other guys would go home, too."

I hugged her to me tightly. "Oh, baby. I'm so glad you're ok."

"I'm ok. But mommy isn't." She pointed behind me. Sherry was rocking and sobbing on the ground. I finally could let something else in and saw everyone was waiting for something. I realized what it was.

"It's over," I told them. "They're gone…for good. Lily sent them home."

"Over, over? Like….over?" Danny asked and wrapped his arms around a smiling Celeste from behind.

"Like, over, over," I confirmed.

He laughed and then his chest started to shake. He was crying. He ran and gave me one of his big hugs, taking Lily from me and holding her in the air as she squealed and laughed. Then he yelled and laughed and whooped as he swung Lily around. Celeste was jumping up and down clapping as she watched Danny. Miguel started next and by the time I reached my Sherry, the whole yard was erupting in cheers and tears. There wasn't a dry eye in the place.

I bent down on my knees and lifted Sherry's face with my finger under his chin. "It's over, baby."

"I'm so sorry," she begged. "I saw Mrs. Trudy! She told me I had to let Lily go. I didn't want to, but I…."

"Baby, Lily saved the day. Do you understand what happened here? Not only did the Lighters and Markers leave this place, they left the world. Honey, our little girl just saved the human race."

She sniffed. "You're not angry with me for putting her in danger?"

I chuckled, almost hysterical with everything that had happened. "I'm not sure she was. She seemed to be pretty good at what she was doing."

She let her breath go slowly. "I thought you were never going to be able to forgive me."

I pulled her up and pressed her chest to mine. Just as I was about to tell her exactly what I wanted to do to her, a warmth hit my chest. It spread rapidly and when I felt the wind on my face that only touched me and not Sherry, I knew what this was. I looked over my shoulder to see Jeff and Kay and Ryan. All of us Keepers. We were being called home.

Piper began to scream and I looked over just in time to see her disappear. I closed my eyes and shut my mind to where she was going. I told them in my mind that I was happy. I wanted to stay with the woman in my arms that somehow had it in her mind that it was possible for me to hate her.

I waited for their disappointment, for their shame, for their judgment, but it never came. I got this feeling come over me. I heard the voice in my mind. "Contentment and happiness are two different things." I nodded and looked at my Sherry whose silver dollar sized eyes were trained on my face. They certainly were two different things. The warm feeling left me peacefully, with blessings my way.

It was over. I was human. I was here to stay. I'd never see the After and I'd die one day as a human. It was everything I wanted and I smiled through my unshed tears and pulled Sherry to me.

Simon stood and went to Cain. He hugged him hard and Cain seemed to understand somewhat that this was a goodbye. "Cain, I've never been more proud of a charge. Thank you for allowing me to watch over you."

"Take it easy, Simon," Cain said in return and nodded to him. "You're a good guy."

Simon nodded and then closed his eyes. His body fell to the ground and he was gone. Jeff must've made the same decision I had because he looked as peaceful as I'd ever seen his human face look. Marissa was crying into his shoulder and he held her gently and smiled.

Kay went to Celeste and we knew what her decision was. Celeste shook her head a 'no', but Kay hugged her to her. "You don't need me anymore." She cupped her face. "Celeste, thank you." She looked between Danny and Celeste. "Take care of each other."

"We will," Celeste said, but still asked, "You have to go?"

"I have to go. I'll miss you. You were always my favorite. Maybe I'll check in on you from time to time." She looked at me. "Breaking the rules isn't unheard of."

I smiled and took Sherry with me as I went to give my sister a final hug. I bid her farewell. "Guard you in all your ways, sister."

"And you in yours, brother." She teared up. It was a mix of happy to go, but sad to want to stay.

All the Keepers followed suit and bid her farewell, and then we bid Max farewell as well. And then Ann and Patrick and all the rest. In the end, only Jeff, me and Ryan were left.

I held my breath and realized that I could no longer hear Ryan's thoughts. I wasn't tied to him any longer…because I was a human. I had chosen a mortal life and it made me the happiest to feel that I didn't feel much different. In my mind, I'd been human with Sherry all along.

He stared at Ellie and then glanced at Calvin before settling on Ellie again.

"Ryan," Ellie began, "we talked about this remember?" Her chest bucked with a sob that she tried to stop. "Go. Be with your kind and be happy. I just want you to be happy."

He stared at her longer before nodding. The warm light left his face and I knew he'd made his decision. "I'm happy right here."

"Are you sure?" she said in hysterics. "It's permanent, Ryan. I don't want to be a burden or..or a…or a regret-"

He covered her mouth with his and she cried happily into their kiss and she got her answer. I turned to my wife and she looked at me like I was an alien. That thought stung after everything we'd just been through. She whispered the words like a prayer, "You stayed with me?"

"Of course I did. I told you I always would."

"But....I just thought you said that because the day would never come. You actually...chose me, over everything you've waited your whole life for."

"You are my life," I told her sternly in a growl against her forehead. "You are my life, baby. I'm here to stay."

Her sobs may have been the loudest of the whole bunch. It was almost funny how we all sat around and cried like a heap of babies for the ones lost, for the ones gone home, and for the ones who stayed who gave up one paradise for another kind.

I pulled her face up once more and kissed her eyes, tasting the tears that were shed for me and no one else. God...thank you for this gift, for this girl, for this opportunity at having my everything, for letting me feel the difference between content and happy, for letting me have this family that loved me to my core and vice versa. Thank you for making me just to end up in the arms of the girl I watched when I wasn't supposed to. The girl who stole my heart and saved it all in the same moment. The girl who I'd grow old with and die with, happily, blissfully, contently.

The end was looking pretty good. Brown eyes met mine and I was looking at my future. My brown eyed everything that saved us.

My Sherry.

The Beautiful End
Chapter 31

Sherry

His skin was warm, but not as warm as it had been. It really was true. He was here to stay, he'd chosen us.

He'd chosen me.

I felt…torn again. I wanted him to stay, but he'd given up so much. I looked up into his green eyes and tried to tell him everything with my stare. My mouth would never utter the words, but I wanted him to know. The tears wouldn't stop either. He kissed my eyes. Such a sweet gesture and gave me a look that told *me* everything.

That I was an idiot if I thought he'd ever leave me.

We were on our knees in the sand and it bit into my skin, but I was focused on other things. I wrapped my arms around his neck and breathed him in. He squeezed me to his chest and said into my ear, "I can't believe this."

"I know," I agreed and leaned back a fraction. I gazed at his face with nothing but love. "It's over, finally."

"No," he said and chuckled. It sent goose bumps all over me. "No. I can't believe…I got everything I ever wanted."

"Stop," I told him and sniffed. "You're going to make me cry again."

He smiled. "I'll be here to wipe them away. Forever."

I melted in more ways than one. He kissed my forehead. His smile was pure happiness, but when we heard a scream behind us, we both turned.

Chesser was still kneeling in the sand in a stupor, but apparently had woken up. He was screaming at the sky. I felt my heart lurch thinking of all of the horrible possibilities. Was he still the Taker? Was he something else? But then he started to laugh. A deep, hysterical laugh and he bent down and kissed the dirt. He held his hands up and let two fistfuls of sand go and they blew over us in the wind.

He looked over at us. *Us* being all of us who had stopped what we were doing to watch the maniac.

"We did it!" he yelled and laughed again. "And you!" he pointed at Lily and got up, running to her. Her swung her around and hugged her to him. "You brought me back, you darling little thing!"

She smiled at him and tilted her head. "Did you like Mrs. Trudy?"

"Was that her name?" He smiled, too. "She sure was bossy." I laughed. I couldn't help it. I covered my mouth to keep it to myself as he continued. "She said it was over." He looked around at all the bodies littering the ground. "I guess she was right."

"What are we going to do now?" Rylee spoke up. She was dirty and her arm was bleeding. "What about the town?"

"Let's go inside," Miguel said. "We'll clean up and see what the next step is." He took Rylee's hand. "Come on, ginger."

"I love it when you call me ginger," she crooned. He grinned smugly, but then she socked him in the arm. "Not. Stop calling me that, Aussie, or we're gonna throw down again."

He laughed and threw his arm over her shoulder. "You got it, sheila. You got it."

"Well," Danny sighed, "I wonder what Mom and Dad would say about all this." Celeste sat stoic in his lap. She understood that Kay needed to go, but after just recently losing her mother, naturally she was upset. He stroked her arm and let her snuggle in for comfort. I was proud of him.

I rubbed the bandage on Merrick's foot that I had applied, making sure it was still stuck and watched Frank and Calvin chase Bones around the crates, playing fetch with my wooden spoon.

"I don't know," I confessed. "I'm actually afraid of what they'd say." I leaned back into Merrick as we sat on the floor, leaning on the crates. He kissed the side of my neck and I sighed. "What do you think they'd say, Merrick?"

He pressed his mouth to my bare shoulder, right over my Marker's scratch and his words were muffled. "Don't get me started on those two."

"Things are so different now," Celeste said. "I can feel it. Things are going to be so…normal. It's weird."

"Normal," Merrick mused and smiled. He leaned down to whisper into my ear. "No more Keeper talk, no more being oblivious to the cold, no more speed. You sure you still want me when I'm not so fantastic?" he joked.

I laughed. "I do wish you'd gotten to speak to me just one more time in my mind." I looked up at him over my shoulder. "Your real Keeper voice was so sexy."

"Like how? Deep?" He lowered his voice a notch. "Like this?"

I giggled. "Lower."

Lower, he said, "Like this, baby?"

I laughed harder, along with Danny and Celeste, who were listening apparently. "That's it. Keep that up and we'll be fine."

"No problem." He nipped my earlobe. "Anything you want."

"I've got everything I want."

I felt him sigh and knew he knew that I was telling the truth. I couldn't lie.

Later a shaken Cain, which was a sight to see let me tell ya, told us what had happened to him and Daniel. After he hugged me long and hard, he told us about how Daniel had went to the store only to find it ransacked. He guessed that was when they took Piper. He told us about going to the vet doctor because Daniel took him there by mistake. He told us about finding the line maps for the broadcast stations and he told us about what Daniel had done to save him. Lillian must've heard the story already because she sat silently in Cain's lap on the floor and clung to his neck.

She looked unsettled….but settled. It was weird and I felt for her. Marissa spoke up and told us about the vision she'd seen. She debated on whether to tell Daniel or not, but to not let someone do the task that was set out for them was never a good thing. Daniel had been meant to switch sides and save us. In the end, he saved all his brothers as well and they all went home, never to return.

Daniel. The Lighter who saved us all.

"I've got a little surprise," Chesser told everyone when we'd all cleaned up as much as we could and sat in the big room together. "I need to check something out first, but if it pans out, you're going to love me."

"What is it?" Jeff asked, his usual Keeper self. Though he wasn't a Keeper anymore.

"I'll explain later. Mind if I take the van?"

"Sure, mate," Miguel spouted and turned on the TV. "Before you head into town let's…"

The town was a mess. Stores had been destroyed, some things were on fire and still burning. The streets were littered with debris and the wind whipped some of it around into the air. The anchorwoman stood in front of the sign that I had defaced. *Our Town* now blazed behind her as she said what was happening. The sound of yelling could be heard from behind the camera. As she, who was no longer compelled, walked through town and showed the destruction, she also showed the people gathering in the streets. They were…celebrating.

I gripped my husband to me and we all watched enraptured. We'd been fighting here and they'd been fighting *there.*

Even though we hadn't made it to them last night, they'd fought and stood strong. And when the Lighters had been defeated they knew the war was over. Now in the morning light of glorious victory, even though we still weren't together as one body, we all celebrated together as one human race.

The war was over.

A new life was beginning.

A life without Lighters or Keepers or Markers or Takers. A life of humans who were hell bent on rebuilding a world worth living in.

The rebellion may have been over, but the revolution was ongoing.

This was our world, *our town*, and we refused to give up.

Happily Ever After
Chapter 32

Lily

I giggled as I watched Mommy cwy. It always made me sad to see her cwy, but this time, she was laughing and cwying at the same time. Daddy kept kissing her neck. He was her prince charming. Well, that's what Aunt Rissa had said.

Aunt Rissa was going to be a good mommy. She was a good teacher. And Uncle Jeff was a good Daddy. He was her prince charming, too.

Calvin and Frankwin, those meany pants, were not prince charmings.

But I was glad the bad man was gone now. I wasn't scarwed. Mrs. Trudy said not to be. She said everything was going to be ok. And now we could go outside and play! Maybe Daddy could build me a swing, and tell Calvin he's not allowed to play on it 'cause he's too big!

Maybe Daddy would build a doll house. A big one. We might need a big one one day, because Mommy didn't know it, but there was a surpwise in her belly. It was a girl and Mrs. Trudy said to tell Mommy to name her Hope.

Because all the world needed right now…was a little Hope.

Epilogue
One Week Later

Sherry

So, the little surprise that Chesser had been talking about was staring back at us as we all stood in the middle of town. It was beautiful. We'd packed all of our things, which wasn't much, and followed Chesser in our little convoy across town.

And there we were.

It was an apartment complex that had been abandoned. It was right near the radio station and where the Enforcement facility used to be, so people had scrammed and moved on to somewhere not so close.

He said he'd scoped it out a long time ago, checked all the rooms, and that it was as empty as it could be. But the glorious thing was that when people fled, they left most of their furniture and 'stuff'. So we weren't sitting on the floor anymore, or sleeping on concrete anymore, or eating off our laps. And the very, very best part? We got to be separated, but still be technically together.

There were only about twenty apartments, but that was plenty for us. We'd divide it up by families and it would be perfect.

We walked into the first one we saw. It didn't matter what it looked like. It was a place to live and be alone. They were all two bedrooms so we had our room and Lily had hers.

I didn't even remember what privacy was like, but when I walked to the back and saw the washer and dryer, I almost cried right there. I heard Merrick call me into the kitchen. "Don't faint," he said.

"What? Why?"

He took my arm and pulled me around to see a dishwasher. I squealed like a little girl and jumped up and down and into his arms as he laughed. Lily hugged our legs and we lifted her up to squeeze between us.

Later as we sat on our couch - *our couch* - we thought about what we could do to start turning the town back around. Money was a thing of the past. No one had it and no one knew much about what was going on outside of the state except that all the Lighters were gone. We figured there was no point in waiting for the government to come and fix things.

There *was* no government.

So all of us met in the conference room and talked about it until we decided to invite the town, what was left of it, to speak with everybody all at once and come up with a trade system. We needed to start planting crops again and getting the stores back in order. We needed have limits and rules and regulations that everybody agreed to and we needed to start living them.

It was exciting to think about a new society.

That night after we put Lily to bed in her new room, we lay in our own bed and looked at the ceiling. The sheets I had washed were soft and smelled heavenly. Merrick and I had taken a shower for a long time, like we couldn't get clean enough. Then without putting on clothes, he'd carried me to bed.

Lily had told me some news this morning while Jeff and Merrick were talking to the Enforcers in our group about setting up some kind of security, just in case. I was dusting and going through the books left in the apartment and she'd let the secret fall sweetly from her lips.

Now, I was about to let it fall from mine and I had barely been able to keep in my excitement in all day.

I twisted my necklace, rubbing the hearts that were made for me, and sighed.

"What's wrong, babe?" Merrick asked, so predictably.

"Nothing. I was just thinking that this apartment is awfully small."

He frowned. "I thought you loved it."

"I do. It's just small."

"Well," he said slowly, "beggars can't be choosers, sweetheart."

I giggled. "I guess not. But the baby is going to be awfully cranky-"

"What…did you just say?"

I sat up and straddled his lap. "I said…" I smiled and cried for about the millionth time in the past week and whispered, "The baby will be cranky."

His mouth opened and he stared. "You… Really?"

"Really. Lily told me, and I don't think it's a good idea to doubt her when she says something. Plus," I shrugged, "a woman knows her body."

"Are you saying…" his eyes filled and the joy was all over him, "we're going to have a baby?"

"That's what I'm saying, Keeper. Not only did you save me more times than I can count, and come for me, and love me, you gave me the one thing I thought I'd never have."

"But…how?"

"Do I need to give you an anatomy lesson, baby?" I licked his earlobe and kissed his chin. "I think you know how."

He rolled so quickly, it reminded me of the Keeper speed he no longer possessed. He grinned down at me. "Really?"

I smiled and burst. It hurt to have so much joy in my gut. He lay down on me and absorbed my sobs as he stroked and kissed me. It took a while before I realized that he was crying, too.

We held onto each other and dreamed about things of the future. Soon he was tucking me under him in more intimate ways and I arched, and sighed and gave into him.

This was what I had to look forward to for the rest of my life.

And I was one happily content girl.

Ten Months Later

"How's the sign coming along?" I asked.

Merrick and Miguel grinned down at me. Miguel nodded. "It's bloody perfect! Everyone will see this thing from a mile away."

"They better," Billings groaned as he held it up from the bottom. "Are you done yet?" No one answered him and he growled and yelled, "Hey!" at Bones who nipped at his pants legs.

Cain stopped beside me and looked up at it. He whistled. "Looks good." He read aloud the 'In Honor of Daniel. The Lighter whose sacrifice saved us all'. He smiled wistfully, rubbing L's arm as she laid her head on his shoulder, and then smiled down at me. "And how are you doing?"

"Oh, fine," I sighed happily and rocked my hips side to side. "I just don't want you guys to get in over your heads, that's all. There's a lot of people in this town to feed."

"Nah," he shrugged off, "we're fine. We've got lots of help from the other guys in town. And Pap's seeds that he left at the cabin were plenty enough to get us started." He chuckled. "I never thought I'd be a farmer."

Lillian wrapped her arms around him from behind. "Bet you'd look cute in overalls."

He grinned. "I look cute in anything, L."

"True." She smiled at me. "How are you *really* doing?"

"I'm great!" I laughed. "Everyone needs to stop worrying about me."

"Where's Marissa?" Cain asked.

I nodded my head toward the lounge chair. "She's there." Marissa, Jeff and that gorgeous baby were all snuggled up for a nap in the lounger together. They needed the sleep for sure. The baby was keeping them up at night, I knew.

"You could probably do with a nap, too," Lillian said and gave me a look.

"She's right," Merrick said and glanced at Jeff. "I'm a little jealous of Jeffrey right now."

"Ah," I crooned and kissed Hope's little head. "She's not that bad, are you, baby?"

Merrick smiled gorgeously and kissed her head, then mine. "No, she's not that bad." He took her from me, my arms releasing with the ache of being still so long. "In fact, she's perfect. She looks just like you," he whispered, as he'd whispered a million times since she was born. He held her effortlessly and kissed her forehead again.

"Let us take her for a bit," Lillian said excitedly. "The grand opening for the produce farm isn't for a few hours still." She looked at Cain and he nodded with a grin. "Come on, let us," she pleaded.

I kissed my little girl's head once more and Merrick handed her sleeping form over reluctantly. She was exactly two months old today. Merrick took my hand and towed me upstairs toward our apartment. Calvin and Lana's was right at the end of the stairs. I saw Calvin's sheet tent in the living room. Ellie and Ryan's apartment was on one side of us and Jeff and Marissa's was on the other. Ryan's door was open and they were standing in the doorway.

He must've been heading off to help with the opening because he was giving her one heck of a goodbye kiss. Merrick and I smiled at each other as we passed. We entered our apartment, a nap sounding like the best idea ever right then, to find Lily there. She was brushing out her doll's hair and setting them up for a tea party.

We stopped. She'd been so good about sharing us with the baby and all the stuff that needed to be done to get things right in the town again. We both looked at each other at the same time. Even without his Keeper talk, I could practically hear his thoughts.

We both sat down across from her. I picked up one doll and Merrick picked up the other. I laughed at him, because I knew what was coming. He held the Barbie in one hand and the other held out like a diva and said in a high voice, "So girls, what's been going on?"

Lily squealed and moved her Barbie closer. "Nothing, just buying a new fur coat. Wanna see?"

"Do I *ever*!"

We laughed and played with our little girl until it was time to go meet up with everyone at the opening of the produce store.

The men in our group had gotten together with a few others and started a garden. Pap and Margaret had gone back to their cabin on the hill to live instead of staying with us. But not before he told us about his farm supplies, seeds and tractor included. As far as we knew, we were the only farm\garden in the state. No one else had seeds and we planned to start spreading them around when our first big crop came in. And it was in. Today we were open for business, but not for money. We traded things or services with everyone and it worked out perfectly.

And let me tell you, Merrick, shirtless in the blazing sun as he worked in the garden was a sight to see. You thought chocolate made your toes curl…

They were getting a school ready, too. Marissa was going to teach along with a couple of others. It was going to be laid back. Marissa was taking the baby with her and we were starting off with half days. I had agreed to start teaching piano and music once the baby was a little older.

The town wasn't perfect by any means. We'd had a few run-ins with trouble, someone who wasn't too keen on having to go back to the following the common laws of a society, like no stealing. The Enforcers, who were mostly a bunch of cops anyway, had kind of started to keep the peace again. The town clean-up had been massive, but we'd gotten so much done in the last ten months.

Marissa and I had our babies within three days of each other. That had been eventful, but so worth it. Merrick was the best coach ever. We thought Jeff was bad. Merrick turned worrying into a sport for those months, but I loved every minute of it.

Ryan and Ellie were stuck in the lovey stage. The sweet one where all you wanna do is touch and be touched. Miguel and Rylee were still love-hating on each other. Miguel never walked around with anything but a smile though, so I assumed it was working for him. Celeste and Danny lived across the hall from us and were still the same old, same old. He was a great uncle and husband. When kids of his own were brought up, he and Celeste both wrinkled their noses.

Cain and Lillian were as happy as ever and lived down the hall from us. They were the biggest baby hogs of the bunch.

Calvin had grown two more inches. Franklin hadn't and was brooding and irritated. Two teenage boys running around… But Calvin had become extremely protective of Lily lately.

The radio transmissions had been turned back on, but we only had one station. Some older man who used to run one decided he was taking it over. He only played songs from the forties, but it was better than nothing. The news continued to play daily because there wasn't much else, but they talked about actual news and not just Lighters anymore. They did start to play some old movies and re-runs, but again, we only had one channel, so it was that or nothing.

This was our life now. We lived our separate lives in our apartments and then lived together, one big family and community.

Later that night the whole town gathered for the grand opening and listened to Chesser give his speech on the importance of equal giving and taking. We all needed to work together to make this new world work.

They cut the ribbon and everyone went inside the big field for our first time with fresh produce in more than a year. Lily went right to the watermelons.

Afterwards, they held a get together and had live music and dancing in the street. I rocked my hips side to side to keep my Hope asleep and felt Merrick's arms go around me from behind. "Still sleeping?"

"I'm surprised with the loud music that she is, but yeah."

He kissed the side of my neck. "Wanna dance with me?"

I looked out at our family who was already dancing. The band was playing a wonderful acoustic version of Howie Day's *Collide*. It was a perfect song, to a perfect day, to a perfect new life.

The dawn is breaking,
a light shining through.
You're barely waking,
and I'm tangled up in you.
Yeah.
I'm open, you're closed.
Where I follow, you'll go.
I worry I won't see your face light up again.
Even the best fall down sometime,
Even the wrong words seem to rhyme,
Out of the doubt that fills my mind.
We'll somehow find, you and I collide.

I held Hope between us as Merrick took us in his arms and swayed us. He kissed my forehead, his lips warm. *Human* warm. I let him guide me with his hands on my hips.

"I love you, baby," he said to me and closed his eyes. "I could stay right here all night."

So we pretty much did.

Life wasn't perfect, but we found our perfection in it. Our new life in this new world was going to be hard and rough and beautiful. I couldn't wait for my kids to grow up and see what they helped to literally build back up from nothing. This was worth fighting for.

I looked up at my husband and even after everything had happened I couldn't help but be grateful that our worlds collided.

"I love you, too, Keeper." He laughed. He always laughed when I said that. I didn't care what anyone said.

Merrick would always be my Keeper to me.

THE VERY END

Shelly is a bestselling YA author from a small town in Georgia and loves everything about the south. She is wife to a fantastical husband and stay at home mom to two boisterous and mischievous boys who keep her on her toes. They currently reside in everywhere USA as they happily travel all over with her husband's job. She loves to spend time with her family, binge on candy corn, go out to eat at new restaurants, buy paperbacks at little bookstores, site see in the new areas they travel to, listen to music everywhere and also LOVES to read.

Her own books happen by accident and she revels in the writing and imagination process. She doesn't go anywhere without her notepad for fear of an idea creeping up and not being able to write it down immediately, even in the middle of the night, where her best ideas are born.

Shelly's website:

www.shellycrane.blogspot.com

PLAYLIST

(Theme) Collide : Howie Day
(Merrick's flashback) Open Your Eyes : Snow Patrol
(Sherry's dream) Touch This Light : House of Heroes
(Plotting) Angel With A Shotgun : The Cab
(Fight) Skin Graph : Silversun Pickups
(The hard truth) Ann Sun : Walk The Moon
Remember The Empire : House Of Heroes
(Ryan & Ellie) Love Somebody : Maroon 5
You Know Where I'm At : Gavin Degraw
Wide Awake : Katy Perry
Iscariot : Walk The Moon
Keep Your Eyes Open : Needtobreathe
Y Control : Yeah Yeah Yeahs
Stay : House Of Heroes
(Cain in the Sand) Be Still : The Fray
Alibi : 30 Seconds To Mars
Where I Belong : Switchfoot
(Daniel's Goodbye) Broken Angel : Boyce Avenue
We Were Giants : House Of Heroes
Home : Phillip Phillips
(On the road to the station) Roads Untraveled : Linkin Park
Gunnin' : Hedley
This Is Why We Fight : The Decemberist
On The Run : Kaiser Chiefs
(The war) The War Inside : Switchfoot
Daylight : Boyce Avenue
(The End) Vegas Skies : The Cab

Thank you

to my God and my family for supporting me through my endeavors of writing. This book was so hard to write! I'm going to miss Sherry and Merrick terribly. They were my first couple and will always hold a place in my heart. I hope you enjoyed this series as much I enjoyed writing it. This last book, gut wrenching for me as it was, was still fun and reminiscent. Thank you for coming along on this journey with me.

Thank you!

Shelly's other works

Significance series

Devoured series

Stealing Grace series

Wide awake

Smash Into You

Please feel free to Contact Shelly at the following avenues.

www.facebook.com/shellycranefanpage

www.twitter.com/authshellycrane

www.shellycrane.blogspot.com